CW01214532

Red Hammer

V Plague Book Four

DIRK PATTON

Dirk Patton
Text Copyright © 2014 by Dirk Patton

Copyright © 2014 by Dirk Patton

All Rights Reserved

This book or any portion thereof may not be reproduced or used in any manner whatsoever without the express written permission of the publisher except for the use of brief quotations in a book review.

Published by Reaper Ranch Press LLC

PO Box 856

Gilmer, TX 75644-0856

Printed in the United States of America

First Printing, 2014

ISBN-13: 978-1511503976

ISBN-10: 1511503971

This is a work of fiction. Names, characters, businesses, brands, places, events and incidents are either the products of the author's imagination or used in a fictitious manner. Any resemblance to actual persons, living or dead, or actual events is purely coincidental.

Red Hammer
Table of Contents

Author's Note

Thank you for purchasing Red Hammer, Book 4 in the V Plague series. If you haven't read the first three books, I strongly encourage you to do so first. Otherwise, you will be lost as this book is intended to continue the story in a serialized format. I intentionally did nothing to explain comments and events that reference Books 1 through 3. Regardless, you have my heartfelt thanks for reading my work, and I hope you're enjoying the adventure as much as I am. As always, a good review on Amazon is greatly appreciated.

First and foremost, my heartfelt thanks to Katie. For everything you do.

No book is ever complete without thanking Dog. For waking me up in the middle of the night so I'm writing in a daze (makes it easier to think like an infected) and for distracting me when I've been sitting in front of the computer for too long.

Finally, if you're still reading this crap and haven't skipped ahead to Chapter 1, thank you for spending your money to read my work. That is an honor that I didn't fully appreciate until I became an author. It also puts a lot of pressure on me to make sure I'm holding up my end of the deal and producing a quality product that meets or exceeds your expectations. If I've done that, I would greatly appreciate a good review on Amazon. Yes, I know they're a pain to do, but reviews from readers like you are the best marketing in the world!

Also, you can always correspond with me via email at dirk@dirkpatton.com , visit my website at www.dirkpatton.com and if you're on Facebook, please like my page at www.facebook.com/DirkPattonAuthor and Twitter @DirkPatton.

Thanks again for reading!

Dirk Patton

August 2014

Also by Dirk Patton

The V Plague Series

Unleashed: V Plague Book 1

Crucifixion: V Plague Book 2

Rolling Thunder: V Plague Book 3

Red Hammer: V Plague Book 4

Transmission: V Plague Book 5

Rules Of Engagement: A John Chase Short Story

Days Of Perdition: V Plague Book 6

Indestructible: V Plague Book 7

Recovery: V Plague Book 8

Precipice: V Plague Book 9

Anvil: V Plague Book 10

Merciless: V Plague Book 11

Fulcrum: V Plague Book 12

Hunter's Rain: A John Chase Novella

Red Hammer
Exodus: V Plague Book 13

Scourge: V Plague Book 14

Fractured: V Plague Book 15

Brimstone: V Plague Book 16

Abaddon: V Plague Book 17

Cataclysm: V Plague Book 18

Legion: V Plague Book 19

The 36 Series

36: A Novel

The Void: A 36 Novel

Other Titles by Dirk Patton

The Awakening

Fool's Gold

Red Hammer

Take the children and yourself
And hide out in the cellar
By now the fighting will be close at hand
Don't believe the church and state
And everything they tell you

Mike and the Mechanics – Silent Running

1

Army Master Sergeant Darius Jackson stood leaning out over the narrow platform on the edge of the slow-moving locomotive, watching John Chase plummet more than eighty feet to the brownish-grey water of the Mississippi. There was a large splash, then the Major disappeared beneath the swirling surface of the river.

"Crazy motherfucker!" Jackson said to himself, staring at the spot where the Major had gone under.

He wanted to stand there and see if the insane man surfaced, but he needed to get the train stopped and reversed. There were still evacuees back on the Memphis side of the bridge that hadn't boarded when the deserter, Air Force Captain Lee Roach, had hijacked the train. In a struggle with Rachel and Dog, the three of them had fallen off the train, past the bridge and into the flood-swollen river below. Major Chase had immediately gone in after them.

Shaking his head, Jackson slung the Major's rifle with his own and stepped into the locomotive cab to figure out the controls. It only took him a couple of minutes to get the train stopped, but several more to get it in reverse and moving back toward Memphis. While he worked, he was in radio contact with his CO, Colonel Crawford, somewhere above him in a Black Hawk helicopter.

"He did what?" The tone of incredulity was clear in the Colonel's voice.

"He jumped off the goddamn train and into the river, sir. Guess I should have listened to him and killed Roach when we captured him."

"Don't waste time second-guessing yourself, Master Sergeant. We're peeling off to see if we can spot them in the water. Get those people out of there. The Hummers and Bradley are almost out of ammo."

"Yes, sir. Out."

While the train rolled backwards on the bridge, Jackson opened the side door, reached out and tugged the large rear-view mirror into alignment. Roach had knocked it out and down to prevent Jackson and Major Chase from seeing inside the cab as they approached. Mirror in proper adjustment, he was able to see down the side of the train.

Over a thousand people still stood on the bridge decking, as far away from the Humvees and Bradley that were guarding the entrance as they could get. All three vehicles were firing their machine guns, the Bradley also utilizing its chain gun to stop the infected and there was a respectable pile of shattered bodies in a semi-circle around the approach to the bridge.

Eyes on the mirror and hand on the throttle, Jackson slowed the train as the rearmost car reached the part of the bridge that had solid decking beneath the rails. This was where the panicked evacuees waited and he slowed further. Fully on the solid portion of the bridge, Jackson cut the throttle to idle and set the brakes for the train cars and the four locomotives. Immediately, people surged forward, climbing into the waiting cattle cars that were all that was left of the original train.

The people loaded themselves quickly, frightened, but still willing to help each other. Jackson watched them climb on in the big mirror, willing them to move faster. The chain gun on the Bradley fell silent and a moment later one of the Hummer's machine guns ran dry as well. That left one Humvee-mounted machine gun and the machine gun on the Bradley still in the fight. The greater destruction of the Bradley's chain gun had equaled the firepower of at least three machine guns, and with it out of ammo the wall of infected quickly pushed forward. The semi-circle of clear space around the entrance began rapidly shrinking.

Jackson got on the radio with the soldiers holding the line, asked a few questions then started issuing orders. Momentarily, he saw the majority of the men and women manning the vehicles exit and start running for the train. Once they had a hundred-yard head start, the Hummer that still had some ammo, and the Bradley, started following them out onto the bridge deck, machine guns still firing to keep the infected at bay.

By the time the running soldiers reached the rear of the train, all the civilian evacuees were loaded. Even in the cab of the giant locomotive, Jackson could hear them screaming for him to start moving. The two military vehicles came to a stop twenty yards behind the rearmost car, the Hummer's machine gun going silent. The infected surged, but only covered a few yards before a Black Hawk swooped in and opened up with its door mounted minigun. The helicopters were very low on ammo and Jackson had held them in reserve for just this moment. He was determined to get all the soldiers on the train.

The leading ranks of infected fell under the withering minigun fire. The heavy, high-velocity slugs tore through bodies, the steel of the bridge, anything they touched. The remaining soldiers wasted no time in abandoning the two vehicles and running for their lives. As soon as Jackson saw their boots hit the bridge deck, he throttled up the diesels, ready to go the second the running defenders were on board.

They had only covered half the distance when the minigun ran out of ammo. Dozens of female infected screamed and immediately sprinted past the devastated bodies. They didn't make it far as the Black Hawk peeled off and dropped towards the river as an Apache took its place and opened up with its chin mounted chain gun. Jackson smiled, watching the leading edge of infected dissolve as the explosive rounds hit in their midst. Pulling his attention back to the fleeing soldiers, he released the brakes when he saw the last man climb on.

Managing the controls, he advanced the throttle. Jackson didn't know what he was doing and was a bit intimidated by the complicated control panel, scanning the myriad gauges and warning lights. But, he figured that as long as he kept everything in the green, he was ok. Manipulating the throttle and the controls that fed the electricity generated by the diesels to the drive motors, he successfully kept everything working and soon the train was moving at twenty-five miles an hour. That was fast enough to prevent any infected from catching up and boarding, which was good as Jackson wasn't comfortable with pushing the speed any higher.

The bridge across the river was four miles long and it took nearly ten minutes to cross the span. On the Arkansas side, the infected were not nearly as numerous and had been held back by a

Black Hawk and Apache helicopter. Bodies were piled several feet high on the track, but the heavy train pushed them aside without so much as a shudder. They continued on into the flat countryside, rice paddies stretching out as far as the eye could see on either side of the tracks.

Jackson looked over his left shoulder, through the thick windows of the locomotive. Above the middle of the river, more than a mile downstream from the bridge, a pair of Black Hawks were slowly moving south, apparently still searching for the people in the water. They were too high to be conducting a rescue. Jackson had been raised in Mississippi, not too far down the river and he well knew the power of the water. Very few people had ever gone into the river and come out alive.

A rumble of explosions sounded over the heavy throb of the locomotive's diesel. Shifting his gaze to the large, external mirror, he watched as two Apaches fired multiple hellfire missiles into the mid-span of the bridge. The structure was no match for the warheads which cut through the steel with ease. Less than a minute after the bombardment began, nearly a mile of girders and tracks broke free and fell into the river below, preventing the hundreds of thousands of infected in Memphis from crossing to the west. Reaching to his neck, Jackson worked his fingers under his uniform to grasp the small, gold cross his mother had given him the day he enlisted in the Army. Saying a prayer, he rubbed the cross with his thick thumb, turning his attention back to the track in front after a heartfelt Amen.

2

"Oh, SHIT!" flashed through my head a half a second after I leapt off the train. The bottom of the bridge was sixty-five-feet above the surface of the Mississippi River, and with the height of the bridge deck and locomotive, I was going to fall at least eighty-five-feet before hitting the water. From that height, it was likely I could be seriously injured or killed if I impacted the water on my back or stomach. Rachel had gone in feet first. I hadn't seen how Dog impacted and didn't give a shit about Roach. Well, actually I hoped he did a face plant and the river finished him off.

I recalled from jump school, when I was learning to use a parachute, that there's something called terminal velocity. That is, when a falling object cannot fall any faster because of the resistance of the atmosphere as the object passes through it. Wind resistance, in other words. A human who is positioned horizontally will reach terminal velocity very quickly, in about the first forty or fifty feet of the fall, since there is a large area of the body creating drag. Falling feet or head first greatly decreases drag and you fall faster and take longer to reach terminal velocity. I couldn't remember the numbers, but knew I needed to go in feet first to have a decent chance of surviving.

The drop seemed to take forever. I had time to notice how the surface of the river appeared swollen. It roiled with eddies and looked like dirty, liquid steel. I tried to spot where Rachel and Dog had impacted, but the water wasn't giving up any clues. As I continued to fall, I clamped my ankles together as tightly as I could and pointed my toes down. A couple of moments before impact I raised my arms straight over my head so they wouldn't be yanked up when I hit and leave me with two dislocated shoulders. In the last moment before hitting, I squeezed my butt cheeks together as hard as possible. I've heard stories of water being forced up a jumper's anus upon impact, and while I didn't know if that's true, or even possible, I sure as hell didn't want to find out by getting a Mississippi River enema.

Hitting the water was far less dramatic than I expected. Perhaps my body position was exactly as it should have been, or maybe it's really not that bad from eighty-five-feet. Either way, I knifed through the surface and deep into cold darkness. Immediately upon entering the water, I twisted my body and spread my arms and legs to create drag and slow my decent. The river was shockingly cold. Much colder than I ever would have expected for the middle of summer. My body wanted to gasp in reaction to the sudden temperature change and I barely managed to stop myself from inhaling as I continued to sink.

The current was strong. I could feel it pulling me along and I quickly became disoriented as I tumbled into the water. Forcing myself to stay calm, I started swimming. I was heading for a lighter looking area, even though I had initially thought the surface was in the opposite direction. With enough light to see, I let a few air bubbles trickle out of my nose and was glad to see them rush in the direction I was already going. Lungs burning, I swam harder, suddenly breaking through the surface and gulping air.

Looking around, I had to dive and swim frantically to avoid a large log that was spinning in one of the surface eddies. Breaching the surface again, I swam to it and hooked an arm over its top, using its buoyancy to hold me up while I surveyed my situation. I was on the western side of the middle of the river and the current had already carried me a couple of hundred yards south of the bridge. That was about all I could see other than water. My head was only a foot or so above the surface and, while I could see land on either side of the river, I couldn't see the banks from that low in the water.

Holding on to the log, I let it spin me through a full three hundred and sixty degrees, hoping to see a head bobbing in the water. Nothing. I tried climbing up onto the log to gain elevation and a better view, but it had been in the river a while and was slippery with slime. I couldn't get a grip on it to pull myself any higher. Still spinning and watching, I started shouting Rachel's name, pausing to listen every few seconds. No answering shout. I didn't know what to do. I had jumped without thinking, panic and fear at seeing Rachel and Dog go into the water driving any reasoning out of my head.

My makeshift raft was still spinning slowly and as I faced to the north once again, I was surprised at how much farther downstream I was. Absently noting that the train had reversed and was heading back to the east, I forced myself to calm down and think through my options. Rachel and Dog had gone off the train about fifteen seconds, at the most, before I had jumped. That meant they were likely to my east as the train had been rolling west at the time. Was the current stronger or weaker where they'd entered the water? Were they ahead of me or behind me? I had no way of knowing.

I was preparing to abandon the log and strike out across the water to the east when a Black Hawk roared into a hover directly above me. I looked up and could see two heads leaning out of the side door, staring at me. One of them waved and I waved back with my free arm. Moments later, a weighted rope splashed into the water twenty feet downstream. Riding the log, I released just before coming abreast of the line and swam a few strokes before grabbing on. The rotor wash was fierce, churning up the water and blinding me, but this was an old drill and I soon had a foot firmly shoved into a loop and a death grip on the rope. I released my hold long enough to twirl a hand in the air, then grabbed tight as the pilot gained altitude and plucked me out of the river.

The Black Hawk headed straight to the western shore where I was deposited on a tall levee that separated the river from what looked like endless miles of rice paddies. Stepping away from the rope, I shielded my eyes as the helicopter descended to pick me up. It came to a hover a few feet off the ground, dirt and debris swirling around it and I dashed forward. Hands reached out the open side door and pulled me in as I scrambled up, the pilot spinning us around and gaining altitude over the river before my legs were all the way inside the aircraft. Captain Blanchard reached out and snapped a safety tether onto my vest before dragging me the rest of the way in where Colonel Crawford waited. One look at his face and I knew I was in for an ass chewing.

"Are you dumber than a fucking box of rocks, or do you just have a death wish?" He roared in my face, clearly audible over the noise of the helicopter even without benefit of headphones. "I've seen some fucked up shit in my day, but you take the goddamn cake! Twenty fucking helos flying around up here that can *actually fucking see* what's in the goddamn river, but like a dim-witted moron, you go and jump in the fucking water. I swear to God; you don't have the brains of the turd I flushed this morning. If I didn't need you, I'd bust your ass back to no-nuts Private and let you clean latrines for the Jar Heads!"

I looked back at him for a few moments, watching him breathe heavily as the anger boiled inside.

"Wow, sir. You sound just like my old Command Sergeant Major. He could chew ass and spit it out like no one I've ever met."

I grinned, calculating my response would defuse the situation and not prompt the Colonel to carry through with his threat. Oh well. I've been a Private before. There're worse things in the world. Captain Blanchard stared at me with his mouth hanging open in disbelief. Crawford clenched his jaw, his face going even redder for a moment before barking out a laugh and letting out a huge sigh.

"You are a pain in the ass, Major. A five star, big balled, tiny brained pain in my ass."

The Colonel turned away with a shake of his head to speak to the pilot. Blanchard sat there like he was at a tennis match, head moving back and forth as he looked from me to the Colonel. Dismissing the incident from my mind, I turned and stuck my head out of the door to look down at the river. We were now about a mile south of the bridge and moving slowly downstream no faster than the current was flowing.

To my east, I could see another Black Hawk matching our speed and direction. I was mildly surprised that Colonel Crawford was devoting two of his assets to search for one woman and one dog, but wasn't about to look the gift horse in the mouth. I looked to the north when a rumble of explosions reached me, watching as two Apaches fired missiles at the bridge. Moments later a huge section of the mid-span collapsed into the water with a massive splash.

Movement to the west caught my attention and I turned my head to look at a large flight of helicopters approaching, skimming the surface of the rice paddies. There were at least two dozen aircraft in the flight and I wondered why the Colonel had called in more air support. As the helos approached the river, they broke into three groups, two of which quickly gained altitude while the third appeared to be accelerating directly at the train which had just reached the western shore. They looked like they were on an attack run, which didn't make sense. You didn't make runs on the infected, you hovered and hosed them down.

Glancing around the interior of the Black Hawk, I spied a pair of tethered binoculars, scrambled across the deck to grab them and returned to the door. Focusing on the newly arriving helicopters, I was completely unprepared for what I saw. So unprepared that at first I didn't believe what I was seeing. Thinking I had to be mistaken, I shifted the glasses to an Apache to compare. I wasn't mistaken.

The design was similar, but these weren't Apaches. Lowering the binoculars, I reached out and grabbed Colonel Crawford, pulling him to the open door and shoving them into his hands. I pointed, and he looked, freezing when he saw the helos. The Apache pilots in the area had noticed the intruders and turned to meet them, several of them firing missiles as they raced forward.

"What's going on?" Captain Blanchard had moved to squat right behind me and was peering over my shoulder.

"The goddamn Russians are here," Crawford answered before I could say anything.

3

Russian President Alexie Barinov looked around the large conference room adjacent to his office in the Kremlin. The room was filled to capacity with senior politicians, Generals, Admirals and all of the associated aides that came with busy, powerful men. Barinov was not young, but his hair was still a thick mop of white that framed a broad, peasant face. He was short with a blocky build, the eight thousand dollar, custom-tailored Armani suit he wore managing to make him seem almost elegant. Glancing at the gold Rolex on his left wrist, he compared it to the *official* clock on the wall of the conference room, satisfied that his aide had properly synchronized them, down to the second.

Alexie had grown up in a poor village on the slopes of the Ural Mountains during the time of Soviet rule. He may have been born a peasant, but he had been blessed with a very high IQ and a canny mind. At only five years of age, he had watched as the KGB rolled into his tiny town to arrest a man who had complained about the government's seizure of the meager crops he had produced on a small plot of land. He had only been trying to feed his family. Rather than frightened or aghast, Alexie had been in awe of the men dressed all in black, driving a shiny black Volga sedan. He decided that day to become one of them when he was old enough.

Barinov joined the right youth groups, consistently impressing the group leaders with his vocal and rabid support of the Kremlin and all things Soviet. By his early teens, he had been noticed by the right people and plucked out of abject poverty to attend the Stalin School for Boys in Moscow. He soon became the school master's favorite, regularly informing on his classmates that exhibited anything less than absolute zeal for the Soviet way of life. Upon graduation, he received a glowing recommendation from the schoolmaster, who happened to be the brother-in-law of a Colonel in the KGB. Young Alexie realized his dream at the tender age of seventeen, taking the oath of loyalty to the most brutal intelligence agency the world had ever seen.

His rise in the ranks of the KGB was meteoric, joining the Communist Party and becoming a full Colonel by his thirty-fifth birthday. Alexie was on the cusp of becoming a Major General when the Soviet Union fell. Suddenly, the power he had wielded was so diminished it was as if it had never been. Not one to despair, he aligned himself with the criminals that quickly took all but political control of Russia in the absence of the heavy boots of the Soviet government. He grew enormously wealthy, cultivating friends and assassinating enemies in the shadows.

When Vladimir Putin came to power as Russia's strongest leader since Brezhnev, Barinov rode his coattails into the Kremlin. The hammer and the spear behind Putin, he was ruthless in silencing any dissent and quickly became the most feared man in Russia. Alexie blamed the Americans for ultimately causing the fall of his beloved Soviet Union, and had been plotting his revenge for decades. Unable to reconcile that the United States had won the Cold War, he approached his counterpart within the Chinese government with a plan to finally destroy America. Science had finally progressed to the point where he felt he could achieve his goal without risking the destruction of Russia by American nuclear weapons.

Diverting hundreds of millions of US dollars, the Chinese wouldn't accept Rubles, Alexie seduced highly placed men within the Chinese communist party to participate in his plot. Not only to develop the nerve agent/virus combination, but to execute the actual operation. To take the blame and the brunt of the American response. But for his plan to work, Barinov needed to have control of the Russian military. While even Generals trembled at the mention of his name, he couldn't order the armed forces to do anything. For that, he needed Presidential authority.

A year before the Chinese launched the attacks, Alexie found an opportunity to have a private, late night meeting with Putin. A vodka drinker in public, Putin preferred single malt whiskey in private. Barinov arrived for their meeting with a hundred-thousand-dollar bottle of Glenfiddich single malt whiskey in hand. The alcohol had already been laced with a lethal dose of polonium-210, a radioactive isotope that was undetectable by the Kremlin's radiation detectors as it gives off no gamma rays and the alpha rays emitted are so weak they couldn't pass through the heavy glass bottle that held the whiskey.

Alexie abstained from drinking during his meeting with Putin and three weeks later the Russian president died of a mysterious ailment. Alexie ensured there was no investigation into the cause of death. Within twenty-four hours of Putin's passing, Barinov seized control of the Russian government and installed himself as the new President. Within a week, he had removed all opposition through a series of assassinations and bribes. The last part of his plan was in motion.

"Comrade President, the missiles are within one minute of targets. Operation Red Hammer is on schedule."

Air Marshall Ludnikov, a staunch supporter of Barinov, spoke from the chair immediately to the President's right. Alexie looked up at the Chinese made OLED screen that covered an entire wall of the conference room. It was divided into five sections. The left half was a real-time satellite image of the United States, zoomed so that an area stretching from West Virginia to Colorado was in frame. The right half of the screen was spilt into four, equal parts. Each quarter was the view from the nose of an orbital launched, deep penetrator missile carrying an eighty-kiloton nuclear warhead.

Newly developed, each missile accelerated out of orbit, reaching near hyper-velocity speeds prior to impact. Tests had confirmed that the weapons were capable of penetrating over one hundred feet into Earth, or up to forty feet of hardened concrete. Everyone in the room was anxious to see the results of the fabulously expensive development effort that Barinov had started more than a decade ago.

Two targets within the continental US were digitally circled in red on the left-hand screen. Target 1 was a hardened bunker deep inside Mount Weather in the West Virginia Mountains. Well paid spies within the White House staff had confirmed that this was where the US President and the surviving members of Congress had fled. Target 2 was Cheyenne Mountain in the Rocky Mountain range in Colorado, where the Vice President and military leadership from the Pentagon had taken refuge after the Chinese attacks.

In each of the quarter screens that showed the view from the missiles, a small digital timer blinked in the corner, counting down time to impact. The two upper screens read 00:00:10, ten seconds, the two lower screens exactly one minute behind. Alexie kept his eyes on the upper screens, shifting to the real time satellite view when each of the missile's video feeds blanked out and their timers reached zero.

On the larger screen, there were brilliant flashes, but from within the red circles identifying the targets, huge plumes of dust billowed into the atmosphere as the warheads detonated well below the surface. Millions of tons of pulverized rock, steel, and hardened concrete blasted into the atmosphere, creating a two-hundred-foot deep crater for the follow-on missile to strike.

Mount Weather and Cheyenne Mountain had both been constructed at the height of the Cold War, but when they were built neither the US nor the Soviet Union possessed the technology to build penetrator missiles. The two bunkers were intended to provide a survivable environment that could withstand a direct surface strike from a Soviet ICBM. Not a subterranean detonation within the protective rock that surrounded them. Mount Weather was breached and completely destroyed by the first penetrator. The second missile, when it arrived, wasn't needed.

Cheyenne Mountain, carved out of solid rock, fared better from the first strike. Electricity was knocked out and numerous cave-ins killed dozens of personnel, but the hard, Colorado granite held. Until the second penetrator arrived. The stone that had withstood the first missile had cracked from the unimaginable force of the nuclear explosion. The second penetrator dove into the crater created by the first, impacting the fractured rock and burrowing deep into the mountain before detonating. Every living thing within the bunker ceased to exist less than half a second after detonation.

A cheer sounded in the conference room as more plumes of dust obscured the satellite view of the two targets. There were no iconic mushroom clouds since the detonations were below ground, but even on the monitor it was obvious that dust and debris were being thrown all the way into the upper atmosphere.

"Congratulations, Comrade President!" Air Marshall Kuchenko said from across the table, standing to address Barinov. "With your permission, I will have the technicians adjust our view so we can watch the next phase."

Barinov nodded and Kuchenko turned and barked orders to three Russian Air Force Captains seated at a side table laden with computers. A moment later the giant screen blinked, then displayed a single image. They were looking directly down onto Canada and the northern United States, the extreme upper edge of the display showing the polar ice cap.

Flying in formation over Canada, nearly into US airspace, were twelve-hundred Sukhoi and Mig fighters, two hundred aerial tankers for refueling, and nearly two hundred transport planes. Looking like toys on the display, everyone in the room knew that the cargo planes were the massive Antonov AN-124 aircraft, loaded with troops, helicopters, and supplies for the invading army. In 2001, Barinov had acquired the Antonov aircraft manufacturing enterprise and had been building the massive planes, capable of lifting nearly a quarter more weight than the venerable American C-5A Galaxy, preparing for this day. Every man in the invasion, as well as three-quarters of the Russian population, had been vaccinated against the virus that had been unleashed on the Americans. He smiled as he watched his planes enter American territory, unopposed.

4

Two of the Russian Mi-28 Havoc strike helicopters exploded in mid-air, along with one of the Apaches, before our pilot reacted. A Havoc was coming down the river, straight for us, and he spun us into a nose dive for the water, flaring and jinking to the left at the last second. A missile streaked by close enough that it seemed I could touch it, then we were gaining altitude and turning so fast I was pinned at the end of my safety tether. A moment later a hellfire missile leapt off the right pylon with a roar, tracked the Havoc for a couple of seconds and detonated as it impacted the Russian's tail rotor. The back half of the helo sheared off, the remainder of the aircraft spinning out of control and crashing into the Mississippi River.

The pilot continued to fly an evasive pattern and I crawled my way to the door mounted minigun and started trying to strap in. Blanchard saw what I was doing and made his way across the tilted deck to help. Finally secured in place, I grabbed the headphones Crawford held out to me and slapped them on my head.

"Come on you fucking bastard, hold still for Daddy!"

I heard the pilot's voice over the intercom a moment before another missile roared off its pylon, destroying a Havoc that was pursuing a Black Hawk. Unfortunately, the Russian had launched at the same time we had, the Black Hawk exploding into a ball of fire a heartbeat before the Havoc died.

We headed north, following the river, directly towards the main air battle that had quickly developed. I wasn't able to count aircraft, but it looked at first blush like the Russians were getting the worst of it. Roaring under the bridge, we cut speed and suddenly popped straight up a couple of hundred feet, two more missiles streaking away and finding their targets. Another Black Hawk and an Apache exploded, and both fell burning into the tightly packed mass of infected at the eastern entrance to the bridge.

Tearing my eyes away from the dogfight, I looked for the train. After a moment, I spotted it still rolling west. Whoever was driving, Jackson I presumed, had the diesels at full throttle. Thick, black smoke belched from each of the locomotives and the train appeared to be rapidly gaining speed as it fled the battle. Two Havocs peeled away from the fight after dropping another Apache into the river, pursuing the speeding train.

"Two hostiles going after the train," I shouted into the intercom.

Immediately the pilot threw us into a stomach clenching turn and we accelerated to fall in above and behind the Russians. Ahead I could see the lead Havoc launch a pair of missiles. I followed their smoke trail with my eyes, holding my breath as they closed on the back of the train. The first missile struck the tracks just behind the rear car.

The explosion shredded the metal sides of the car and lifted the rear of it into the air. The second missile arrived, slamming into the undercarriage. Bodies, body parts, and metal shards flew in every direction as it disintegrated.

Four missiles sped away from the Black Hawk, two for each Havoc. The Russian closest to us reacted almost instantly, pulling up and to the right while deploying magnesium flares in an attempt to decoy the missiles away. As he tried to evade the attack he kept pulling through his turn, speed bleeding off, and lined up beautifully with the Black Hawk's open side door. I had a perfect sight picture on him and squeezed the trigger on the door mounted minigun and held it down.

My aim wasn't as perfect as I thought, red tracers flying underneath the desperately maneuvering helo, but I kept firing and adjusted until I pumped a couple of hundred slugs into the helicopter. Engine knocked out and black smoke billowing, he started falling and I turned my attention back to the train just as the other two missiles impacted the lead Havoc and blew it out of the sky.

Dodging around the plume of smoke from the destroyed helicopter, we caught up with the train. All that remained of the rear car was a few feet of the steel frame at the front, still on its wheels and coupled to the next car. I wondered how many people that Russian pilot had just killed, but put the thought out of my head as we spun around and headed back east. I leaned forward as far as possible, trying to see ahead of us, but I couldn't get a view of the battle we'd left behind to save the train. Tilting my head back, I hoped for a view out the windscreen, but couldn't see around Colonel Crawford whose broad back completely blocked the narrow access into the cockpit.

I wanted to ask what was going on, but since I didn't need that information at the moment I decided to stay off the intercom and not distract the pilots. Instead, I busied myself with checking over the minigun to make sure it would be ready when needed. Satisfied with its status, I leaned forward and scanned all of the sky that I could see.

No other aircraft were visible, ours or Russian. Our direction and speed changed a few moments later and I found myself looking down at the Havoc I had shot up. The helicopter was sitting in a rice paddy at a severe tilt, rotor slowly turning and black smoke billowing from the destroyed engine. I knew helicopters that lost power could uncouple their rotor from the engine and let the air flow of their fall spin the rotor and slow them down so they would have a relatively soft landing. This is called auto-rotation, and my best guess was the Russian pilot had pulled it off.

Three Russians stood in knee deep water a hundred feet from their downed aircraft, heads tilted up watching us as we orbited the crash site. I tracked them with the minigun, hand on the trigger, ready to reduce them to pulp if they did anything I didn't like.

"Hold fire." I heard Crawford's voice over the headset. "We're going to have a chat with our visitors."

We orbited two more times, then stabilized into a hover with the side of the Black Hawk with the minigun towards them. I held them in my sights as we landed fifty yards away, the pilot keeping the rotor spinning at full speed.

"Major, you and the Captain switch places and let's go greet the Russians," Crawford ordered.

Blanchard stepped up and quickly unstrapped me. When I could move freely, I vacated the door gunner's spot and the Captain quickly slipped in and gripped the minigun. I strapped him into place and looked around for the

Colonel. He was standing behind me, holding out an M4 rifle. Grabbing it, I pulled the sling over my head and dropped the magazine to check the load. Satisfied, I slapped it back into place, made sure a round was chambered and set the selector to burst mode. A quick pat-check of my vest to make sure I still had spare magazines on my body and I was ready to go.

Moving to the edge of the cabin, I jumped to the ground, splashing into two feet of water and stepping forward to make room for Crawford. Rifle up and sighted on the three Russians, I heard the Colonel splash to the ground. He stepped next to me and raised his rifle. We started wading towards the waiting men.

"How did we fare?" I asked as we walked, referring to the air battle.

"All the Russians are down. We lost eleven aircraft."

As he spoke an Apache roared into a hover a hundred yards to the left of the enemy soldiers, chain gun trained on their position.

Moving across the flooded rice paddy wasn't easy. Footing was slippery, and the uneven ground beneath the water kept us from moving very fast. Treading carefully, we crossed the open space, spreading apart as we approached the men and finally stopping a dozen feet from where they stood waiting. My rifle was up and trained on the senior man present, a Captain if my memory of Russian insignia and rank was correct.

He stood holding his left arm tight across his body, the limb obviously broken. He bled from numerous cuts on his face. The other two were a Sergeant of some rank and an enlisted man that I guessed was the equivalent of a Corporal or Specialist in our Army. Each of them was banged up and bloody, but neither seemed to have any broken bones.

"Do you speak English?" Crawford addressed the officer. He glared back for a moment before nodding his head. "Good. Then you'll understand this. I'm Colonel Jack Crawford of the United States Army, and you are my prisoner. Any resistance or failure to immediately cooperate and I'll put a bullet in your head. I don't give a fuck about the Geneva Convention. Do you understand?"

The Russian's eyes shifted from Crawford to me, looking down the barrel of my rifle which was solidly trained on his face. He glanced up at the hovering Apache before turning his attention back to the Colonel.

"Da. I understand." He spoke in surprisingly good English.

5

Captain Lee Roach struck the surface of the Mississippi at a bad angle, getting the wind knocked out of him. He plunged deep but didn't try to swim or reach the air. The shock of first the impact, then the cold of the water had stunned him, slowing his racing mind. Water that was at first cold was now comforting, and for a moment Roach didn't care if he lived or not. But, like any predator, he was first and foremost a survivor and eventually started stroking towards the light. Breaching the surface, he looked around for the bitch but didn't see her or the damn dog anywhere. Just steel grey water in every direction.

The current was strong, the river swollen from the storms upstream, and he was swiftly carried south. Something bumped hard into his back and turning his head he saw a wooden shipping pallet, floating low in the water. Grabbing on, he was able to pull his upper body onto the pallet, grasping each edge and shifting until he was balanced. The wood sank a few inches deeper into the river, then its buoyancy overcame the added weight of Roach's body and he rested as the mighty river swept him along.

It wasn't long before the sound of high explosive ordnance reached his ears. Using his legs as a rudder, he was able to steer the pallet into a spin in time to see the mid-span of the bridge collapse into the river. Relieved to have escaped, but frustrated that he hadn't had time to play with the bitch, Roach relaxed and watched the shoreline slip by. He guessed the river was moving him at four or five miles an hour and decided to stay in the water no more than an hour. He wanted to get away from the Major, but not too far.

It wasn't long before he heard a helicopter approaching, but there was nothing he could do, caught in the current in the middle of the river. But the helicopter never came as far downstream as he was floating. Spinning the pallet, he watched it hovering, a long rope dangling into the water. After a moment the aircraft rose and headed for the western shore, a figure clinging to the end of the line. Was it the bitch? Had she survived the fall? He couldn't tell, then the pallet spun again and he lost sight of the rescue.

He entered a sharp bend and started paddling and kicking frantically as the current took him within a dozen yards of the eastern shore which was lined with a wall of infected. Coming out of the curve, the river immediately bent again, the current sweeping him close to the western shore. This time, he paddled and kicked, aiming for a sandbar that stuck out into the water.

When he realized he couldn't free the pallet from the force of the water, he slipped off and swam as hard as he could, angling for the sand. He had a bad couple of moments when it looked like he was going to be swept past his goal, but suddenly he was out of the pull of the current and able to swim the final few yards.

Crawling onto the dry sand, he collapsed face down and rested. Catching his breath, he lifted his head at the sounds of an aerial battle to the north. Who the hell was fighting? Roach was curious, but not too curious, standing up and running across the sand to the shoreline where he disappeared into a narrow strip of trees growing along the edge of the river. Pausing, he checked himself over, dismayed to find he had lost every weapon other than a small, four-inch folding pocket knife tucked into a pouch on the vest he still wore.

Roach pushed through the trees and came up against the slope of a tall levee. He crawled up it, cautiously poking his head above the edge to look around. To the south a few hundred yards, sunlight glinted off the windshield of a vehicle. It was too far away to make out details, but it was sitting on the gravel roadway that ran along the top of the levee, and Roach needed transportation. He knew his limitations, and walking across open country, living off what he found and fighting the infected with a four-inch pocket knife was not something he even imagined he was capable of doing.

Following the river south, he walked along the lowest edge of the levee to stay hidden from any of the vehicle's occupants. When he thought he'd covered enough distance, he slowly crawled to the top and looked around. His estimation had been good and he was pleased to find that he had walked past the vehicle's position by only ten yards. As he hid in the weeds and surveyed the area, he detected a faint electronic beeping sound. Carefully he looked all around, but couldn't identify the source of the noise.

Ignoring the sound for the moment, Roach concentrated on the vehicle. It was a fairly new, four-wheel-drive Ford pickup, painted white with an orange lensed light bar on top. A large spotlight penetrated the roof in front of the light bar, two smaller ones sticking out from the pillars on either side of the windshield. The truck was facing north, the passenger side towards Roach, and in big, red letters on the door closest to him he read "St. Francis Levee District – Official Use Only."

When Roach saw the lettering, he smiled. No one was going to be checking on the levees after everything that had happened. What was the point? Even if they found a major problem, there wasn't anyone left to fix it. This truck had to have been abandoned, or maybe the driver got infected and wandered off. Regardless, his usual good luck was back. He'd just found the transportation he needed to survive.

Climbing to his feet, he fished out the folding knife, flicked it open and carefully walked to the truck. As he approached, the beeping sound grew louder, the source becoming apparent when he was close enough to see the driver's door standing open. Smiling again, he trotted the rest of the way, hopped into the cab and closed the door, silencing the alert tone for keys having been left in the ignition. Roach twisted the key and the truck's engine rumbled to life. A quick scan of the dash showed he had a nearly full tank of gas. Now. Where to go?

The road on top of the levee was narrower than the truck was long, so there was no way to turn around and go back. That meant there was either a turn-around on ahead, or a way off the levee. Shifting into drive, Roach accelerated down the gravel road, keeping his speed low to prevent creating a dust plume that could be seen for miles in the flat terrain. As he drove, Roach kept an eye on the river below, hoping to spot the bitch. If she was in the water, he didn't know how he'd get to her, but he still wanted to feel her squirm under his hands as he violated her in every way imaginable.

6

Rachel came out of unconsciousness with a start. Face down in mud. She was cold, shivering, her body screaming in protest when she tried to roll over. Her head pounded and every inch of her ached, making her catch her breath and stop trying to move. Slowly, she gently started moving different parts, just a couple of inches, testing for injury. When everything seemed to move ok, even though it hurt to even wiggle a finger, she steeled herself for the pain and rolled onto her back. She wanted to cry out, but bit down on her lip and stayed silent. With no idea if there were infected close by, she wasn't about to announce her presence.

Lying there, Rachel managed to get her breathing under control and looked up at the night sky. Night? It had been early morning the last thing she could remember. What *was* the last thing she remembered? The train derailing. Fighting through the infected as they ran for the bridge. The terrifying helicopter flight back to get the train. Driving the train to the bridge, then being attacked by Roach. Roach!

Rachel involuntarily sat up in fear, stifling a groan of pain as she wrapped her arms around her bruised body. Dealing with the pain, she looked around frantically, terrified that she would see

Roach standing there with a smile and a knife. Not seeing any immediate threats, she climbed onto her knees and slowly raised her head up to survey her surroundings.

She was kneeling on a narrow strip of mud, the waters of the Mississippi lapping against the bank only inches from her feet. The shoreline was on the outside edge of a sharp bend in the river and Rachel could only assume the current had washed her onto the bank. But where was she? How far downstream had the river taken her before mercifully depositing her in the mud? And which side of the river was she on?

The sun wasn't up to tell her east from west, but as Rachel sat there shivering, she realized all she had to do was look at the river. As she faced it, it flowed from her left to right, which put her on the western bank. Thank God for that small mercy! She didn't know how many infected were on the west side of the river, but she sure knew how many were to the east.

Dog! Where was Dog? His rescue of Rachel from Roach's knife was what had knocked all of them off the train and into the water below. Where the hell was he? And why hadn't John found her? Rachel felt herself slipping into despair and mentally chastised herself. She didn't have time to feel sorry for herself or worry about why something hadn't happened. Even if they weren't right on top of her, there were likely infected in the area and she needed to start thinking and acting before she became a late night snack.

Checking her holster, she breathed a sigh of relief to find the pistol still firmly secured to her body. She had learned a few things from living with John for the past few weeks and drew the weapon to make sure it hadn't become fouled or blocked by mud and debris. Satisfied with the results, she ran her hands over her body and found three of the five spare pistol magazines were still with her.

She carefully checked each of these, first unloading then reloading the magazines to ensure they were operating properly. Her knife was gone. Rifle was still in the locomotive's cab, and she had no idea where her pack was. She had no food, no water, nothing other than the clothes on her back and a pistol with sixty-four rounds of ammunition. Reminding herself that she wasn't very good with a handgun, Rachel decided she would use it only as a last resort. Besides her lack of skill, it was loud and would draw more infected to her, so it was for emergencies only.

Finger combing the wet and muddy hair out of her face, Rachel stood, stifling a groan. She felt like she'd been beaten with a baseball bat. In a way, she imagined that was a good analogy. She had already been banged up when she fought with

Roach, then the fall to the river and who knew how many new bumps and bruises as the water had carried her downstream. She wished she knew how long she'd been on the bank so she could have an idea how far south from the bridge she was.

Rachel tried to remember what she had heard about the Mississippi River over the years, finally settling on a vague memory that the current ran at about three miles an hour on average. But it was swollen from the heavy rains and moving much faster than that. If she had gone into the water in the early morning, more than twelve hours ago, she could have been carried anywhere from a couple of miles to nearly fifty. It all depended on how long she'd been unconscious, and she had no way of knowing.

Looking around now that she was standing, Rachel could only see a few yards in the darkness. The moon was up but it was new, so there was very little light. To her west, she could see a tall levee looming in the darkness. It appeared to be straight, following a direct north-south path as it paralleled the river. Stumbling forward through the mud and thick vegetation, Rachel made her way to the base of the tall mound of earth and started climbing the gentle incline. Quickly reaching the top, she was surprised to find herself standing on a gravel roadway that stretched in each direction for as far as she could see. It was hard to tell in the dark, but in front of her the land stretched away to the west, appearing as flat and featureless as a billiard table.

Drawing on lessons learned from watching John, Rachel closed her eyes after making sure there were no infected anywhere within her limited sight range. Breathing quietly, she listened to the environment around her. She could hear the river making a shushing sound as it flowed over and against its banks. What was surely thousands of frogs sang, nearly masking all other sounds, but she could also hear the occasional night bird. The buzzing of mosquitoes and stealthy rustlings of small animals in the grass were the only other sounds. Absolutely no man-made noises. Rachel imagined this must have been what it was like to stand here a few hundred years ago, before the first European settlers reached this part of America.

What to do? Follow the gravel road on the levee to the north until she reached the train tracks? Then what? The chances that John or Dog was waiting for her at the bridge were so slim as to be nearly non-existent. Heading south didn't seem like a good idea. There were supposed to be large herds of infected in all the gulf coast states and Rachel sure didn't want to go find out. West, cross country? But how was she going to find John?

Rachel wasn't ready to contemplate thoughts that she might never be reunited with him. The last few weeks, her time with John, fleeing and fighting the infected, felt like a lifetime. She had fallen in love with him. There was no use in denying that any longer. But now he was gone. Would he be trying to find her? How did he even start looking? It was hard enough to survive in the new world, let alone search for one lost woman. Starting to slip back into despair, Rachel struggled to calm her racing mind. Then it hit her.

Oklahoma City! That's where the train was headed. If he couldn't find her, that's where John would go! How far was it? Rachel had never been west of the Mississippi before and had only a vague idea of the geography of the western US. Could she make it? Straightening her back with a grimace, she made her decision, crossed the gravel road and descended the steeper side of the levee to the rice paddy below.

7

The sun was setting, sporadic rifle fire in the distance reaching my ears as soldiers and the surviving civilian population mopped up the remaining infected in the immediate area. We were in West Memphis, Arkansas, a few miles west of the Mississippi River. Actually, we were a few miles west of West Memphis, occupying the public airport just south of US 70. Two Apaches were on station a hundred miles farther to the west, acting as an early warning if any more Russian aircraft headed our direction. Eight Black Hawks and half a dozen Apaches sat on the tarmac, refueled, rearmed and ready to go. But go where?

Two fat C-130s sat at the far end of one of the pair of runways, empty after having disgorged their cargo of soldiers, missiles, ammunition and maintenance crews for the helicopters. Both aircraft had been on stand-by at Little Rock Air Force Base, waiting for Colonel Crawford's call. When they arrived, the first one on the ground had delivered a hundred Army Rangers in full battle rattle. They cleared all the airport's grounds and buildings before spreading into the adjacent town where they linked up with the remnants of civilian law enforcement to finish the job. The second one was heavily loaded with all the ordnance needed to completely re-arm the helicopters, resupply all the ground troops with ammunition and give everyone a hot meal courtesy of the mess hall at LRAFB.

The train Jackson had driven across the river sat on a siding a quarter of a mile from the airport, guarded by a couple of dozen Rangers. The evacuees had been allowed to disembark, but the Lieutenant in charge at the siding had orders to keep all of them within a hundred yards of the train in case we needed to get them moving in a hurry. They were eating the same chow as the rest of us and sat in subdued groups as the light faded.

Crawford, Captain Blanchard, Jackson and myself had commandeered the small air traffic control tower. We sat around a folding table, eating. The tower provided a commanding view of not only the entire airport, but miles in every direction. The terrain here along the flood plain of the river was almost perfectly flat. Earlier, I'd taken a pair of large binoculars from the controller's workstation and looked to the east, across the river. Hundreds of thousands of infected lined the shore, all staring directly into the setting sun.

This was our first opportunity to have a meeting. Jackson and I had spent much of the day in the field with the Rangers, rooting out and killing infected. I was hungry, tired, and nearly obsessed with worry about Rachel and Dog.

"Hell of a day," Crawford commented, tearing into a large piece of fried chicken. "Let's all get on the same page. Captain, you've been running SAR flights all day and getting our remaining train ready to roll. What's our status?"

Blanchard placed his fork down next to his plate, finished chewing, drank some water and wiped his mouth with a paper napkin before he started talking. Jackson and I kept right on eating, devouring the food on our plates like starving dogs.

"Sir, we've had multiple search and rescue operations underway all day. First mission was to look for survivors from the battle with the Russians. I'm sorry to report that the only survivors on either side were the three men you captured. Next, we ran two operations. The first operation was a Black Hawk detailed to search the river for the woman and dog." Blanchard turned to me before continuing. "We have searched for fifty miles downstream from the bridge, two passes over the water and one pass each on the two shorelines. So far we have had negative results and I'm not optimistic we will find them."

I started to open my mouth, but Crawford beat me to it.

"Put up another Black Hawk now that the sun is down. Maybe we'll get lucky with FLIR."

I nodded my thanks to the Colonel and went back to my food. I had lost my appetite but forced myself to eat. Food is fuel, and without it the body will suffer. I needed to be in as good condition as possible.

"Yes, sir."

Blanchard made a quick note in a small, spiral notebook before continuing.

"The second train out of Nashville was our large SAR operation. When the air units arrived, the train was almost completely overrun by infected, but there was one livestock car that had been able to keep them out. Using air assets, we were able to clear enough of the infected away from the car to start lifting people. Some were lost, but we did manage to rescue..." he paused to flip through his notebook. "We rescued four hundred and eleven, mostly women and children. They are now with the other evacuees at the first train."

"Four eleven? That's it? There were nearly ten thousand people on that train when it pulled out of Nashville!" Crawford didn't try to conceal the pain in his voice.

"Yes, sir. That was all we could save," Blanchard answered in a quiet voice.

He looked down at his plate of cooling food as he spoke. We all sat there in silence for a couple of minutes, each of us lost in our own thoughts as we processed the number of people that the infected had ripped apart.

"Moving on to the train, with your permission sir?"

Blanchard waited, Crawford finally nodding before taking another bite. The look on his face told me he was only eating because he needed to. None of us were enjoying the meal.

"We have found a retired railroad engineer in Little Rock that is being flown to us. We have also found plenty of passenger and livestock cars on a siding ten miles to the west. When the engineer arrives, Lieutenant Anker will assist him in getting the extra cars coupled to the train so our evacuees aren't having to sit on top of each other. This should take a couple of hours, so before midnight we'll be ready to load and depart on your order. That's all I have, sir."

Crawford nodded and looked first at me, then Jackson to see if we had any questions.

"Can I tag along on the Black Hawk you're sending out to keep looking for Rachel?" I asked, but Crawford was already shaking his head before Blanchard could respond.

"Negative, Major. We've got some Russians downstairs that I want you to have a chat with."

"Me?" I had forgotten he'd read my file.

"Yes. You were trained in enhanced interrogation techniques and I know you've successfully put that training to use. Several times."

"Yes, sir. I have, but that was a long time ago. Surely there's someone with more current training. Better techniques."

I've never liked being the interrogator. It's a brutal, soul sucking job, and you come away from it feeling like you need a shower, no matter how many times you bathe. There are times it is absolutely a necessity, but if I had my choice I'd rather leave it to the guys that actually like doing it.

"Nice try. You're the man. You don't have to like it. You just have to do it. I want to know everything those goddamn Commies know. The two enlisted won't know shit and the Captain may not know much, but he'll know *something*. I've lost all contact with command since before we reached Memphis, and I've got a really bad feeling. Right now, as far as I can determine, I'm the ranking officer out of the entire US military."

I'd been so busy and pre-occupied with worry over Rachel and Dog that I hadn't realized Crawford was working without a parachute. All of command was gone? That most likely meant Mt. Weather in West Virginia and Cheyenne Mountain in Colorado had been compromised. How the hell had that happened?

My first thought was an outbreak, but dismissed that as too unlikely. Both facilities experience another outbreak that is severe enough to knock them completely out, and it happens at the same time? Very doubtful. That left the Russians. But how?

Both bunkers were designed to withstand a nuclear bomb going off on the ground, right above their heads. How the hell could the Russians have penetrated not just one, but both of them? The one thing I knew for sure was the Russian Captain wouldn't have that information. He was way too far down the chain of command. But he might have information about what the Russians were planning, where they were staging, and how many of them there were.

"Yes, sir. I'll take care of it." I said, suppressing a sigh.

"Unless there's anything else, we all have work to do." Crawford looked around the table, but no one spoke up. "Very well. Thank you. Dismissed."

We all stood, collected the detritus from our hasty meal and headed down the spiral, metal staircase. A large, plastic barrel sat outside the control tower door, top cut off so it could do duty as a makeshift trash can. We deposited our garbage and paused in the evening air. A gentle breeze was blowing, blessedly cutting the oppressive humidity of the day. Overhead, stars were twinkling brightly as the sky continued to darken, a thin sliver of a moon providing just enough light for me to see the faces of the men standing next to me.

"Captain, no matter what time it is, please come find me with any news from the search."

"Yes, sir. I will. Now, please excuse me. I need to get that bird in the air."

I nodded and pulled out a pack of cigarettes as he walked away. I'd come across a looted convenience store earlier in the day while clearing infected out of the town. The owner was trying to clean up and I'd struck a bargain with him. I traded the little .380 pocket pistol I had taken off the fake cop I'd killed in Nashville for two cartons of cigarettes and a couple of disposable lighters.

Knowing Crawford was a smoker too, I'd given him one of the cartons. He knew me well enough by now to understand I wasn't sucking up or trying to kiss his ass, just being thoughtful. Now, as Jackson and I strolled out onto the tarmac, I lit a smoke and looked up at the glass-enclosed tower. It was dark inside, but I could see the red, glowing tip of a cancer stick as Crawford inhaled.

"Want some company with the interrogation?" Jackson asked as we walked in the dark.

"I want some sadistic little fucker from the CIA to do this, not me. That's what I want."

"Yeah, never had much of a stomach for it either," Jackson replied. "But we need that information, and we need it fast."

"I think I already know that Master Sergeant," I said much sharper than I intended. "Sorry. It's been a bitch of a few weeks."

"No need to apologize, sir."

We strolled in silence for a few more minutes, winding up at the guarded door into the small office building at the base of the control tower. The three Russians were inside, separated into different offices and each had his own guard assigned. They hadn't been allowed to talk to each other since their capture.

All had received medical attention for their injuries and been given water, but they hadn't been fed. They were probably pretty scared by now. I know if I had been captured on Russian soil, I'd be shitting my pants at the moment. The guard opened the door for us and after crushing the cigarette out under my boot, I led the way inside.

8

Rachel had been walking for an hour but hadn't covered more than a couple of miles. The flooded rice paddies made the going very slow, and while she had crossed some dikes that divided them, they had all run north and south. Suspecting there were also dikes running east to west, she changed direction and started walking north. If she didn't find one within half a mile, which was about how often she had been crossing them, she'd turn back west again.

About fifteen minutes later, Rachel breathed a sigh of relief when she spotted the ten-foot tall berm of dark soil that made up a dike. Splashing through the last of the paddy, she gratefully climbed out of the water. The top was flat, hard packed earth, wide enough for a vehicle, and she imagined farm hands driving along them to check on the crops.

Rachel paused to catch her breath and waved her arms around her head, wishing for mosquito repellant. There was a cloud of the damn little pests swirling around her, feeding on every inch of exposed skin. She already itched from the hundreds of bites she had received and worried briefly about West Nile Virus. With a start, she wondered if the genetically engineered virus the Chinese had released could be transmitted by mosquitoes. There was no doubt they were feasting on the infected.

The only thing Rachel could think to do was to cover her exposed skin. Skidding back down to the water below, she bent and scooped up handfuls of black mud and spread it on her arms, face, and neck. Soon she had a thick coating on her skin and, while the insects continued to swarm, drawn by the carbon dioxide in her breath, they couldn't find skin to bite.

Back on top of the dike, Rachel took a moment to survey her surroundings from the elevated perspective. First, she looked for any sign that infected or survivors were in the area and tracking her. There was a small amount of moonlight and in every direction she looked it reflected off the perfectly calm water that flooded the paddies. Raising her eyes, she looked at the horizon. In nearly every direction, it was completely dark. To the north, she could just make out a faint glow that had to be electric lights. The quality of the light was too steady and too close to the white end of the spectrum to be a fire.

Rachel was debating the wisdom of approaching other survivors when the sound of a helicopter reached her ears. Turning quickly towards the sound, which seemed to be coming from the river, she peered intently into the darkness. Where was it? She couldn't see it, but she could hear a heavy rotor beating the thick, humid air. Black Hawk, she thought, having spent enough time around helicopters in the past couple of weeks to be able to accurately identify them by sound alone.

Black Hawk meant Army, and that meant John was looking for her. Her heart leapt in her chest, both at the prospect of rescue and the fact that John hadn't given up on her. Hadn't abandoned her. Even though the river and helicopter were two miles away, and the aircraft was apparently operating without showing any lights, Rachel turned to the east and started to run in the direction of the sound.

She had only covered a short distance before skidding to a stop. A couple of hundred yards east of her position, the surface of the water in the flooded paddy was no longer glassy smooth and reflecting the moonlight. Looking carefully, she could just make out a dozen figures stumbling in her direction. They had to be males since they were moving so slowly, but at a point between her and the approaching infected she could see water being violently displaced as something moved through it at a much faster pace. A female, and she was coming fast!

Abandoning hope of reaching the river and being spotted by the helicopter, Rachel turned back to the west and started running. She knew she had improved dramatically with a rifle and could probably have held her ground against a single female and a dozen males, but all she had was a pistol. She knew how to use it, but hadn't fired at anything more than ten feet away and had no illusions about being able to fight with it. If they cornered her and were close, she would use it, but shooting at anything at much more than arm's length would be a waste of ammunition.

Rachel ran hard, boots pounding on the dirt. She'd never been a runner, preferring to get her exercise from dancing and yoga, but since the attacks she'd had no choice. Running was survival now, not something to just burn calories after indulging in too much chocolate or a few extra fries. In good condition to start with, she'd grown stronger and faster and now she pushed herself to quickly gain some separation from the pursuing infected.

She had no doubt she could easily outdistance the males, but was worried about the female. The adrenaline-fueled and rage-enhanced females could run at a full sprint for long distances. They never seemed to tire, though Rachel knew they had to. No matter what the nerve agent and accompanying virus did to them, they were still limited by basic, human biology, and the human body would eventually tire. Unfortunately, she would tire well before the infected without benefit of what seemed to be a nearly limitless supply of adrenalin.

Having covered close to half a mile, Rachel slowed to a fast walk and looked over her shoulder. In the darkness, at the limit of her vision, she saw a human silhouette climb onto the top of the dike and start sprinting in her direction. Guessing the female was now a quarter of a mile behind her, Rachel faced front again and ran. She knew she couldn't outdistance the female, would have to turn and fight, but the more ground she covered before that moment, the farther away she was from the males.

As she ran, Rachel remembered one of the lessons John had tried to teach her. One of the many that she'd listened to, but not really focused on what he'd been trying to convey. At the time, she hadn't contemplated being on her own and having to fight. It had seemed like he'd always be there to protect her.

He had been talking about shooting under stress and how your aim and control was affected by a pounding heart. Not remembering everything he'd said, but understanding the concept, Rachel slid to a stop and turned to face the female. Breathing deeply, she focused on calming her body as she drew the pistol and made sure a round was in the chamber and the safety was off.

With her feet shoulder width apart, Rachel held the weapon in her right hand, relaxed, and watched the female approach. When the infected closed to within fifty yards, she screamed. Rachel's blood ran cold when there was an answering scream from the rice paddy to her left.

Snapping her head in that direction, she saw another female fighting through knee deep water, not more than twenty-five yards from the base of the dike. Smart infected? Smart or not, they had hunted her, flanked her, and she was about to have two of them arrive at the same time.

Raising the pistol into a two handed grip, Rachel aimed at the female sprinting along the top of the dike and fired her first shot. The infected was still about thirty yards away when the round punched into her stomach. She slowed for one step, then kept on coming. Not daring to risk a glance at the female in the water, Rachel maintained her stance. She began squeezing the trigger every second, slow and steady, just like John had shown her. Her second shot missed, but the third and fourth struck the female in the chest. She staggered, slowed, but kept on coming.

Sweating under the mud, skin crawling with fear, Rachel held her ground and fired two more rounds. The first one tore through her attacker's shoulder, the arm flopping uselessly at her side. The second round ripped her heart in half and the infected's body crashed to the ground close enough for Rachel to stick her foot out and touch. Swiveling to her left, ready to fire, she had to twist her body out of the way as the second female leapt at her.

Rachel made her miss the tackle, but the infected reached out as she flashed past, grasping for any purchase on her prey. The female managed to grip Rachel's right wrist for a moment, then her hand slipped down Rachel's and seized the pistol, yanking it free and sending it skidding across the dirt. Off balance, Rachel fell to the ground and scrambled forward on hands and knees to retrieve the dropped weapon. The female was faster, recovering from her miss and leaping with a scream. Rachel changed direction, trying to avoid the infected's grasping hands, but knew she was too slow.

Raising her arms to deflect the attack, she flinched away as a body slammed into the attacking female. The two bodies crashed to the ground next to her and she rolled away from the fight, going too far and tipping over the edge of the dike. She couldn't stop her momentum and continued bouncing down the steep slope until she splashed into the paddy. Disoriented and experiencing a bit of vertigo, Rachel fought her way to her feet and looked up at the top of the dike. Dog stood at the edge, looking down at her, tail wagging hard enough to make his whole body shift back and forth.

9

Rachel climbed the dike and fell to her knees, arms wrapped around Dog, face buried in the matted fur of his neck. Sobs of relief racked her body for a few moments. Relief that Dog was alive. Relief that she wasn't alone. For the first time since waking up in the mud on the river's shore, she felt a stirring of optimism that she might survive long enough to be reunited with John. Hearing the growl in Dog's powerful chest, she snapped her head up to look around. He was facing east, nose twitching as he scented the air. It was time to move.

Rachel grabbed the pistol out of the dirt and they started walking west, Dog close by her side. Occasionally, she glanced to the north at the glow of lights just over the horizon, but experience with other survivors tempered her desire to seek the company of strangers. Ignoring the lights, they continued on through the night. They hadn't encountered any more infected, but Rachel knew it was only a matter of time. She smiled and patted Dog's back, happy he was with her for the company and also because he'd know there were infected in the area long before she would.

After a few hours of walking, they reached the end of what had seemed like endless rice paddies. Pausing, Rachel was momentarily surprised to see broad pastures with the occasional tree and a narrow road paved with crumbling asphalt. The road ran to the west, picking up where the dike ended. Taking advantage of her last opportunity to survey the area with a height advantage, Rachel took her time and turned a slow circle but could see nothing other than empty terrain. They had left the lights to the north behind over an hour ago, and now it was completely dark in every direction.

Her stomach rumbled, and she was thirsty. Dog had drunk from the irrigation water that flooded the paddies on several occasions, but Rachel wasn't thirsty enough yet to risk consuming the plethora of bacteria and organisms to which a dog would be immune. She knew she could wind up with E Coli, Dysentery, or a dozen other ailments, any of which would be crippling and leave her unable to run or fight. She also knew that eventually her system would develop a resistance and she could drink water that hadn't been filtered and purified, but wasn't in any hurry to get there.

Dog bounded gracefully down the sloping face of the dike, Rachel sliding and winding up on her ass for the last few feet. He stood looking at her, panting, and for all the world appearing to be laughing at her lack of coordination. Smacking him lightly on the rump, Rachel started down the road, sticking to the middle of the narrow ribbon of pavement.

They walked for another hour, their pace slowing when the moon set and the small amount of light they had been relying on faded to nothing. Dog seemed unaffected by having only starlight by which to navigate and, again, Rachel was thankful to have him with her.

Pushing on, they covered another three miles, stopping when the road dead ended into a slightly larger one that ran north and south. Rachel looked to Dog to see if he was detecting any infected, but he was just a slightly darker form on the road to her eyes. He wasn't growling or trying to get her to start moving again, so she relaxed a notch.

Looking north and south, Rachel could see nothing except more darkness. No sign of habitation. Which way? Trying to picture a map of the United States in her mind, she finally gave up. The central part of the country just wasn't geography that Rachel had any familiarity with. She knew her destination, Oklahoma City, was to the west, but it could have been hundreds of miles farther north or south as far as she knew. Tossing a mental coin, she turned to her right and headed north.

Within three hundred yards, she smiled and congratulated herself as the road curved to the west. Hoping this was a sign that her luck was on the rise, she nearly cried out for joy when she spotted a squat building ahead of them. It was too dark to make out any details and all she could see was the outline of the structure against the stars on the horizon. But that was enough for her to tell it was a building. Approaching cautiously, she kept her hand on Dog's back, ready to turn and run if he sensed any danger.

Dog remained calm as they neared the driveway to the building. Moving off the road, Rachel froze when the ground under her feet changed from asphalt to gravel. Her first two steps had crunched as the gravel shifted under her boot soles, so loud that she was certain any infected hiding in the building would know she was there. Remaining frozen for a full minute, Rachel listened intently and watched Dog for any reaction. Finally, hearing nothing and not getting a warning from Dog, she resumed moving towards the building.

The gravel that made up the driveway had apparently been recently put in place. There was a thick, loose bed of the stuff. She was making a lot of noise walking since it wasn't packed tightly into the ground like old gravel driveways. Cringing with every step, Rachel forced herself to keep moving, finally coming close enough to the building to recognize it as a gas station. In front of the garage and office was a small area paved with concrete that held a single gas pump. Happily stepping off the gravel, Rachel paused again to listen and give Dog a chance to sniff the air.

Her heart skipped a beat when Dog growled deep in his chest. He was looking directly at the office portion of the building, ears straight up as his nose twitched. Rachel slowly drew her pistol, somewhat more confident in her ability to defend herself with it after having killed the infected on the dike. If John was here he'd caution her to not get overconfident, but he wasn't, and she needed all the spirit she could muster at the moment.

Dog stopped growling and moved forward, leaving Rachel standing alone. Surprised, she stayed put as he walked up to the glass door and started wagging his tail. Not enthusiastically like he had when they'd been reunited, but still a wag to let someone know he was friendly. Friendly greeting or not, Rachel raised her pistol and aimed at the door, preparing herself for a screaming infected to come charging out and across the concrete apron. She almost pulled the trigger when the door started to open, and if not for Dog continuing to stand there calmly, she would have.

Two figures stepped out, both moving timidly towards Dog. Expecting infected, Rachel was caught by surprise when she realized these weren't even adults. She lowered, then holstered the pistol as the shorter of the two walked forward and started petting Dog. They hadn't seen Rachel in the darkness, shrinking back towards the door when she came forward.

"It's OK. I'm not going to hurt you," Rachel called softly, afraid to make any noise, but not wanting them to disappear back inside.

They stopped moving when they heard her voice, but stayed poised to run. Dog took a step forward and sat down next to them, looking for more petting.

"My name's Rachel. This is Dog. Are you here alone?"

Rachel slowly covered the distance to where Dog sat. When she was within a few feet, she could tell the two were both girls, and based on their size guessed their ages at eight and ten, but couldn't see any details in the dark.

"We're alone." the older of the two spoke up. "They came to take our Ma and Daddy. Ma made us hide so they wouldn't find us."

"Who took your parents?" Rachel asked. "The infected?"

"No. The bad men. They said it's time for our kind to go back to the fields where we belong," the little girl said.

"What do you mean, back to the fields? What are you talking about?" Rachel was completely confused.

"On account of we's niggers!" The younger girl said, her voice hard and dripping with venom, belying the way she was gently petting Dog's head.

10

Jackson and I stepped out of the office building, through with my interrogation of the captured Russians. It was well after midnight and I was momentarily refreshed by the cool, night air. Looking up at the sky as I dug for a cigarette, I absently noted that the moon had already set and the stars were twinkling brightly. I hoped that Rachel and Dog were somewhere safe, looking up at the same sky.

"What did you learn?"

I was startled when Colonel Crawford spoke. He had found a cheap, plastic lawn chair and was sitting in the dark, looking up at the night sky, waiting for me. Apparently he'd been waiting for a while as there was a fairly impressive pile of neatly stacked cigarette butts on the ground next to him. He gestured to two empty chairs and Jackson and I gratefully sat down.

"Some, but they don't know much," I answered. "The Captain says they were told that the American government has requested assistance from Russia to put down an uprising within our military."

Crawford snorted when he heard this.

"That's actually brilliant," he said. "Tell your troops they're saviors, not invaders. Everyone gets to be a hero."

I nodded agreement. I'd had exactly the same thought when the Russian Captain had told me.

"What else?"

Crawford field stripped a cigarette by pinching just below the filter and rolling it back and forth until the burning tobacco dropped out of the paper and onto the ground. He crushed the smoldering cherry under his boot before adding the butt to the neat pyramid he was building.

"Got an idea of troop strengths, where they are, equipment brought in, which units were deployed and a few other tidbits." I handed him the legal pad Jackson had made notes on during the interrogations. "The enlisted don't know many details, but based on what they saw as the Russians made preparations, I think the Captain is telling the truth."

"Speaking of truth, did you set him straight about what's really going on?"

"No, sir. Didn't see the point, even if he believed me, which I doubt he would." Crawford nodded his head in agreement. "Any luck reaching Command? Or anyone for that matter?"

"I finally spoke to an Admiral Packard. He's CINCPACFLT (Commander in Chief Pacific Fleet). The Navy's still got some command and control capabilities in Pearl Harbor and on a couple of ships. They monitored four nuclear detonations within the continental US, yesterday morning. Two at Mt. Weather, two at Cheyenne Mountain. They can't confirm it was the Russians, NORAD is in pieces, but that's the educated guess."

We all sat quietly in the dark, Crawford lighting another cigarette. I had lit one but had wound up just holding it in my hand and not smoking it. I stripped it and carefully added on to the Colonel's project.

"Are we retaliating?" Jackson spoke up.

He had been unusually quiet through the whole interrogation. I didn't blame him. It hadn't been pleasant.

"We can't." Crawford drew deeply on his smoke and leaned his head back to look straight up at the stars. "The Russians successfully decapitated us. All civilian leadership is dead. All senior military leadership is dead. The arming and launch codes for all our nukes are gone. There're fail-safes built into the system to allow deployment even if this happens, but they require three senior military officers to coordinate, and Admiral

Packard is the only officer on the list that is still alive. Or at least that we know of."

I leaned back and let out a deep sigh. The Russians had finally done what the Soviets had said they would do shortly after the end of World War II. America was on its knees. No, that's being too generous. We were on our backs and gasping for air. It wouldn't take much more to finish us off. But if the Russians thought they'd just be able to waltz in and settle down, they were in for a rude awakening. Americans may argue and fight amongst ourselves, appearing weak and divided to outside observers, but don't underestimate us. Well, if there were any of us left, that is.

"There's something else you should know." Crawford interrupted my train of thought. "The devices that were detonated in New York, DC and LA. Admiral Packard says his analysts have finished going over the data and have concluded they were Soviet, not Chinese."

"What? How can they tell?" I asked, stunned by the news.

"Something to do with the signature of the initial detonation which was recorded by satellites, and analysis of the fallout. They are confident these were not only Soviet, but had been smuggled into the US during the Cold War. Probably in the 60s or 70s."

"So you're saying the Russians are behind this? Or that at the very least, they were cooperating with the Chinese?" Jackson asked, sounding as caught off guard as I was.

"If I had to guess, I'd say the Russians played the Chinese. Got them to do the dirty work, take the hits from us to knock them out of the picture and are now stepping in to seize the spoils of war. I've spent a lot of time studying the Chinese. After the Cold War, it was popular wisdom that the next eight-hundred-pound gorilla on the block to challenge us would be China, so there was a focused effort to understand them. One of the things I learned is that the Chinese have always been masters at playing the long game. Setting things into motion years, if not decades in advance, then manipulating others to get their plans to come together.

"But they got greedy. They got a taste of capitalism. The money, luxury, power and prestige. They probably played right into the Russian's hands. The new Russian President, Barinov, is a billionaire. Between his own money and control of the Russian government, it's not a stretch to imagine him buying the right Chinese officials to make this happen. Old, hard-line China? Never would have happened. The new China? If you've got enough money, anything you want is yours. But this is just the musings and guesses of a middle-aged Army Colonel. If I was that bright, I'd have stars on my collar, not eagles."

I sat there thinking about what Crawford had just told us. It made sense. More sense than the original belief that China had attacked because they wanted our land and natural resources. They may have needed these things, but without the consumerism of the US, their economy would tank beyond repair. Why would they give that up, unless the men in control thought they had a replacement in their pockets? How many billions had the Russians invested in this gambit? We looked up as Captain Blanchard appeared out of the dark, snapped a salute and stood there at attention, waiting for the Colonel.

"Jesus Christ, Captain. It's oh four fucking hundred and I'm too goddamn tired to stand up and salute. Relax and have a seat."

Blanchard completed his salute, but didn't sit, instead choosing to stand.

"Sir, we've completed four full searches of the river and both river banks. The pattern began at the bridge and terminated sixty miles south." He paused and turned to me. "I'm sorry, Major. We didn't find any sign of her or the dog. Unfortunately, if they came up on the eastern shore..."

"I got it. Thanks, Captain. And tell the air crews thank you for me."

This time, I lit a cigarette and started smoking it. I was exhausted and pissed at myself. If I had killed Roach when I first saw him on the train, Rachel and Dog would be sitting here with me. Were they really gone? I had to acknowledge the likelihood, but the same part of me that believed Katie was still alive refused to give up hope. Rachel was a survivor, and Dog was... well, Dog was one tough son of a bitch. One could argue that Rachel had survived as long as she had because she was with me, and to a degree that was true. At first. But she had shown a toughness that many men I'd known couldn't have matched.

"Thank you, Captain. Now go get some rest. All of you."

Crawford lit another cigarette.

"What about you, sir?" Blanchard prompted, falling into the role of a good aide.

"I want to look over these interrogation notes. Then I've got to talk to the Admiral again. Figure out what we're going to do about these fucking Russians that are stinking up our country."

"Yes, sir," Blanchard answered as we all stood to head for our makeshift beds.

"Oh, Captain. Do we have early warning pickets out? For the Russians and the infected?" The Colonel asked, turning on a small flashlight and digging out a pair of reading glasses.

"Yes, sir. Air assets up at all four points and a platoon of Rangers keeping an eye on the river. Just in case the infected figure out how to swim."

We all looked at him for a moment after he put that thought out there. They can't swim. Then, a few days ago, I didn't think they could coordinate their efforts to hunt us, either. Crawford thought about that for a moment, nodded his head and waved us away as he started reading from the pad.

11

I woke several hours later, bathed in sweat. The small airport didn't have much in the way of accommodations, so Jackson and I had unrolled a couple of thin, foam ground mats in the back of a tin-roofed hangar. We had gone to sleep with the hangar door open. A cool night breeze had been blowing through the opening, but when the sun came up the humidity returned and the metal roof had quickly heated up. Now it felt like I was in a sauna.

A few feet away, Jackson lay on his back, snoring loud enough that I wondered how I had slept. I'd have to get him and Dog together to see who was worse, I thought, then remembered I didn't even know if Dog was alive or not. The thought soured my mood, more than it already was, and I climbed to my feet with a groan. I may have stayed in shape, but my knees, back, and shoulders weren't as young as they used to be. Working the sore joints, I thought about kicking Jackson and telling him to get his ass up and moving, but didn't see the point. Let him sleep while he could.

Wandering out into the bright Arkansas sunshine, I wished for a pair of sunglasses as I headed for the trench some of the Rangers had dug on the far side of the runway to serve as a latrine.

Business complete, I set out in search of the Colonel. I intended to ask him to send out another helicopter to search for Rachel. If he wouldn't, I was going to slip away and start looking myself. Of course, I didn't have a clue where to start, but that didn't matter.

Trudging across the hot tarmac towards the control tower, I had time to think. In my heart, I knew I wasn't going to desert to go look for Rachel. I was many things, but no matter how good the reason, I wasn't a deserter. Men were fighting and dying. Brother soldiers who most likely had someone they cared about who was missing, too. I knew I'd be fighting until I was dead, or we won, and winning wasn't looking like it would get very good odds in Vegas right about now.

Reaching the base of the control tower, I returned the guard's salute, pulled the door open and stepped into blessed, nearly orgasmic quality air conditioning. I had forgotten that the FAA required emergency generators for any airport with a controller assigned. Apparently, the Colonel hadn't. I could faintly hear it purring away, providing power to the building. Climbing the staircase to the upper level, I found Crawford seated at the same folding table where I'd eaten dinner the previous evening.

In the far corner of the room sat a folding cot, a thin Army issue blanket folded into a perfect square sitting precisely in the center. Crawford looked freshly showered, shaved and wore a crisply pressed uniform. He was drinking a cup of coffee from an Arkansas Razorbacks mug, satellite phone pressed to his ear. He looked up when I walked in and waved me into a chair on the opposite side of the table. Before sitting, I looked around for the coffee pot, but couldn't spot one so sat down and enjoyed the cool air blowing out of the ceiling vent directly over my head. Crawford wrapped up his call and hit the end button on the sat phone.

"Before you even ask, I've got two Black Hawks out looking for her. Well, not just looking for her, they're also scouting for Russians and infected, but I put a Ranger on each bird and tasked them with looking for her specifically."

He noisily slurped some coffee and picked up his reading glasses and the legal pad with the interrogation notes.

"Thank you, sir."

"Don't like to leave anyone behind," he said. "That was Admiral Packard and his staff I was just talking with. Briefed them on what you got out of our prisoners last night. They still have access to our satellites and are re-tasking several of them for surveillance of the US. What we do know is that the Russians have taken Malmstrom Air Force Base in Montana, Ellsworth in South Dakota and Kirtland in New Mexico. Malmstrom gave them access to our Minuteman III inventory of ICBMs. They're consolidating their hold on us and we've got an idea to ruin their day."

"I'm all ears, sir," I said when it was obvious he was waiting for me to respond.

"SADMs."

At first, I was sure I hadn't heard him right. SADM stands for Special Atomic Demolition Munition. In plain English, a nuke that fits in a backpack. I had trained on these devices at one point in my military career, preparing to carry them into the Soviet Union if the President ever decided it was time. But that was a lot of years ago. Technology had made them obsolete, or so I thought.

"We still have some? Weren't the last ones built in the 70s?" I asked.

"60s, to be accurate, but you know the US Government. Nothing ever gets thrown away, just stuck in storage and forgotten about."

"Will they still work?"

"Admiral Packard checked with his staff that maintains the Navy's nuclear arsenal, and they assured him that the devices will work as well today as when they were built. Sounds like they have a pretty long shelf life."

"So, what's the catch? If I'm remembering right, these things are variable yield from ten tons all the way up to a full kiloton. Couple of these at each base they took over, cranked all the way up and there's a lot of fried Russkies."

I was getting a sinking feeling about where he was going with this.

"That's our thought. Do you still remember how to adjust the yield?"

"Yeah, I do. Once you're shown how to operate a nuclear bomb, it's not something you tend to forget."

I said this with more sarcasm than I probably should have when talking to a superior officer, but at the moment I didn't really give a shit.

Crawford ignored my tone and continued. "The problem is, there are only three locations we can identify where these are in storage. The Navy had some at Little Creek in Virginia and at Coronado out in California. Unfortunately, no one can find any records to confirm they're still there, or even exactly where they are on the bases, and there's not someone to call up and ask to go check. The third location, and we have found inventory records from less than a year ago, is Los Alamos."

I looked at him and stayed silent. I knew what was coming and I wasn't going to help him. The room was quiet other than the rush of cool air from the air conditioning vents and a large analog clock ticking away on the wall over the north-facing bank of windows.

"I need you to lead a team into Los Alamos and retrieve the devices. Records indicate there's ten of them in storage. Captain Blanchard has all of the details you'll need."

I knew I was going to accept the mission before he even asked. Yes, asked. Crawford was a good officer, a good leader. He could have ordered me to go, but that wasn't his style. He knew me well enough by now to understand that he didn't need to order me to do anything. Just explain to me why it needed done. I've always been a soft touch that way.

12

The two little girls were named Lindsey and Madison, Madison the younger. Rachel's guess of their ages had been close. Madison was seven and Lindsey ten, almost eleven as she proudly announced. Their parents owned the small gas station, the only place to buy gas for forty miles in any direction, Madison assured her. They had only lived in Arkansas for a few months, their parents having sold everything they owned to come up with the money to buy the business from a distant relative. The girls missed their friends, but said their mother was very happy to have left the crime in their Memphis neighborhood.

They huddled with Rachel in the back of the office area, Dog lying protectively between them and the door. He was close enough for the girls to touch him and both kept a hand on his back, gently rubbing. Tired, but unable to sleep, Rachel got them talking about what had happened to their parents. While they talked, she kept an eye out the glass front of the office even though it was too dark outside for her to see anything. She trusted Dog to warn her if there was any danger.

Shortly after the attacks, the local Sheriff had come around and talked to their daddy. They weren't able to hear the conversation, but when the man left their father was very upset. He used a lot of bad words when he was telling their mom about what the man had to say. Their mom was frightened and begged their daddy to take them away to somewhere safe, but he said there wasn't nowhere safe anymore. He said that the monsters were everywhere, and the river was all that was keeping them safe, and they couldn't leave it.

It wasn't long before the first monsters showed up. It was late evening and the girls were playing in front of the gas station while their parents sat watching. Madison was on her fourth game of hopscotch when she hopped out of the last block and looked up. Three men were walking down the road in her direction. They were still a short distance away, a small stand of trees screening them from their parents' view. It wasn't uncommon to see field hands walking long distances in the area, so Madison didn't pay any attention to them and went back to her game.

Back and forth she went, happy with how well she was doing. She had just started another game when Lindsey screamed. The three men were much closer now, just coming around the edge of the trees, and when Madison looked up, she screamed too. One of them was missing most of his face, bone and teeth clearly visible in the evening light. Their mother screamed and ran to protect them while their father dashed into the small office and grabbed the shotgun he kept under the counter. Gathered up in their mother's arms they cried as she hustled them to safety, wailing harder when they heard the booms of their daddy's gun.

After that, they weren't allowed to play outside anymore. There was a small two room shack behind the gas station, which was where they lived, and their mother stayed there with them while their father kept watch from the office. They never saw any more monsters, but every day or two they would hear their daddy's shotgun and their mother would start praying that he was OK. Then, two days ago, the bad men came.

There were six of them. Peeking out through a crack in the wall, the girls recognized the Sheriff who had upset their daddy so much. There was a lot of shouting and the men pointed guns at their parents and made them climb into the back of one of their pick-ups. The girls, terrified, had stayed hidden in the shack like their mother told them. They watched as the trucks drove away, two men sitting in back with shotguns pointed at their daddy. There hadn't been much food left in the shack, and they had finished it off quickly, wandering out to the office to search for more. That's what they were doing when Madison had looked out the window and seen Dog.

Now, the girls sat on either side of her, Madison finally lying down and putting her head in Rachel's lap. Rachel was shocked and saddened by their story. She knew racism was still alive and well in the world, probably would be as long as there were humans that weren't identical to each other, but never dreamed that there were men who would take advantage of the situation to start enslaving other men. Where the hell was John? Why hadn't he found her yet?

Gently stroking the child's hair as she drifted off to sleep, Rachel cursed the circumstances that had separated her from John. These innocent little girls needed his help, and she just needed him. At first, Madison started softly snoring, then Lindsey fell asleep with her head resting on Rachel's shoulder. It wasn't long before Rachel's eyes grew heavy and she joined them in a dream haunted sleep. Dog was aware that all of them were sleeping, but he didn't take his eyes off the windows that looked out at the road. Remaining still and silent, he watched the small pack of infected males approach from the east and stumble slowly past the turn-in to the small gas station.

13

Little Rock Air Force Base, just outside of Little Rock, Arkansas, was a hive of activity, despite having been nearly decimated by the second outbreak a few days ago. I was just arriving from West Memphis on a Black Hawk. It would take a few minutes to refuel, then return to where Colonel Crawford had his temporary headquarters. Captain Blanchard was along for the ride, briefing me on what was known about the conditions in Los Alamos. Where the SADMs were stored in the city and calling ahead with his satellite phone to coordinate the equipment and personnel I needed. I would have liked to have Jackson with me to watch my back, but I had asked him to stay in West Memphis and help with the search for Rachel and Dog. Crawford left the decision up to him and he had grudgingly agreed.

I had several problems to deal with to get my hands on the nukes. First off, Los Alamos was crawling with infected. The small city had avoided the initial release of nerve gas, but Blanchard's best guess was that due to the relative proximity to Denver, which had been attacked, the virus had arrived and wreaked havoc.

Problem number two was the whole reason I was even going. The goddamn Russians. They had captured Kirtland Air Force Base, which is on the southern edge of Albuquerque, giving them effective control of a large swath of the American southwest. Los Alamos, no more than seventy air miles from Kirtland, was within the protective bubble of the CAP – Combat Air Patrol – the Russians were flying around the clock. There was no way to get an aircraft inside the CAP and on the ground in Los Alamos without being spotted.

Problem two exacerbated problem number three. Once I had the nukes in my possession, how the hell did I get them out where they could be used by American forces? I hadn't seen them but had been assured we had satellite imagery that showed plenty of vehicles available that could be commandeered. The SADMs were so small and light, I didn't even need a truck. A small SUV or even a sedan with a decent sized trunk would fit the bill if that was all I could find. I refocused on the moment as the Black Hawk's tires touched the tarmac. With good luck wishes from Captain Blanchard, I jumped out the side door onto the concrete apron.

Fifty yards in front of me a man stood next to the door of a squat office building. He waved and I headed in his direction. As I approached, I had a moment to look him over. He was younger than me, by more years than I cared to acknowledge, and close to my height with a broad chest, powerful arms, and shoulders. Dressed in desert camouflage cargo pants and a tight, black dri-fit T-shirt with a holstered pistol and slung rifle, I could tell he wasn't an officer. Both arms were almost fully sleeved in tattoos, artfully done with the result making his already powerful build appear even more intimidating. When I closed to within a few feet, he straightened his stance and snapped a salute which I returned, surprising him when I stuck my hand out to shake his.

"John Chase," I said, looking him in the eye and trying to get a sense of who he was.

"Tech Sergeant Zach Scott," he replied with a small grin. "Welcome to Little Rock. Heard you had some excitement in Memphis."

"Yeah, and I didn't even get to see Graceland," I answered with a grin of my own.

He smiled, either because I'm genuinely funny or because I'm an officer. He didn't look the type to suck up and didn't encourage me to say something else witty, so he passed my first little test.

"We're getting set up inside, sir. If you'll follow me, we'll get started."

He turned and pulled the door open, leading the way inside and turning into the first doorway we encountered. The room was large, appearing to be a pilot's briefing room. Two large tables at the back were stacked high with equipment being checked over by another man dressed similarly to Scott, and a woman wearing a standard Air Force flight suit with Captain's bars on her collar. Scott called them to attention as we entered and I walked over to meet them, telling them to stand at ease.

The woman was small and looked to be in outstanding physical condition. The name tape on her uniform blouse read Martinez, and when I looked in her eyes, I recognized something that told me she was not a woman you wanted to mess with. The other man was an Air Force Staff Sergeant named Yee, nearly as short as Martinez and whip thin. He looked like the type that could run a marathon as a warm up for the day.

The two Sergeants were part of a very small and elite group in the Air Force called SOF TACP or Special Operations Forces Tactical Air Control Party. They normally run with Army SF units to coordinate any air support that may be needed to complete their mission. To be able to do that, they had trained to the same level as their Army counterparts and in most, if not all cases were just as capable. I was glad to have them along for the fight.

Martinez didn't have the same level of training, though she looked like she could have made it through the selection process. But she was a helicopter pilot. Her job was to ride along with us and if we found the opportunity to get our hands on a helo, she'd fly us where we needed to go.

Looking down at the gear, I couldn't help but smile. New weapons, clothing, radios, jumpsuits, parachutes... the list went on and on. Everything was neatly separated by category and I was happy to find a change of clothes and lightweight but very warm long underwear. It was going to be cold where we were going.

"No night vision?" I asked, hoping there was some that just wasn't out in the open.

"That's the one thing we couldn't get our hands on." Scott shook his head, looked at me and shrugged his shoulders.

Glancing up at the clock I was surprised to see it was already 1500 – 3 pm. We needed to get our asses in gear. But, first things first.

"Have any of you fought the infected, face to face?" I asked, looking at the three Air Force personnel. All three shook their heads.

"Not like you have." Sergeant Scott spoke up after glancing at Captain Martinez. "We've had some on base and also been into parts of town to help clear them out, but we've always had superior numbers."

"OK, then you know some of the basics. These are just humans. They aren't zombies or vampires that can't be killed. That said, they are so pumped up on adrenalin from the infection that they don't feel injury. Body shots are all but useless unless you hit the heart. Headshots put them down instantly, and if they're really close, a good knife thrust to the heart or brainstem works well too.

"I've seen infected take injuries that would completely incapacitate one of us and keep on coming like nothing happened. Those injuries will eventually kill them, but they don't feel pain or go into shock. They go until their body completely fails. Questions?"

There were none, so I continued.

"Have you been briefed on the smart infected?"

Nods all around this time.

"I won't beat a dead horse, but the smart ones, which seem to be just the females, are scary as hell. I've encountered a few and they understand death and the concept of self-preservation. They are also able to work together and set up ambushes as well as form hunting parties. They don't just scream and run at you, they stalk you and strike when you're vulnerable. Heads on swivels out there. Got it?"

There were more nods, and I was happy to see that while they were taking me seriously, none of them were looking like they were going to freak out.

"One final thing. They are strong as hell, both male, and female. Remember, they're in a rage. I've fought females that were the size of Martinez here, and they were nearly as strong as I am. You *cannot* engage with multiples in hand to hand. They will overpower you, especially since nothing you've been trained to do will stop them short of a knife or a bullet.

"The males are slow, but the females are fast as hell. They don't tire. I imagine they'd run at a sprint until their heart exploded, but I've never seen one get to that point. You won't outrun them. You won't outlast them. No one will, no matter what kind of shape you're in. If you find yourself being pursued, find a defensible position and start killing them. That's your only option."

I looked at each of them in turn. Sergeant Scott met my look, steely resolve in his eyes. I saw the same thing in Martinez and Yee and decided I had a good team going in with me. I was opening my mouth to ask where the mess hall was when a strident alarm began blaring. Martinez dashed to a phone hanging on the wall next to the door and snatched the handset off the cradle. Apparently listening to an announcement, she stared intently at the floor with the phone held tightly to her ear, slamming it back in place after about twenty seconds.

"Russian air raid," she said in a surprisingly calm voice. "Our CAP is engaging them a hundred miles to the west, but there's more of them than there are of us. We're going now!"

She ran to the tables, and with the two Sergeants helping, started stuffing equipment into waiting duffel bags. Stepping over, I joined in and soon we had eight very large and heavy duffels ready to go. Each of us grabbed two and Scott led the way outside and around the building to where an Air Force pickup was parked. We tossed the bags into the bed, Scott and Yee piling in on top of them as Martinez jumped behind the wheel and I joined her in the cab.

The alarm was louder in the open air and she didn't hesitate to floor the accelerator as soon as the truck started, leaving twin, black patches of rubber on the concrete. Driving fast, she swung onto a road that paralleled the runways and quickly pushed our speed to over one hundred miles an hour. Next to us on the runway, a pair of F-35s screamed into the sky, quickly followed by two more. Ahead, I could see more lining up for takeoff, waiting behind half a dozen F-18s that were already starting their takeoff roll.

As Martinez drove, I watched fighter after fighter leap off the runway and into the air, pilots immediately going nearly vertical to gain altitude as quickly as possible. Beyond the sortieing jets were several massive hangars. A couple of them had the tail sections of cargo planes sticking out as the aircraft were having maintenance performed on them, but the three largest hangars were buttoned up tight, each with its own chain link fence topped with coiled razor wire.

Martinez pulled out a small, handheld radio and spoke briefly into it. Moments later, I saw the doors of the closest high-security hangar crack open and two figures ran across the large apron. The rolling gate in the fence started moving and Martinez pointed the front of the truck at the opening. I'm pretty much a fearless driver, but don't do well when someone else is behind the wheel. It took every ounce of my self-control to not scream at her that we weren't going to make it. The gate was opening much too slowly and we were going way too fast.

Somehow, we did make it, roaring through at over a hundred miles per hour. If there was more than two inches of clearance on either side of the truck, I'll eat my beret. Fucking pilots!

Approaching the hangar doors, which were still trundling open, Martinez braked sharply and cut our speed to a sedate pace as she drove into the cavernous building. She made a sharp right before coming to a screeching halt, parking the truck out of the way of the menacing looking plane that sat in the middle of the hangar. I'd never seen a stealth bomber up close before.

14

It turned out that the bomber wasn't even officially an Air Force plane, yet. It was a prototype of the next generation stealth bomber, the replacement for the B-2 that had been undergoing performance testing when the attacks happened. Now it had been pressed into service, being flown by a Boeing test pilot who had retired from the Air Force ten years ago and started a second career with the giant aircraft builder. He was in control in the pilot's seat, an active duty Air Force pilot flying co-pilot. The rest of us were spread out in the back of the aircraft.

One of the requirements the Air Force had for the new bomber was that it could do dual duty as a transport and covert insertion platform for SF units. To accommodate this, Boeing had made it easy to reconfigure the inside of the plane and had also added a ramp at the rear. I'd had a conversation with the test pilot after we were in the air and cruising along at forty-thousand-feet. He had assured me that the Russians could not detect us.

According to him, we had the radar cross section of a sparrow, and the IR – infrared – signature of a duck. When I asked him what that meant, he laughed and told me that a duck farting would release more heat into the atmosphere than the bomber's engines did. The only risk was being visually spotted by a very observant pilot. That is until he opened the bomb bay doors or lowered the rear ramp. Then, due to the change in the profile of the aircraft, we would be detectable on radar for the amount of time either was open.

Currently, we were flying south, the Gulf of Mexico eight miles beneath us. The pilot may have been confident that the Russians couldn't detect us, but at the same time, we didn't want to tempt fate by taking a direct route from Little Rock to Los Alamos and fly directly over territory already occupied. Instead, we headed south over the gulf and would soon be turning west over Mexico before turning to the north and coming back into the US over Arizona, after the sun had set. From there we'd proceed northeast to Los Alamos. I can't say the thought of asking him to put down at the airport in Phoenix for a couple of hours didn't go through my head, but I had a lot of people depending on me and didn't have time for personal missions.

When we reached Los Alamos, we'd descend to thirty-five-thousand-feet. The pilot would lower the rear ramp, and we'd jump. This is called a HALO – High Altitude Low Opening – insertion and was the only option we could come up with on short notice and with even shorter resources. Lots of things could go wrong.

Just like divers have to worry about the bends, nitrogen bubbles forming in the bloodstream because of rapid pressure changes, high altitude jumps face the same issue. In extreme cases, the jumper can suffer from hypoxia, fall unconscious and fail to open their chute. There's also concern over frostbite. At thirty-five-thousand-feet, the temperature outside the aircraft is about minus fifty degrees Fahrenheit. And that's just the first few items on the list of things that can go FUBAR when jumping out of a plane nearly seven miles up. Oh, and I haven't done a HALO jump in about ten years.

The two Sergeants were crashed out. Heads pillowed on their parachutes. Martinez sat a few feet away from them, honing a wicked looking dagger on a small sharpening stone. I was tired but too keyed up to sleep, so I made my way forward to talk with the pilots.

"Where are we?" I asked, poking my head into the cockpit. They both looked around, surprised to see me.

"About three hundred miles south of New Orleans at the moment." The pilot answered. "I'm going to turn us west in about ten minutes. Just killing time right now. I don't want to re-enter US airspace while the sun is up. The fucking Commies will have patrols up and the last thing we need is for a Mig pilot to see the sun glint off this baby."

I nodded in agreement.

"Any word from Little Rock?" I asked.

"They fought the Russians off, but took heavy losses and a lot of damage to the field. Only one runway left in operation." The Air Force officer answered.

I thanked them, asked them to let me know when we were crossing into Arizona, then headed for the back to get some sleep. Curling up in a space that would normally hold a stick of bombs, I rested my head on my parachute and closed my eyes. The bomber was surprisingly quiet in flight and I could clearly hear the rasp of blade on stone as Martinez kept working the dagger's edge to razor sharpness.

Normally, I can fall asleep on a plane at the drop of a hat. It was a useful skill I learned early on in life when I'd spend hours in the belly of a C-130, being flown to whatever part of the world the Army chose to send me. Later, when I started traveling for work in the civilian world, I'd usually be asleep before we were even off the ground. It's the only way to fly if you ask me. Keep your in-flight movies, drinks, snacks, and chatty seat mates. Let me sleep. But I couldn't. I had too much I was worried about.

Katie. Rachel and Dog. The impending jump with a parachute that had been packed by

God only knew who. I had toyed with the idea of pulling it open and repacking it myself, but there just wasn't room in the plane. I was worried about the jump. I've got a ton of jumps under my belt, and a fair number of both HALO and HAHO – High Altitude High Opening – but like I said, it's been ten years since the last time I threw myself out of a perfectly good aircraft. I thought I remembered everything I needed to remember, but the rub is the stuff you don't even realize you forgot until it was too late.

I'd had time to chat with the three Air Force personnel after we took off from Little Rock. The two Sergeants had five HALO jumps between them, which meant they were still rookies, but at least they'd done it in a combat environment. Martinez had none. She'd jumped before, but from a nice, sedate ten thousand feet on a calm, sunny day. When you're falling at night, from seven miles up, to my targeted opening altitude of fifteen hundred feet, lots of things can happen. Updrafts, downdrafts, and cross winds can push you around and you end up coming down miles away from the rest of your unit.

We would be wearing special suits with flaps of fabric sewn in between the arms and body and between the legs. We used to call these bat suits and for the life of me, I couldn't remember what the proper name for them was. If you knew what you were doing, they helped you steer and, to a degree, fly well enough to compensate for any winds that might push you off target. If you knew what you were doing. I had no doubt Martinez had been trained on how to control her body during a descent, but this was going to be like nothing she had ever experienced.

These may have sounded like petty concerns, but I'd been to Los Alamos before. It was built on the top of several mesas which are nothing more than tall, flat-topped mountains surrounded by fairly deep and rugged canyons. If one of us missed and dropped into a canyon, we were screwed. A broken ankle would almost be assured and would probably be the least of the injuries sustained.

The terrain in the area was unforgiving and very difficult to navigate. Exactly the reason the government had chosen this location for the development of the first atomic bomb during World War II. Instead of dwelling on these concerns and worrying over something I couldn't control, I let them roll around in my head for a bit, finally falling asleep to the steady rasp of Martinez' blade.

15

Rachel startled awake when Dog growled. She'd lived through enough danger in the post-apocalyptic world to know to stay perfectly still and see if she could detect what had upset him. Movement could reveal her position and might very well draw an attack that would have passed her by if she had just remained motionless. Madison's head was still pillowed in her lap, the small girl snoring softly. Lindsey had slid down the side of Rachel's body in her sleep, head resting against Rachel's hip.

Moving only her eyes, Rachel scanned the area but saw nothing. The sun was up and shining brightly, the small office already hot and humid. Dog was lying perfectly still, facing the windows, ears stiffly alert. About to sit up straighter for a better view, Rachel froze when she saw movement in the field on the far side of the road. Three females.

At first, she wasn't sure if they were infected or not. They were walking slowly, looking down at the ground as if they'd lost something, but when one of them ticked her shoulder up before twitching her head, she knew they were infected. As Rachel watched, they kept moving forward slowly, one of them suddenly freezing in place and snapping her head to stare at a spot on the ground a few feet in front and to the side. She stayed still for a moment, then with inhuman speed and agility, leapt forward and reached for the spot she had been watching. Rising back to her feet, she held a small, squirming rodent. The creature was quickly devoured.

Trying to suppress a shudder of revulsion, Rachel failed. Lindsey stirred from the movement and changed position, stretching her leg out and bumping an ancient table that served as a desk. A large, metal ashtray sat on the edge of the table. Nearly half of it extended out into open space, having been pushed there by the piles of receipts and paperwork that cluttered the surface. Rachel held her breath as the table shook and the ash tray wobbled. Seeing what was about to happen, she reached out to catch it, but the two girls restricted her movement and she could only stare in horror as the heavy object tipped beyond the point of no return and fell off the table.

Six inches across and an inch deep, with a wide lip around the perimeter, the aluminum clattered like a gong when it struck the concrete floor. Dog grunted in surprise and leapt to his feet. Both girls snapped awake with sharp intakes of breath. Rachel groaned internally and looked up to see all three females staring at the building where they were hiding. First, the closest one, then all three broke into a sprint in their direction.

Not trusting the glass windows to stop the infected, Rachel scrambled to her feet and snatched Madison into her arms. To her right, a battered steel door led into a small garage area and Rachel dashed through the door, yelling for Lindsey and Dog to follow her. In the service bay, she set Madison down on her feet. As Lindsey and Dog ran through the opening, she slammed the door and frantically looked for a way to secure it. The door swung into the garage and there was only a standard door knob without a lock to hold it shut. She didn't think the females could turn the knob to open the door, but they might be able to ram their way through, especially if they were hungry enough.

The garage was dim, the only source of light a set of grimy windows set in the single roll up door, and stunk of grease and motor oil. Rachel cast around for anything she could use to brace the door, drawing her pistol when she heard one of the windows in the office shatter. On the far side of the room, she saw a short handled shovel and dashed across to grab it. She had just picked it up when the door from the office rattled in its frame as one of the females began crashing into it.

Rachel was three steps away from the door when it burst open under the assault of the infected. The female that had broken through stumbled into the garage and Dog slammed into her, taking her to the ground. The other two were right behind, appearing in the doorway, and Madison and Lindsey both screamed in panic. Both infected heads swiveled in their direction and they ignored Rachel in favor of the children.

Raising the pistol, Rachel fired three shots, the first two missing but the third destroying one of the female's heads. She tracked the second one but didn't pull the trigger for fear of hitting Madison, who was shrinking away from the grasping hands. Lindsey stepped protectively in front of her little sister and was knocked aside as the female lunged and grabbed onto Madison's arm. Holstering her pistol, Rachel raised the shovel over her head and charged.

"Get away from her, you bitch!"

She screamed as she stepped in and swung with every bit of strength, fear and frustration she possessed. The edge of the metal head of the shovel impacted the crown of the female's head, crushing deep into her skull and sending her crashing to the floor.

Panting, Rachel looked around to make sure they were safe, then dropped the shovel and dashed to Madison, folding her up in her arms. The small girl was crying and wrapped her arms around Rachel's neck. Holding her arm out, Rachel gathered Lindsey in and held both of them as they cried. Dog had killed the female he had fought and quickly sniffed the other two to make sure they were dead, then sat down facing the open door with his back pressed against Rachel.

The girls regained a degree of composure and after giving Dog a quick hug, Rachel stood and drew her pistol. She didn't want to walk through the door back into the office. It was one of the last things in the world she wanted to do, but she needed to know if the sound of the fight had drawn other infected that were about to attack. Breathing in short, shallow pants, Rachel walked to the door on the balls of her feet, pistol held in two hands in front of her just like John had taught her. Reaching the door, she held her breath, carefully peeking around the frame to get a view of the office.

Nothing moved, so she kept inching forward until she was standing in the doorway, weapon up and aimed at the front of the office where a pile of shattered safety glass lay on the floor. Dog came and stood with her, sniffing the air. Rachel didn't see anything moving, but when Dog growled quietly, she knew he was smelling more infected. She had no idea how he could tell the difference between ones that were approaching and the dead ones behind him in the garage, but wasn't about to fail to trust his warning.

"We have to go," Rachel said to the girls, glancing back at them to make sure they were ready. "Madison, tie your shoes so you can run without tripping."

Madison looked down at her feet and back-up at Rachel with a confused expression on her face.

"I'll do it." Lindsey volunteered, kneeling on the dirty floor to tie her sister's shoes. "But why don't we just take my daddy's car, so we don't have to run?"

Rachel turned and looked at her with her mouth hanging open. A car. She hadn't even thought about there being a car. Living all the way out here, of course there would! And the parents had been taken in their captor's trucks, so it should still be sitting here. Getting a taste of how John felt sometimes when he overlooked the obvious, Rachel smiled at Lindsey.

"Where is it, honey?"

"In back, behind our house. The keys are right there."

She pointed at a split ring with two big silver keys on it hanging from a nail that had been partially pounded into the wall. Rachel grabbed them and stuffed them in her pocket, resuming her two-handed grip on the pistol.

"Lead the way, Lindsey."

Holding her sister's hand, Lindsey went to a sturdy steel door in the rear wall of the garage and pointed. Leaving Dog to watch the front, Rachel joined her and undid the heavy deadbolt. Keeping the pistol up and ready, she turned the knob and gently pulled it open. No infected were waiting for them, so she stepped through, the girls on her heels, calling Dog to follow.

Lindsey kept her grip on Madison, and they moved quickly through knee-high weeds, crossing a narrow gravel driveway that led to a small, rickety shack. Walking around the house, Rachel was momentarily dismayed to see the vehicle that sat under a large shade tree.

The car was an ancient and battered Ford LTD. Rachel didn't even recognize it, having been a small child when Ford ceased production of the model. There was more rust than paint, and the rear bumper was missing, but the glass was intact and clean, all four tires looking to be in decent shape and fully aired up.

Quickly unlocking the door, Rachel put the girls in the back seat then she and Dog piled into the front. The engine started easily and settled into a smooth idle. A glance at the dash showed a full tank of gas. Breathing a small sigh of relief, Rachel shifted into drive and headed down the gravel driveway to the road.

16

Rachel nosed the big Ford around the gas station, letting it idle down the gravel drive. To her left, she could see a couple of males stumbling along, zeroing in on the rumble of the big V8 engine and crunch of the tires on the gravel. Stopping at the edge of the pavement, she looked around but didn't see any other infected.

"Lindsey, do you know how to get to a big highway, like the Interstate?" Rachel asked the older girl, hoping she had paid attention when her parents drove.

"Turn right," Madison answered, sounding absolutely certain with her directions.

Smiling, Rachel turned the wheel and accelerated onto the asphalt. Having never owned an American car, Rachel was surprised at how well the old sedan drove. She couldn't help but continue to smile as she pushed the car up to fifty miles an hour. The throaty rumble made her feel confident and powerful, unlike the buzzy four-cylinder Japanese engine in her hybrid.

The road was perfectly flat and straight as an arrow except when it occasionally made two consecutive, opposite direction ninety degree turns to adjust for the corner of a new rice paddy. After the second set of turns, she had to keep her speed down to steer around infected males that were stumbling across the pavement, alerted to her presence by the burbling exhaust.

The girls were quiet as she drove and Dog stuck his head out the open window, enjoying the wind. Rachel was starting to relax a notch, growing more comfortable with the power of the car under her control. After a few more miles, they reached a three-way intersection, the road they were on continuing straight ahead, a larger road heading ninety degrees to her left.

Braking to a stop, Rachel looked at the faded signs posted on a pipe that leaned drunkenly in the weeds. Straight ahead was West Memphis, five miles away. To their left, the new road was state highway 18. There was no indication where it led, but Rachel was sure she didn't want to go anywhere near Memphis, or West Memphis, or anything Memphis. She turned left.

"You should have gone straight," Lindsey spoke up from the back seat.

"We're not going anywhere near Memphis, honey. It's full of monsters," Rachel said, meeting Lindsey's eyes in the rear-view mirror. The girl stared back at her for a moment before nodding and looking out the side window.

The new road was slightly wider, with a yellow line painted down the middle. Soft dirt came right to the edge of the pavement on either side and the asphalt was barely wide enough to turn the big car around if needed. Driving off onto the shoulder was a certain recipe for getting stuck. Rachel's tension level raised a couple of degrees as she thought about this, her foot backing off the accelerator until their speed slowed to thirty.

Slowing for an upcoming ninety-degree jog, Rachel glanced at the open window Dog was enjoying. She thought about reaching across and rolling it up, but decided it wasn't necessary. Nothing was coming through with Dog sitting in the passenger seat. Negotiating a right-hand turn, Rachel drove for a hundred yards before having to turn ninety degrees back to the left. Her view in the new direction was blocked by a tall dike like she had walked along the previous night. She didn't see the roadblock until she was already most of the way through the turn.

A large pickup and SUV, painted brown with gold stars on their doors, sat across the road. Both vehicles were labeled as Crittenden County Sheriff. Four men dressed in jeans and white T-shirts leaned on the vehicle's fenders, pistols on their belts and rifles in their hands. A month ago, the sight of law enforcement might have made Rachel cringe and look at her speedometer, worried she was about to get a ticket. Now, she was immediately suspicious and slammed on the brakes, bringing the car to a halt thirty yards from the men. She shifted into reverse, keeping her foot on the brake when two of them raised their rifles and pointed them at her.

From the back seat, the two little girls started crying and Dog growled, staring at their ambushers through the windshield. Rachel debated flooring the throttle and trying to steer around the bend in reverse. Could she do it without putting the car into the ditch or getting stuck in the soft dirt of the shoulder? Would the men really start shooting, and if they did, were they good enough to hit her? But if they didn't hit her, they might hit Dog or the children.

One of the men who hadn't raised his rifle stepped forward and lifted a small, powered megaphone to his mouth. He claimed he was with the Sheriff's Department and ordered Rachel to turn the car off and step out with her hands over her head.

"Girls, get down on the floor. Now!" Rachel said without turning her head.

She heard them scrambling behind her, flicked her eyes to the mirror to make sure they were down, then took her foot off the brake and floored the accelerator. The engine bellowed and the rear tires screamed as the heavy car shot backwards. The men were caught off guard for a moment. They could tell the driver of the vehicle was a woman and the last thing they expected was for her to run. Women were supposed to cry and beg and eventually do what they were told to do. They weren't supposed to go screeching away in a cloud of tire smoke.

The first bullet punched through the windshield as Rachel was turning the wheel to steer around the bend in the road. It blasted a hole just below the rearview mirror and went on through the back window. That was the only bullet that hit glass before they disappeared behind the protection of the dike. The car was going fast and Rachel fought the wheel, trying to straighten them out. But, every time she corrected their direction of travel, she over corrected.

By the time she thought to take her foot off the gas, it was too late. The car went into a spin, ending up with both rear and one front tire in the soft dirt on the left shoulder. They were facing the way they had come and Rachel shifted into drive and pressed on the throttle. The car moved a few inches before the rear tires dug deep into the dirt. In seconds, the wheels were buried all the way to the axle.

17

Master Sergeant Jackson sat in a web sling, behind the pilots of a Black Hawk, staring out the open side door at miles and miles of nothing but rice paddies. Two Rangers sat farther back, lost in their own thoughts as the big helicopter pounded through the humid air. A door gunner was strapped in behind a minigun, an Army Private sitting to his side, ready to provide any support he might need.

They had been searching for Rachel and Dog for hours. Jackson had promised the Major that he would personally take charge of the search, and he was keeping that promise. He doubted they would be found alive if they were even found, but he knew the mission the Major was on and looking for lost friends was the least he could do.

The search had gone up and down the river several times, high passes for a broader view of the area and low, slow passes looking for bodies washed up on shore. Someone had suggested to Jackson that they had probably been washed all the way to Louisiana by now, but he had grown up in this part of the country and knew that wasn't how the river behaved. The Mississippi twisted and turned like a snake, and in every twist, there were sandbars that formed when the river current slowed for the bend and dropped the soil it had carried down from upstream.

All kinds of debris, including bodies, washed up and grounded on the sand on a regular basis. In fact, without constant steering by a knowledgeable pilot, the river wasn't nearly as easy to navigate as most people thought. A boat or barge without power might be carried downstream for a short distance, but it would quickly end up on the shore or a sandbar. This knowledge was the only reason Jackson held out even the faintest hope of finding Rachel and Dog.

They hadn't bothered to search the eastern shore of the river. For miles in either direction from Memphis, thousands of infected lined the shoreline. If they had washed up within wading distance of them, well, Jackson didn't want to think about what would have happened. After thoroughly searching the river and western shore as far as eighty miles south of the bridge where they'd gone in the water, he'd directed the air assets to start moving inland on the western side of the Mississippi. Currently, the Black Hawk he was riding in was flying a search pattern a few miles to the south of their temporary base at the West Memphis airport. Two more Black Hawks divided up the area farther south, all of them slowly working their way west.

"Master Sergeant, we've got some activity on our forward camera."

The pilot's voice over the intercom snapped Jackson out of his reverie. He turned to look at the high-resolution screen mounted in the cockpit.

They were currently flying at a thousand feet, and with the flat terrain had a good line of sight in all directions. Two miles ahead, and a little to the south, the cameras were zoomed in on a narrow strip of blacktop that bent around an earthen dike. A large, four-door sedan was stopped in the road a short distance from two police vehicles that were parked diagonally to each other, creating a roadblock.

As Jackson watched, he could clearly see two of the men he assumed were police officers, raise their weapons and point them at the vehicle. A moment later it shot backwards, fishtailed around a bend before losing control and spinning off the pavement. Jackson wasn't sure but thought the officers had been firing at the car as it started backwards.

The co-pilot adjusted the camera and zoomed tighter onto the car. A moment later the driver's door popped open and a woman with long hair leapt out and yanked the rear door open. Jackson's pulse started pounding when he saw the woman, but as good as the resolution was, it wasn't good enough for him to tell if it was Rachel.

Back door open, the woman hustled two children out of the back seat and seemed to be yelling at someone inside the car. She scooped the smaller girl into her arms and started running into a flooded rice paddy. When a dog jumped out of the passenger window and started following them, Jackson nearly let out a whoop of excitement.

"The guys from the roadblock are pursuing," the pilot said, looking at another screen fed by a different camera that was still focused on the police vehicles.

"The woman, dog, and children are our search targets. Consider everyone else hostile!" Jackson had to make an effort not to shout into the intercom.

The pilot responded instantly, lowering the nose of the helicopter and accelerating. The Black Hawk surged forward, losing altitude until they were only fifty feet in the air, screaming along in excess of the aircraft's published top speed of a hundred and eighty miles an hour. Jackson watched the monitor as they quickly closed the distance, glancing around briefly to satisfy himself the two Rangers and door gunner were ready. Turning back to the monitor, he could see Rachel was running as fast as she could through the flooded field with a child in her arms. Another girl ran in front of her, Dog bounding along at her side.

The men in pursuit were sixty yards behind, having covered the distance to the abandoned car quickly, but were also being hampered by the water as they pursued into the paddy. The helicopter was still nearly a mile out and apparently not yet detected by anyone on the ground. One of the men came to a stop and raised his rifle in Rachel's direction. They were approaching from an oblique angle and the pilot didn't hesitate to shoot. A hellfire missile roared off the left pylon and almost instantly accelerated to one thousand miles an hour, covering the distance to the parked police vehicles before the man could pull the trigger on his rifle.

Both vehicles erupted in a massive explosion, everyone on the ground stopping and turning to see what had happened. As the fire burned, the pilot flared to bleed off speed and roared into a nose down hover, twenty feet above the ground. The helicopter was protectively positioned between the four men and where Rachel and Dog stood with the children. Jackson didn't need the cameras and monitors to see the shocked looks on their faces. It's not every day you find yourself face to face with a fully armed Black Hawk.

18

I opened my eyes to see Martinez standing over me, hand outstretched towards my shoulder.

"We're just crossing out of Mexico, into Arizona," she said before turning away and resuming her seat.

I groaned softly, stretching my back and shoulders, then sat up and looked around. The two Air Force Sergeants still slept. Catching Martinez's eye, I tilted my head in their direction. She scooted across the deck and nudged them awake with the toe of her boot.

Checking in with the pilot, I asked him to let me know when we were over the Phoenix area. I might not have been able to stop, but this new bomber had some pretty advanced imaging equipment on board and I wanted to spot my house and see if I could get any idea of what might have happened to Katie. Depending on what I saw, I might be heading to Arizona once the mission was completed in Los Alamos.

As we flew over the southern part of the state, we all began getting ready for the jump. First order of the day was to strip down and don the polypropylene underwear that would protect us from the intense cold when we first exited the aircraft. For a few minutes, we all looked like big kids wearing Doctor Denton footy pajamas at a party. But kids didn't wear skin tight, thermal underwear, and sure didn't look like Martinez.

Scott and Yee were doing their best, but couldn't help but steal appreciative glances at her. Grinning and ignoring all of them, I finished dressing in my combat fatigues, finally slipping into the bat suit which also was well insulated. Boots back on, I packed everything else away into my pack, then stacked a helmet, insulated hoodie, goggles and my rifle on top.

Next, I inserted a small earpiece for a tactical radio then slipped into an oxygen mask that covered the lower half of my face, plugging the end of the supply line into a narrow tube that was mounted to a bulkhead. The tube supplied pure oxygen which was all we would breathe until on the ground in Los Alamos. To prevent the bends, it is necessary to purge your bloodstream of all the nitrogen that is naturally occurring in the atmosphere.

To do this, you need to breathe pure oxygen for at least half an hour before jumping. We had more time than that, but I knew a SEAL years ago that hadn't properly pre-breathed and was hit so hard with the bends on the way down that he couldn't control his jump and wound up dead. I might die in Los Alamos, but it sure as hell wasn't going to be because I hadn't prepared.

Checking on the other three, I received a thumbs up from each of them as they plugged into the plane's oxygen and confirmed it was flowing into their masks. Moving forward, careful to make sure I didn't snag my O2 line, I stuck my head into the cockpit.

"I was about to call you. Phoenix coming up on our left," the pilot said when he looked around and saw me.

It wasn't practical for me to switch places with the co-pilot to gain access to the imaging controls, so I talked the man through finding my house. It was dark below, much of the sprawling metropolitan area showing no signs of life. There were occasional pockets of electric light that looked like small neighborhoods, but they were few and far between.

The monitor was displaying the feed from a high-definition night vision camera and I was easily able to identify landmarks. The co-pilot made adjustments with a small joystick, finding Sky Harbor airport in the middle of the city, then following the ten lane freeway that ran right past it.

The same freeway I'd driven to the airport a few weeks ago when I'd left on my trip to Atlanta.

For a moment, I idly wondered if the car was still where I'd left it in long term parking. Dismissing the thought, I watched as the camera panned along the freeway, which was clogged with wrecked and abandoned vehicles.

As the view continued to the eastern suburbs, it struck me that there was no movement. No people. No infected. Not even animals. Where the hell did four and a half million people go? That wasn't a question I could answer from forty thousand feet in the air.

Eyes glued to the monitor; I spotted the freeway exit for the area of town I lived in and the camera adjusted to a new angle as I gave directions to the co-pilot. Soon, I recognized neighborhoods, my stomach clenching when all I saw were burned out husks that had once been houses. Following the streets, I counted the number of turns and saw the iron gates that controlled access to my neighborhood.

The gates were torn out of the stone columns they had been mounted to, lying to the side of the road on the front lawn of the president of our HOA. That house had burned as well. Following a couple more streets, I started counting, still seeing nothing other than the remains of large homes that had burned.

Then I spotted my house. Or what used to be my house. I made sure I was looking at the right one by checking the shape of the pool in the back yard. Katie and I had put a lot of time into designing the perfect pool for us, and my heart sank when I saw it was only half full of water, debris from the house piled around the edge from the back wall having collapsed.

I stood there staring for a long time. Until this moment, I had refused to accept that Katie wasn't sitting at home waiting for me. Getting up early every morning, doing yoga for an hour then running five miles before taking a swim in the pool. While I knew that I had been clinging to hope and fantasy, reality didn't hit me until I saw the destruction. And reality hit hard. I couldn't talk. Couldn't move. Couldn't do anything except stare at the monitor.

We were moving northeast and would soon be out of visual range. The co-pilot made adjustments with the joystick to keep my house centered in the image, clicking a button to enlarge and enhance the image. He zoomed in a bit more, leaned forward to stare at the screen then turned to look at me.

"There's no vehicles in what's left of the garage. Should there be?"

I didn't understand what he was saying at first, then leaned forward to look at where he was pointing. No vehicles! I had driven Katie's car to the airport the day I'd left because my truck won't fit in the low-ceilinged parking garage. She always bitched about it, usually preferring to drop me off and pick me up so she had her small Mercedes and didn't have to drive my behemoth. This time, she'd had plans to meet a friend for coffee, so I'd driven myself, leaving my truck at the house. And the truck was gone! Had she gotten out?

She and I had spent a lot of time four wheeling in the Arizona desert and mountains, and we lived so far out of the city that it was just a five-minute drive to Tonto National Forest. She had access to guns and a very capable four-wheel drive truck. And she was smart, tough and practical. I'd always thought she would have made a hell of an SF Operator. Well, if she didn't get pissed off and shoot a superior for telling her what to do. Very early in our marriage, I'd made the mistake of trying to assert my male dominance and tell her the way something was going to be. I'd never repeated that error.

While I was thinking this, we moved out of camera range and the co-pilot shut down the display. I thanked him for helping and returned to the back, sitting down and feeling hope displace the despair that had washed over me when I'd gotten my first look at the house. Was I being foolishly optimistic? Perhaps, but perhaps not. Katie was tough enough to survive. Sometimes she could act like a pampered princess, but if she'd had time to arm herself, gather up food and water and get in the truck, there was a reasonable chance she was alive.

19

"Ten minutes!"

The pilot's voice was clear over our secure earpieces.

Ten minutes to jump. We were over northern New Mexico, flying at thirty-five thousand feet AGL or Above Ground Level. I slipped the insulated hoodie over my head and attached it to the collar of the underwear. Goggles and helmet were in place, heavy gloves held in my left hand. I triple checked the altimeter and GPS unit attached to my left sleeve, ensuring that when the altimeter read ZERO, it was actually seventy-three hundred feet above sea level, which is the elevation of the mesa Los Alamos sits on. Get this wrong and you either open your chute too early or too late. Too early is bad. Too late is generally fatal.

Satisfied with the altimeter, I triple checked the GPS. Captain Blanchard had provided me with high-resolution coordinates for the building where the SADMs were stored, and I planned to come down on its roof. Ten years ago, I would have felt confident that I could pull that off. Now, I'd be satisfied to come down within the city limits. Without any broken bones.

Moving through the plane, I went to each of the Air Force personnel and had them show me their altimeters and GPS. They were all set correctly, as they had been the first two times I'd checked. Scott and Yee looked at ease, having made jumps with Army SF units in Afghanistan. Martinez tried to show a calm exterior, but I could hear her rapid and shallow breathing over the radio. I stopped and stuck my face in front of hers, peering at her through my goggles.

"Just another jump, Captain. Remember your training, keep your body under control while we're falling, and pull at fifteen hundred feet. Good to go?"

She licked her lips nervously and nodded. Reaching out, I placed a hand on her shoulder and left it there. She looked me in the eye and I said nothing, just looking back at her until I heard her breathing even out. When it did, she nodded again and I gave her a smile and moved on.

"Five minutes!"

The lighting inside the bomber changed from white to red. Light in the red spectrum does not affect human night vision and would allow us to still see, but at the same time adjust to the darkness waiting outside the aircraft.

Disconnecting my air supply from the line attached to the bulkhead, I connected to the small aluminum bottle strapped to my body which would supply oxygen during the fall. Shuffling to the back of the aircraft, I stood facing the rear. My pack was heavy and cumbersome, strapped as it was to my lower abdomen and upper thighs. The parachute was light on my back and I took a moment to check all the straps, pulling them as tight as I could get them, especially the ones that went between my legs. Many years ago, I had failed to make sure those two straps were tight before jumping. The looseness allowed one of my nuts to shift underneath the strap, which wasn't a problem until my canopy opened and those straps suddenly snapped taut to slow my descent. Definitely, a lesson I will never forget.

I pulled my gloves on and looked at my GPS. A small red dot pulsed at the bottom edge of the screen, meaning the target was behind me, in the direction we were traveling. The bomber had slowed to just above stall speed when we'd descended to thirty-five thousand feet, and we would go out the back door a few seconds before the plane flew directly over our target. Our forward momentum would bleed off very quickly when we hit the air. Then we would form up and *fly* ourselves down to fifteen hundred feet, where we would open our chutes and steer to the drop location.

The automated weather unit at Los Alamos airport was still transmitting and the pilot had let me know there was only a two-knot wind out of the east at ground level. That was nice to know, but I was also worried about what we would encounter on the way down. It was summer time and the barren terrain below had been baking in the sun all day. Now that it was night, the rock and sand would be radiating heat, creating updrafts which in turn would create downdrafts. A strong updraft could cause us to miss our target by miles. A strong downdraft could cause us to fall thousands of feet in a couple of seconds, or worse, collapse a canopy.

Putting all of this out of my head, I glanced over my shoulders to make sure my small team was ready. Sergeant Scott stood a step behind and to my right, Yee in the same position on my left, Martinez sandwiched between them. I would lead the way off the ramp, the three of them tight behind me. If Martinez hesitated, Scott and Yee were ready to each grab an arm and bring her with us. Her best chance of making this successfully was staying right behind us and doing what we did, when we did it.

"De-pressurizing now." The pilot spoke over the radio.

Moments later, my ears popped as he equalized the pressure within the aircraft to the thin air outside. Both pilots were now wearing oxygen masks as well as having sealed the door to the cockpit, which remained pressurized. Their wearing of the masks was just a precaution in the event the seal on the door failed while the main part of the plane was open to the outside environment.

"Thirty seconds. Opening now."

I felt a slight vibration in the soles of my boots as the sloped back wall directly to my front went into motion. A thin gap opened between the ceiling and the wall, quickly widening as the ramp extended back into space from the main body of the bomber. I stepped forward, stopping with six feet of aircraft decking between me and a seven-mile drop. Scott, Yee, and Martinez moved forward to keep us tight, Scott and Yee placing a hand on my shoulder briefly to let me know they were ready. I was depending on them to monitor the Captain.

"Ten seconds. Good luck and God speed, gentlemen and lady," the pilot said before going into a countdown.

When he said "five," I leaned myself slightly forward and shifted my weight to the balls of my feet. When he said "one," I took a deep breath, let it out and stepped off with a fast stride as he shouted, "Go! Go! Go!"

In two steps, I covered the six feet to the edge of the ramp, launching myself out into space as I ran out of the aircraft. I immediately spread my legs apart and reached my arms out to each side to stabilize my body. The surfaces of the bat suit caught the thin air and allowed me to make a sweeping turn so I was facing in the same direction as the departing bomber. I took a second to look up, catching a quick glimpse of red light as the ramp closed tightly, then it disappeared from my sight.

"Report," I said over the radio.

"Boomer 2 in pattern." Scott answered.

Moments later both Yee and Martinez checked in. Martinez sounded a little breathless, but nothing too concerning. If she wasn't scared, she wouldn't be human.

"Doing OK, Martinez?"

"Time of my fucking life, sir," Martinez panted.

I smiled, knowing she was scared but glad to hear her sarcasm. She was doing great for her first HALO jump.

Below us was nothing but darkness. Far to the south, I could see lights and guessed that was Kirtland AFB and the Russians. Glancing at my GPS, I was glad to see us on target, and a check of the altimeter showed we had already fallen five thousand feet. Another check of the GPS to satisfy myself and I relaxed a notch and tried to see anything on the ground beneath me. Nothing. No lights, candles, campfires...nothing.

As we passed through twenty-five thousand feet, I issued the command to spread our spacing over the radio. Each of them acknowledged, Martinez sounding a little shaky. We were falling in a stack, me at the bottom and Martinez at the top, and were too close together to safely deploy our chutes when we reached the target altitude. To deal with that, we'd start spacing ourselves out now.

I would adopt a slight head down position for a few seconds, causing me to fall faster and pull away from my jump mates who would flatten their bodies in the horizontal plane and use wind resistance to let me gain separation from them. When I was far enough below, Sergeant Scott in the number two slot would do the same thing, then finally Yee. All Martinez had to do was not fall faster than the rest of us and we'd pop out of the fall and touch down within seconds of each other.

Checking the GPS, I noted we had drifted a little off course and made a correction. By ten-thousand feet, we were back on target, and that's when the first updraft hit. I had been falling smoothly through calm air, the altimeter winding down at a constant pace when suddenly I was pushed hard and knocked off course. Curses over the radio a heartbeat later told me I wasn't the only one. As fast as the updraft hit, we were out of it, and after I stabilized my body, I checked the altimeter and GPS. Eighty-five hundred feet and off target.

"Check GPS!" I called out to my team and twisted my body to get back on course.

I hadn't fully compensated when I flew into a downdraft. For a fraction of a second it seemed like I had stopped falling, then it felt more like one of those amusement park rides that drops you and leaves your stomach behind. More curses over the radio.

It only took a few seconds for me to pass out of the downdraft, but when I did, I checked the altimeter and wasn't happy to see how much my rate of descent had been affected. I was passing through four thousand feet and the GPS told me I was off target by almost four miles.

I had been to Los Alamos before, while in the Army and later as a civilian just playing tourist. I knew the mesa the small city sat on wasn't very large, and four miles off our target could easily cause us to miss the mountaintop completely and wind up in a several thousand-foot-deep canyon. As so often happens, the plan had to change to deal with new circumstances.

"Pull now!" I shouted into the radio. "Pull! Pull! Pull!"

Following my own order, I reached behind and pulled the pilot chute from its pocket, releasing it into the air. I heard it flutter in my slipstream and a moment later it inflated, pulled the pin and released the main canopy. The black fabric made a snapping sound when it filled with air and I let out an involuntary grunt when my fall was suddenly arrested. I heard two more snaps above my head, waited for the third and looked up when I didn't. Above and behind, I could see two canopies, darker patches against the dark, starry sky, then a body fell past me.

20

The four men hadn't wanted to lay their rifles down, but Jackson convinced them by having the door gunner fire a one-second burst from the minigun into the ground near their feet. Water and mud erupted into the air. After that, they couldn't disarm themselves fast enough. With their rifles in the water, the pilot descended to a hover with the Black Hawk's tires just brushing the green tops of the rice plants, its rotor whipping up a maelstrom of water, mud, and debris. Jackson and the two Rangers jumped out of the open door, rifles immediately coming up to cover the men.

"Disarm them and get them up on the road."

Jackson issued orders to the Rangers before turning to check on Rachel. She was wading through the paddy, using big strides to move easier through the water while looking intently at the door of the Black Hawk as it climbed and went into a low orbit around the area. Dog trotted up to Jackson and nuzzled his hand.

"You OK?" Jackson asked as Rachel walked up to him.

"We're good, but we wouldn't have been if you hadn't shown up. Thank you."

She was talking to Jackson but looking up at the orbiting helicopter.

"You're welcome, and he's not here. He's on a mission to retrieve some equipment we need to deal with the Russians. Before he left, he made me promise to keep looking for you."

Rachel smiled a sad smile then a confused look passed across her face.

"Russians? What are you talking about?"

"They've invaded. Attacked us right after you four went into the river. That's why it's taken us so long to find you."

"Four? John came in after us?"

"Didn't even hesitate. Couldn't have been more than a few seconds behind you, but it's a big river, and he couldn't find you. We plucked him out and that's when the goddamn Russians showed up."

Rachel stood there, tears threatening to start, thinking about John risking everything to come in the water after her. Well, her and Dog. The damn obstinate man had more feelings for her than he was willing to admit.

"And who do we have here?" Jackson asked, smiling at Madison who was on Rachel's hip with her arms locked around her neck.

"This is Madison, and that's Lindsey. And they have a story you need to hear."

Jackson gave her a quizzical look, then moved all of them out of the paddy and onto dry land. Rachel had Lindsey tell the story of what happened to their parents. He listened closely without interrupting until she was done. Resting on one knee so he was eye level with the girls, he asked a couple of questions to make sure he was getting the whole story. Rachel filled in the details from after she and Dog had found them.

"Lindsey, would you recognize the bad men that took your parents if you saw them again?" He asked.

"That's one of them right there!" Madison said, pointing at the group of men sitting on the asphalt with the two Rangers guarding them.

"Which one?" Jackson asked.

"The one on the left, with the tattoo on his arm. I remember him. He's the one that slapped my mommy and called her a nigger!"

Madison's voice left no room for uncertainty. She was certain of her identification. It also left no doubt what she'd do to the man if she were only a little older. Jackson looked up at Rachel and she nearly took a step back when she saw the expression on his face. He stood and started to turn to where the men were sitting, but Rachel reached out and placed her hand on his arm. He stopped and turned to face her and she could feel the tension and anger rolling off him. Putting Madison on her feet, she told the girls to stay with Dog and walked Jackson a few yards down the road.

"I don't pretend to understand how this makes you feel, but it makes me sick to my stomach. You don't know this, but I was taken by a group of men in Georgia and raped while we were trying to escape. John killed every one of them and rescued me. These men aren't any better and deserve whatever happens to them, but we must do this right. If you go over there, pissed off and ready to start breaking bones, we may not get the answers we need. Perhaps you'd better call the Colonel?"

Rachel kept her hand on Jackson's arm as she spoke, her eyes looking into his. She saw his intent to commit murder and mayhem, then saw it tempered when she suggested contacting Crawford. After a moment, he took her hand in his and nodded.

"Thank you. That's probably best."

He gave her a tight smile, released her hand and turned away to use his radio in private. While he was busy speaking with the Colonel, Rachel went over to where Lindsey and Madison sat on the edge of the road. Dog was between them, soaking up attention from his two new best friends. Rachel sat down in front of them and Madison crawled into her lap, shifting around so she could still pet Dog. A few minutes later, Jackson walked over and sat down next to Rachel, smiling at the girls.

"Who's hungry?" He asked, pulling an MRE out of his pack.

Both girls' eyes got big, and Dog's ears went straight up. Jackson laughed and started preparing the meal, sharing it out between the girls. They finished every bite quickly and he brought out another one, giving half of it to Dog before letting the girls wipe out the remainder.

As they were finishing the meal, he reached to press his earpiece deeper into his ear before standing and looking to the north. Four specks were fast approaching, quickly resolving into a pair of Black Hawks escorted by two Apaches. The Apaches and one of the Black Hawks went into an orbit, the second Black Hawk swooping in and landing on the road fifty yards from where they sat. It hadn't even settled on its landing gear before Colonel Crawford jumped out the door, escorted by four more Rangers. He turned and helped a woman in civilian clothing step onto the ground.

"Good to see you, ma'am," he said to Rachel. "Was starting to think we weren't going to find you."

"Thank you, Colonel. Thanks for not giving up on me."

"I'd like to take the credit, but it was that hard headed maniac you run around with. I think he would have shot me if I'd tried to call off the search," Crawford said with a grin, then shifted his attention to the girls.

"Girls, this is Mrs. Maybach. She's going to keep you company in that helicopter over there while I go talk to these men about where your parents might be. Is that OK?"

"Are you going to get our parents back?" Lindsey asked.

"I'm going to do everything I can, sweetheart. I promise. Now, go with Mrs. Maybach and I'll see you real soon."

Rachel got the girls on their feet, hugged them and assured them she would see them before they knew it. They held hands with the woman, one on either side of her, and the three of them walked to the waiting Black Hawk, which took off and headed north as soon as they climbed inside.

"Who's she?" Rachel asked as they headed over to where the four men waited nervously.

"She was on the train. Is, or was I guess, the principal of an elementary school in Nashville. She just happened to be talking to me about caring for the children on the train without parents when the Master Sergeant called. Thought it might be good to bring her along and have her get the girls away from here."

By now they were standing in front of the prisoners and Rachel pointed out the one that Madison had identified. The tattoo on his arm was a large swastika overlaid with the twin lightning bolts of the Nazi SS.

"I'm Colonel Jack Crawford, US Army. I'm going to ask you some questions and I expect nothing less than full and truthful answers. Do you understand?" He addressed them, looking each in the eye as he spoke.

"Fuck you." A wiry, balding man sitting next to tattoo man spoke up. "We're the goddamn Sheriff's department and the Army ain't got no fucking authority here. That's illegal. So why don't you take this cunt and your pet nigger there and get the hell out of here."

Crawford looked at the man for a long moment, saying nothing. Without a change in expression, he drew his pistol, shot the man in the head, then calmly holstered the weapon. The other three shrank away from the body, shocked expressions on their faces. Jackson and the four Rangers exchanged glances but said nothing and didn't move a muscle.

Rachel was caught completely unprepared. Not because of the violence or seeing a man die, she had grown used to that, but because she hadn't thought of Crawford as the type of man that could calmly execute a prisoner. She wouldn't have been surprised in the least if John had done it. In fact, she had killed a defenseless man back in Nashville, but she hadn't thought of Crawford in those terms. You don't wind up in charge of men like Jackson and John if you're not one of them, she reminded herself.

"Let's try this again," Crawford said his tone as congenial and calm as if he were ordering lunch.

21

An hour later, Jackson climbed aboard an idling Black Hawk on the tarmac at West Memphis airport. The helicopter was already stuffed with Rangers and four other helos, equally full, were ready to go. Crawford climbed in behind him, taking the small, folding jump seat attached to the forward bulkhead that had been left open for him.

"Let's go," he said over the intercom as soon as he pulled a headset on.

In a coordinated ballet, the five helicopters lifted into the air and turned to the southwest, quickly accelerating as they climbed to five hundred feet. Four Apaches flew cover at fifteen hundred feet, keeping an eye out for any Russians that might want to crash the party. One of the Rangers, a young Corporal, was fiddling with an iPod and nodding his head to whatever music he was listening to.

Crawford looked around, found a spare intercom cable and after getting the Ranger's attention, handed it to him with a nod. The Corporal grinned, unplugged his headphones and inserted the cable into the jack. A moment later, Satisfaction by the Rolling Stones blasted across the intercom, the pilot flipping a switch that also played it over speakers inside the cabin. Having expected rap, or anything other than a fifty-year-old song by The Stones, Crawford smiled and enjoyed being in the company of his soldiers.

After he had shot the first man, the other three were so eager to talk they kept stumbling over their words. It turned out they weren't really Sheriff's deputies, but had taken the vehicles when the world fell apart. They were part of a white supremacist group that had settled in Arkansas a few years ago after having been run out of Kentucky. Their leader claimed to be related to Hitler and routinely preached that someday they would rise and join forces with all the other white men to rid their country of its racial stain.

Until the attacks, they'd been held in check by law enforcement to a degree, as well as the disdain of whatever community they found themselves in. They supported their quest by dealing drugs stolen from pharmacies, sometimes breaking in after closing time, but more often through violent, armed robberies. They stayed in touch with other fanatical organizations as well as outlaw motorcycle clubs, moving guns, drugs and underage prostitutes along the interstate system in the southeastern United States. All of them had done time in prison and were members of the Aryan Brotherhood.

Now, after the apocalypse, they were two dozen heavily armed men living in an isolated compound on the edge of Arkansas rice country. Seeing the vacuum of authority and taking it as an omen, their leader decided it was time to start cleansing the countryside of impure races. The first victims were blacks, taken to work as slaves in their fields and animal pens. If someone was too old, too young or too sick to work, they executed them.

With a good number of slaves, they had decided to branch out and start taking white women so they could start building the next generation of the master race. Since none of them had an IQ greater than double digits, they all failed to see the flaw in that plan. But, while they may not have been very smart, they were very dangerous.

With help from the prisoners, Crawford and Jackson had located the compound, sending a Black Hawk on a reconnaissance flight to confirm. The pilot had flown at twelve thousand feet, using the onboard imaging equipment to verify their target. The video stream had been beamed back to West Memphis, clearly showing three large structures, a barn, fields, and close to forty people working out in the hot sun. Zoomed images identified the workers as black, with heavily armed guards standing watch over them as they toiled away.

Crawford hadn't even had to think about the decision to go get the captives. The government might be gone, but this was still the United States and he wasn't about to let assholes like this get away with what they were doing. He had briefly wondered if he would have been as incensed if this was happening in another country, but dismissed the thought. Like most men who are drawn to the military, and especially any form of Special Operations, he had no tolerance for people who forced their will on others. These guys were about to find out what happens when you try to do that.

The flight continued on to the west, past the target, turning and approaching from out of the sun. This wasn't a military enemy that would have early warning radar or IR sensors. These were just a bunch of dumb, white trash morons. The only tactical advantage Crawford needed was to not be seen until they started their attack runs.

"Five minutes, Colonel," the pilot said over the intercom; the music silenced when he pressed the transmit button.

Jackson waved at the Ranger and he unhooked the iPod, carefully wrapping it in a towel before returning it to his pack. He might be able to walk into any abandoned electronics store and pick up a replacement, but it wasn't so easy to download music any longer.

The Rangers busied themselves with a final check of their weapons. The five Black Hawks shifted into a pattern where they flew abreast of each other, spread out across half a mile of airspace. The Apaches set up a five-mile picket line around them. The helicopter Jackson was riding in had two mounted door guns and both gunners slid the side doors open, settling in behind their weapons.

The attack plan had been thrown together quickly, but it didn't need to be complicated. Everyone knew what they were doing and they knew the situation hadn't changed. They were still receiving a real-time video feed from the Black Hawk that was orbiting at twelve thousand feet.

"Commencing run!"

The pilot spoke, the vibration already increasing as they accelerated and dropped to one hundred feet. Ahead, a large square plot of land, growing corn, was being worked by a dozen men and women. On each corner of the square, a man with a rifle stood watch over them. To the left, another field was being worked by close to twenty people, another four guards positioned to guard them. Beyond, a few black men were working on some vehicles under the watchful eyes of a group of six armed white men, seated on chairs in the shade of a large oak tree. There were supposed to be twenty Aryans and, counting the four that had ambushed Rachel, they had accounted for 18 of them.

"Weapons free," Crawford said as they screamed towards the compound.

The first shot of the battle was a hellfire missile targeted on the base of the tree where the six men sat. As it roared off its pylon, door gunners on all five Black Hawks opened up. The missile arrived before the first bullet, slamming into one of the men a fraction of a second before detonating against the trunk of the tree. The resulting explosion destroyed everything within a thirty-yard radius, shattering the tree trunk and sending it toppling to the ground.

There was a mix of miniguns and 7.62 mm machine guns mounted on the five aircraft, and as all of them opened up, the guards along the two fields were shredded. The ones struck by the machine gun fire had limbs blown off and holes blasted through their bodies. The ones hit by minigun fire mostly vaporized into a pinkish mist. In less than twenty seconds, they had all been wiped out. The people in the fields stood and stared up at the helicopters, some of them cheering as it was obvious they were being rescued.

Jackson's Black Hawk was the first to land on the hard-packed dirt in front of the main house, the pilot coming in over the roof of the structure and dropping the final thirty feet to the ground. The door gunners scanned the area while Crawford, Jackson and the Rangers leapt out of the open doors and quickly spread out. Jackson had argued with the Colonel, not wanting him to be on the ground until the area had been cleared, but Crawford overruled him.

"You don't lead from the safety of a hovering helicopter, Master Sergeant," he'd responded, putting an end to the discussion.

As soon as the last soldier exited the aircraft, it roared back into the sky, two more landing and disgorging their loads. Directly ahead of Jackson was a large house that was in dire need of maintenance. The paint was peeling badly and the wooden siding had warped away from the frame due to exposure to the elements. A sagging porch ran the length of the front of the house, its roof seemingly ready to collapse at the first strong breeze. Between them and the house were the vehicles the captive men had been working on. Crawford and Jackson ran to them, two Rangers that Jackson had assigned to protect the Colonel staying close on his heels.

The five men that had been pressed into mechanic duty had hit the dirt when the missile exploded and took out their guards. They were still lying on their bellies, two trucks and an ancient Buick sheltering them from the heat of the burning oak tree. Crawford skidded to a stop on his knees amongst them.

"Gentlemen," he greeted them with a nod. "How many of them are left and where are they?"

"There's six of them in the house and two in the barn." One of the younger men spoke up, pointing to the two locations as he named them. He was tall and looked like he was in good shape other than an eye that was swollen shut, a split lip and a large purplish bruise on his jaw. "They've got eight women in the house and four in the barn. Haven't been inside either building, so I can't tell you the layout."

The other men all nodded their heads in agreement. Crawford eyed the man for a moment.

"You serve, son?"

"Yes, sir. Lance Corporal James Lynch. Marine Corps. Afghanistan and Iraq."

"Good, Marine. Get these men out to the fields and get everyone rounded up and down in the weeds. Don't want any friendly casualties if we can help it."

Lynch grinned and, staying low to the ground, motioned the others to follow him as he headed out in a large arc that would get him to the fields without coming too close to any of the structures. Crawford glanced around to make sure all his troops were in place, nodding to himself in satisfaction when he saw they were. Three of the five Black Hawks had dropped Rangers in front of the structures, the other two unloading behind them.

They had the remaining eight men surrounded. Six more than the prisoners had told him about. He wasn't surprised. Fire from one of the upper windows of the house started up, bullets smashing into the ground around the men Crawford had just sent to safety. One of the Rangers was using the Buick for cover and a shooting rest. He fired a single shot, silencing the sniper. Seven to go.

Jackson and Crawford had a brief conversation, then Jackson started relaying orders over the radio. The Rangers were already in place and on a nod from the Colonel, Jackson transmitted the execute order. Cover fire immediately erupted all around the structures, more Rangers leaping to their feet and running towards their assigned buildings.

They ran with their rifles up, spread into covering formations with each one aimed at a different window or door. Another sniper popped up in the barn, shooting through a small opening at the end of the loft, but his bullets didn't find their target before the same Ranger at the Buick shot him through the throat.

Crawford led the assault on the house, Jackson on the barn. They breached each structure within moments of each other, the Rangers on their heels spreading out as they entered each building. The Aryans didn't surrender and they didn't survive very long. They had spent a lot of time *training*, but it consisted of shooting rusting cans at the edge of one of the fields while they were drinking beer. Several of them got shots off, none of those finding their mark before they were killed. In less than a minute, the assault was over, all of the captors dead or dying of multiple gunshot wounds.

The Colonel stood in the middle of the main room on the first floor of the house, looking down at the two men he'd personally killed while the Rangers brought down the women they'd found locked in bedrooms on the second floor. While he waited, Jackson called him on the radio to let him know the four women in the barn had been executed. Crawford grimaced, taking the death of those women personally.

22

I was reaching to cut away my main canopy to go after whoever was still falling when another body flashed past me, head down and arms tight along the torso.

"Who's still up?" I called out on the radio.

"Yee here. Scott just went after Martinez. Think she's hypoxic."

He meant she had passed out, probably due to a malfunction of her oxygen supply, or perhaps she'd hyperventilated. Scott had cut away from his main chute and was trying to save her.

"Steer on me, we'll try to come down close to them."

I pulled on the right toggle to go into a turn and spiral down along the same path my other two teammates were falling. I also released my pack, letting it fall to the end of a long tether and hang beneath my feet. The pack was close to seventy pounds and would hit the ground ahead of me, rather than adding its weight to the impact my legs would have to absorb when I landed.

In the civilian world, and some military jumps, there's a piece of equipment called an Automatic Activation Device, or AAD, that will take control and deploy your chute at a preset altitude, if it's not already open. These are commonly used on equipment drops from high altitude where you don't want the chute opening as soon as the pallet goes out the back door of the aircraft.

I don't like using these and most of the guys I've jumped with over the years don't either. There are reported cases of them malfunctioning and opening too high, leaving you hanging there like an idiot when you need to be much lower to maintain a degree of stealth.

AADs have a built-in altimeter and I always suspected the reports of malfunctions were actually user error, the jumper having failed to set the device properly. Regardless, none of us had one and, if Scott couldn't catch up and deploy her chute very quickly, he would have to pop his reserve and let her fall to her death. Hell of a set of balls on him to do what he was doing.

"Got her!" A moment later Scott's voice came over the radio.

"Both of you under canopy?" I asked, meaning did they have their chutes deployed.

"Affirmative. She's unconscious. I'm following her down. We're under five hundred. Will update when we're on the ground."

I looked below me, trying to spot them. It was a dark night with not much moon for light, the ground dark and the tops of their chutes even darker. I couldn't spot them. Checking my altimeter, I noted I was at two thousand feet and a quick check of the GPS showed I was several miles off target. So much for an easy insertion.

"We're down. Showing light now," Scott called out.

Normally, showing any light was a big no-no, but we needed to find them quickly and stay together. If we had night vision, he could have flashed an IR light at us, but we didn't so he did the next best thing and aimed a red lensed flashlight up into the air and clicked it twice. I didn't see it, but Sergeant Yee did. Pulling on the toggles to slow my descent I let him get lower so he could lead me to Scott and Martinez.

A few seconds later our boots were on the ground, both of us making recruiting video perfect landings in the nearly motionless air. Quickly shrugging out of my chute, I passed it to Yee who added it to his before piling rocks on top of both. I dropped to a knee with my rifle up, scanning the area with the scope while he concealed our gear. We planned to be gone before the sun came up, but in case we weren't, we sure didn't want to leave a big sign behind telling the Russians that someone had jumped in during the night. Rockpile complete, Yee shouldered his pack and raised his rifle. Settling mine on my back, I stood up.

We had come down within fifty yards of the edge of the mesa. There was enough moon and starlight for me to see the sheer drop to our left. That was a little too close for comfort. I hand signed for Yee to take point, since I still didn't know where Scott had come down, stepping off once he had moved ten yards to our right.

Leading the way up a slope, he paused at the crest to use the night vision in his rifle scope, then disappeared over the top. Following, I saw our two teammates below in a shallow depression when I reached the crest. Hurrying down, I dropped to a knee next to Scott, who was leaning over Martinez. Yee stood to the side, surveying the area. A moment later, he returned to the crest above us and went prone to watch over us.

Martinez lay on her back, unconscious. Scott had removed her O2 mask and parachute and was busily performing rescue breathing. While he worked, I checked over her limbs, happy to not find any broken bones. Didn't mean there wasn't a severe ankle or knee sprain that would hamper her movements, but we wouldn't know that until we got her awake and on her feet.

Scott leaned back a minute later, pulled his glove off and pressed two fingers to her neck.

"Pulse is good. Finally smoothed out," he said with a note of relief in his voice.

She was breathing normally again, her chest rising and falling regularly without the help Scott had been providing.

"I know a Colonel that's convinced I'm crazy," I said to Scott in a quiet voice. "I need to introduce you two. That was some hot shit, Tech Sergeant."

Scott flashed a grin, teeth white against the dark makeup covering his face.

"I just hope she's ok. How long do we wait before we wake her up?"

"We need to know her status, and we need to be out of here before the sun comes up. Can't have a Russian patrol fly over and see us running around in the daylight," I answered.

He nodded and dug through his pack for an ammonia ampule. Snapping it open, he thrust it under her nose and held it there until she coughed and tried to bat his hand away. She started moaning and Scott leaned close, placing his hand lightly over her mouth and whispering in her ear.

"Contact."

I heard Yee's voice over the radio and snapped my head around as he fired three shots from his rifle. They were suppressed and quiet. Signing for Scott to stay with Martinez, I moved up to the crest and lay down next to Yee with just my head, shoulders and rifle above the ridge line. Looking through my scope, I spotted three bodies in the dirt, fifty yards away.

"Talk to me," I mumbled to Yee.

"Three females. They looked like they were scenting us. The one in front had her head tilted back like she was sniffing the air."

He sounded a little freaked out and I reminded myself that these three hadn't fought the infected face to face yet.

"You sure they were infected?" I asked, still scanning the bodies through the scope.

"Yes, sir. I'm sure."

Yee sounded like I'd offended him, but I didn't give a shit. I wasn't worried about the possibility of him having shot survivors. I just wanted to know for sure if there were infected roaming around this far from town. If he was going to take offense to every question I asked, he was in for a long night.

"Martinez, ready to move?" I asked over the radio. "We've got infected in the area."

"Coming to you now," Scott answered.

A moment later he suddenly appeared right next to me, Martinez joining him a second later. She didn't look too bad, considering.

"You good to go, Captain?" I asked her.

"I'm good to go, sir."

"OK, we are..." I paused to double check my GPS. "Six point three miles from our target. Infected are in the area and we need to move fast and quiet. Scott, you're on point. Yee, rear security. I'm on right. Let's move."

Scott briefly checked his GPS, then scrambled over the crest and stood up, moving off at a fast walking pace. Martinez and I fell in a few yards behind him. I was glad to see she hadn't needed me to spell out that I wanted her on the left as we moved. Nothing against her, but she was a pilot, not a ground pounder.

Yee fell in behind us and we headed east towards town. Glancing down at the dead infected as he passed them, Scott pointed at one of the bodies but didn't break stride. A few steps behind him, I looked at the body he'd identified as I walked past. It was female, and once upon a time she'd been a Commander in the US Navy. Lots of work was done on military projects in Los Alamos and it didn't surprise me to see the uniform. I expected to see more before the night was over.

23

Scott set the pace. While he may not have looked like someone who could cover a lot of ground quickly, I was surprised when we'd been walking for half an hour and I checked my GPS to find we'd covered two miles. Good pace for having maintained stealth in rugged terrain.

We encountered the occasional male, stumbling about in the dark. They were almost comical, unable to see as they navigated, continually tripping over rocks and scrub brush. We usually heard them falling before we could see them. I was keeping half an eye on Martinez, glad to see she seemed none the worse for wear as she easily picked off the ones in her area of responsibility.

We climbed a small hill, Scott holding up a fist to tell us to stop when he could see over the crest. We froze in place, listening and watching his hand as well as scanning our individual zones. A few seconds later, he snapped his hand fully open, extending all five fingers before making a patting motion towards the dirt.

We dropped to the ground and spread out silently. Scott had also dropped with just enough of his head above the top of the slope for him to see whatever the danger was. He watched for a moment before turning and signing me forward. I belly-crawled up the slope to lay next to him, slowly raising my head to see over a small rock.

Thirty yards away, a wide strip of blacktop cut through the high desert terrain. Three Humvees and two MRAPs sat in the dark, apparently abandoned. MRAPs are Mine Resistant Ambush Protected trucks that look like a Hummer and a civilian armored car had a long night of drinking and sex, giving birth to a cross between the two. They might be ugly, but they were tougher than up-armored Hummers and could take a lot of punishment. But the vehicles weren't why Scott had called a halt. It was the large group of infected that milled around amongst them.

I did a quick head count. Seven males and five females. Carefully I raised my rifle, using the night vision to check each vehicle for occupants. Finding none, I redid my count, coming up with the same numbers, then scanned the surrounding area. Four more males were struggling through the desert a hundred yards to my front, attracted to the sounds the group below was making, but other than that I didn't see anything.

I wanted one of those MRAPs. We would be secure from the infected and there was plenty of room to carry the SADMs we were here to retrieve. But how closely were the Russians watching the area? Had they already checked and found it overrun? If so, were they doing routine flyovers that would spot a moving vehicle? I had no way of knowing, and no way of finding out without taking a chance. Making a decision, I waved Yee and Martinez to the top of the slope with us, outlining my plan when they arrived. With nods of understanding, we spread out.

When they were in position, I gave the execute order over the radio. Our rifles fired simultaneously and four of the five females dropped dead to the road. Shifting aim to the fifth, I cursed as all I saw was her hair billow behind her as she threw herself behind the protection of a Hummer. Los Alamos had been the victim of the secondary outbreak caused by the virus and that meant the females here were the smart ones. The males weren't any smarter, regardless of primary or secondary outbreak, so we started dropping them as they stood there looking around like drunks at closing time on a Saturday night.

Letting myself think this was going to go off smoothly, other than the one female, I spun when I heard a rock shift behind me. A pack of females was running up the slope, the one in the lead no more than five yards away. She saw me turn and screamed. Bringing my rifle around, I knew I wasn't going to get a shot off in time to stop her, but someone was looking out for me. The female slipped on the loose rocks, going to a knee and giving me time to shoot her through the head.

I didn't need to warn the others; the screams of the lead female had done that quite effectively. More were charging in, some of them screaming as they raced towards us through the night. I shot two more before they were too close, then I had to drop the rifle and draw my Kukri to defend myself.

A female leapt, arms extended with hands held like talons to tear into my throat. I was just able to get the Kukri up between us and she impaled herself on the blade. If I was a rookie, I would have expected that to stop her, but I knew by now that while she would eventually die from the wound, she certainly wasn't out of the fight just yet. Jamming my forearm under her chin to fend off her snapping teeth, I pulled the Kukri out of her body and stabbed again from the side, up through her rib cage and severing her heart.

Shoving the body away, I flinched to the side as another charged in, slashing open her throat and severing her windpipe. Letting the momentum of the swing continue, I rolled and came to my feet just as another female arrived. This one came to a stop ten feet away and stood there staring at me. What the fuck?

I was panting from the exertion and adrenaline in my system, surprised into immobility by this totally unexpected behavior. We just stood there, staring at each other for several long heartbeats. Her red eyes flicked between my face and the large blade in my hand. She was filthy, covered in dirt and blood, some of it fresh and some dried onto her skin and clothing.

Neither young nor old, I guessed she was around forty, and was still wearing what had once been a white lab coat. Time stretched out as neither of us made a move. I could hear my teammates fighting on either side, both suppressed rifle and pistol fire, but I was rooted in place by the odd behavior of this female. Unnerved might be a better way of saying it.

"Can you understand me?"

I spoke in a low, even voice. The female's eyes widened slightly when I spoke, but she stayed in place. I didn't know what to do. Was she trying to communicate? Was that even possible any longer? Max had said the females that were infected by the virus retained their higher brain functions. Did that mean they might still be able to speak? This all went through my mind in a fraction of a second, then realization dawned on me when I heard a sound to my rear and the females eyes flicked up to look over my shoulder.

"Clever girl," I said.

I charged her, Kukri at chest level, ready to tear into her throat. Being upslope, I had the added benefit of gravity. As fast as the females are, she wasn't fast enough. Covering the distance between us in less than the blink of an eye, I rammed the blade home before she could do more than open her mouth to scream. I kept my legs churning and shoved her corpse aside, running to the bottom of the slope before suddenly changing direction to my right.

The female that had been sneaking up behind had followed me, finally screaming when I juked away from her attack. She tried to slow and change direction with me, but there was a lot of loose rock at the bottom of the slope. Her feet went out from under her, and I fell on top, stabbing into the back of her head with the Kukri.

Back on my feet, I looked up the slope to check on the rest of my team. Martinez finished off a female with a dagger thrust to the eye that was one of the fastest moves with a blade I had ever seen. The infected dropped at her feet and the battle was over. Scott and Yee had both killed all of the females attacking them, each with four bodies on the ground at their feet. Yee held his left arm and Scott moved to him to check the injury as I climbed back up the slope.

"Nothing serious," Scott reported after examining Yee. "One of them tried to bite a chunk out of his arm but couldn't get through his clothing. A little damage to his forearm, but he's combat ready."

Nodding acknowledgment, I turned to check on Martinez. I was surprised to find seven dead females on the ground where she had been fighting. She met my eyes and for the first time gave me a real smile.

"Damn, Captain. Try to leave some for the rest of us next time," I said and smiled back.

24

Rachel and Dog stood on the tarmac at the West Memphis airport, staring west as the sun sank towards the horizon. There was maybe two hours of daylight left. Lindsey and Madison were inside the control tower, sleeping, wrapped around each other on Colonel Crawford's bunk. They were exhausted, having fallen asleep on the short helicopter ride to the airport after Jackson had rescued them. By the time Rachel had arrived on a different Black Hawk, Mrs. Maybach had carried the girls inside, commandeering the Colonel's temporary quarters.

Crawford and Jackson had left a couple of hours ago with a large contingent of Rangers. Rachel had wanted to accompany them, not one to be content with being left behind, but the Colonel had told her in no uncertain terms that she was not welcome on a military operation. He had softened it a bit by reminding her that if he took her along and something happened to her, there would be one very upset Major to deal with. Rachel had laughed, understanding the man's position, but still not liking it.

And where was John? What was he doing? All they would tell her was that he was on a mission, something to do with the Russians. She was still in a state of disbelief over that bit of news.

Dog whined and Rachel followed his gaze to see Max propelling himself in his wheelchair across the tarmac towards where she stood. A moment later he rolled up and scratched Dog between the ears.

"Good to see you back with us."

He pulled out a cigarette and lit it. Rachel thought about asking for one, but she didn't really like the damn things.

"It's good to be back," she answered with a smile.

"Any word on Roach?" He asked.

Rachel just shook her head. She hoped the son of a bitch had drowned in the river. Better yet, she hoped he'd washed up on the eastern shore and been ripped to shreds by the infected. She tried to think of how John would say it, but could only come up with hoping Roach was nothing more than infected poop by now. She couldn't help but smile at the thought.

"Why won't they tell me where John is?" She asked, hoping Max could help her understand the military's stubborn love of secrets.

"There's no guarantee the Russians won't swoop down on us in superior numbers at any moment." He exhaled a plume of smoke that hung in the still evening air. "And if that happens, the less people that know anything about his mission, the better. You and I shouldn't even know he's on a mission. The Master Sergeant broke protocol just telling you that much."

Rachel understood, but that didn't mean she had to like it or agree with it. Was this how military spouses felt? Not that she was anything to John other than a friend, despite what she felt for him, but this still sucked. How did the *wives* do it? Their husbands gone who knows where for who knows how long, and no one will tell you anything.

Rachel felt a wave of empathy for John's wife, Katie, followed by guilt over her profession of love to him. She couldn't help how she felt, couldn't stop the feelings she had, but finally realized the impossible position she'd put him in. Even if he did love her too, how could...

Muted screams from the control tower reached her ears. Fear for the girls churned in her gut as she turned and ran for the door, Dog racing ahead of her. By the time she reached the building, she had her rifle up and slowed only enough to yank the door open before charging in. Dog beat her up the stairs and before she reached the top the screaming had changed to a whimpering cry. Pounding up the last steps, Rachel stepped into the glassed-in room with the rifle at her shoulder, seeking the danger. She lowered the weapon when she saw Madison curled into Lindsey's lap, sobbing, one arm wrapped around Dog's furry neck.

"She had a nightmare," Lindsey said, looking up at Rachel.

Starting to step forward to comfort Madison, Rachel glanced out the window, seeing several Black Hawks approaching over the flooded rice paddies. Deciding a distraction was exactly what the frightened girl needed, Rachel slung her rifle and scooped the child into her arms. By the time they reached the tarmac, the first helicopter was landing, not far from where Max sat in his wheelchair. Walking up to stand next to him with Madison on her hip, Rachel made sure Lindsey was close, glad to see Dog staying right next to the young girl.

Jackson was the first out of the helicopter, jumping to the tarmac the moment the wheels touched. He waved at Rachel and turned back into the open side door to help a woman climb down. The first two off the aircraft were barely even women, looking more like teenagers. Both were white and even at a distance Rachel recognized the haunted look on their faces, their initial flinch when Jackson reached to help them down. The next one was a black woman of medium height with a regal bearing. She took Jackson's hand as she stepped down, eyes immediately locking onto Rachel's small party.

Lindsey squealed with delight and broke into a run directly at the woman. A second later, Madison squirmed free of Rachel's arms and sprinted after her big sister. The face of the woman broke into a huge smile and she raced forward to meet her daughters. The two girls threw themselves at her, nearly knocking her off her feet, then the three of them wound up on their knees, hugging each other and crying. Tears were running down Rachel's cheeks and when she turned her head to wipe them away, she noticed Max was crying too.

"What? I'm not supposed to be touched by one of the first good things I've seen happen in a long time?" He asked when he noticed her looking at him.

Rachel smiled as she leaned down to hug him, then she and Dog walked over to the small family reunion. Lindsey saw her approaching and excitedly started pointing and talking to her mother. By the time Rachel reached them, the woman was on her feet and walked forward to wrap Rachel in a tight embrace.

"Thank you! Thank you for saving my babies!" The woman's voice broke with emotion as she spoke, still clinging tightly to Rachel.

"You're welcome."

Rachel was unable to stop smiling from ear to ear. The woman finally released her, grasped each of her shoulders and held Rachel at arm's length to look her in the eye.

"I'm Mary Alice. I don't know how I can ever repay you for what you've done."

"I... you don't need to repay me. They're good girls and I'm just happy you're back together with them."

Rachel smiled, uncomfortable with the woman's gratitude. Understanding her discomfort, Mary Alice pulled her into another hug, then released her and turned to her girls. Rachel bent to hug each of them, surprised at the sense of loss she was already feeling. Goodbyes said, their mother gathered them up and followed the other women who were being escorted by a Ranger to the evacuee camp next to the train. Rachel watched them walk away, happy for them and trying not to start crying all over again when a large man that had just jumped out of a different helicopter ran up and scooped all of them into his arms.

By now, the last Black Hawk had unloaded and the flight lifted off to go pick up the Army personnel that had stayed behind to make room for the rescued captives. Jackson wasn't making this trip and walked up to Rachel, rubbing Dog's ears and looking her in the eye.

"You OK?"

"I'm good," Rachel answered, turning her attention away from the happy family. "Now, you're going to tell me exactly where John is, what he's doing and if I'm ever going to see him again."

She circled her arm through Jackson's and led him towards the makeshift mess tent that had been set up.

25

I was more than a little freaked out by the female I had just encountered. I'd seen the same level of intelligence in the warehouse back in Nashville, but it hadn't really sunk in just how effectively they could coordinate their efforts. I wouldn't be caught with my pants down again. As soon as I saw a female, she was going to die. Otherwise, I was going to wind up someone's tough, stringy dinner.

We had quickly finished off the remaining infected with our rifles, then climbed over the crest and down to the road where the abandoned vehicles sat. With Scott and Yee on security, Martinez and I checked them over. The first MRAP had skidded off the pavement, winding up in a ditch. It was deep enough that the two passenger side tires were dangling in the air, the truck resting on its frame. It wasn't going anywhere without a lot of help from another large vehicle.

The second MRAP was sitting in the middle of the road, driver's door open. And it was out of fuel. I looked around and guessed the drivers had felt ill and stopped the convoy. They had apparently managed to get out of the vehicles before turning, but they'd left the engines running, which had eventually consumed all the diesel in their tanks. I expected to find the same problem with the Humvees, and did. OK, Plan B. I lightly thumped on the jerry cans mounted to the back of each vehicle, finding each of them full. It would just take some time to fuel one of the vehicles.

Pointing at a rack of four cans on the back of one of the Hummers, I grabbed one and handed it to Martinez, then picked up another and headed for the MRAP. The fuel transferred slowly and I heard five suppressed rifle shots from behind while I was holding a can up to the side of the big truck. Martinez was busily bringing me more full cans.

"Status?" I asked over the radio, not stopping my work.

"Four males," Scott answered. "The first round was a body shot. Center mass. He didn't even flinch."

"Everyone remember your briefing," I said, lowering an empty can and lifting a full one. "Head or heart shots, or they don't go down immediately."

I received three acknowledgments, then snapped my head up at the faint sound of jet engines. It had to be the Russian CAP. Were they only up looking for other aircraft, or was the pilot bored and scanning the area with FLIR?

"Make dumb!" I said into the radio and quickly lowered the can of fuel to the pavement, spilling half a gallon or so onto my boots.

Make dumb was our pre-arranged signal to try and fool any aerial observers. On FLIR at night, as long as we weren't doing anything other than standing or walking around randomly, we would look just like any other infected. However, fueling a vehicle, or holding a rifle, would give us away to any reasonably sharp observer. I slowly shambled away from the MRAP, Martinez walking over to stumble around with me. I couldn't see Scott or Yee, but they should be doing the same, their rifles hanging from their slings.

The noise grew louder as the jet approached, but the way sound bounced around the adjacent canyons I couldn't tell from which direction it was approaching. Eventually, it passed over us, traveling east to west. It wasn't showing any light, which didn't surprise me for a military aircraft in a combat zone. But even without being able to see it, I could tell when it passed overhead and the direction it was going. Giving it a few minutes to pass out of range, I dashed back to the MRAP when I felt it was safe, calling an all-clear to the rest of the team.

The jet was flying away from Kirtland AFB, most likely on the outbound leg of its patrol. Would it follow the same path back to base? Was I worrying over nothing? No, I wasn't. We had to plan for the worst and hope for the best. Assuming the Russians weren't keeping an eye on the ground this close to their captured base would be foolish. I would, and no matter what one might think of the Russians, they weren't stupid and they sure weren't incompetent. We had to assume they would be back.

Hoisting the can of fuel, I thought about what I'd once known about Soviet military protocol and procedures. They would typically establish a two-hundred-mile CAP around any operating base. I knew we were about seventy air miles from Kirtland, so I could expect that pilot to travel another hundred and thirty before turning around. When any nation is flying patrols, they fly slow to conserve fuel, but fast enough to cover their assigned areas in a reasonable amount of time. I had been able to tell from the sound of the jet that it was just cruising along, not in a hurry to get anywhere. He was probably flying at three hundred knots, or about three hundred and forty five miles an hour.

Lowering the empty can and grabbing another full one, I did the math in my head. It should take him roughly twenty-five minutes to fly the remaining one thirty miles. Fifty minutes until he was potentially back overhead. Forty-five to be safe. I may have mentioned that I'm not one of those people that can do math in their head quickly or easily, and by the time I had figured all this out, the new can of fuel was empty. Sitting it down, I decided we were good with the twenty-five gallons I had poured in.

We were about four miles from the target building. Ten minutes, at the most, in the MRAP. That would give us thirty-five minutes to locate, retrieve and load the SADMs before we needed to either take cover or make dumb again. Calling the team in, I hopped behind the wheel, hit the starter and checked my GPS. We were already pointed in the right direction, so as soon as Scott and Yee piled into the back and slammed the door, I started us moving.

Within the first half mile, we started smashing infected under the armored bumper. There were a lot of males, but there also seemed to be a lot of females charging us out of the dark. A few of them acted like the ones I'd encountered during the original outbreak, running straight at us and slamming into fenders or doors. But there was a large contingent of smart ones that chose to try and run alongside us, watching and waiting for an opportunity. They recognized we were secure inside the big vehicle and weren't going to sacrifice themselves in a futile attempt to get to us through the armor plating. We quickly outdistanced them, but I could see them following in the mirror, the crowd growing as we drove.

Topping a small rise, we were suddenly in town. Los Alamos isn't large, barely boasting twelve thousand full-time residents. Like many small towns, it has a sharply defined edge where all signs of civilization, other than a road, just stop.

This was where we found ourselves, driving by a fenced county maintenance yard, then a small strip mall. Right after the shopping area, the road forked and Martinez checked her GPS, telling me to go right. Turning onto the new road, we quickly entered an area with twelve-foot chain link fences on either side, the coiled razor wire that topped them gleaming faintly in the moonlight. On each fence, at fifty-foot intervals, groups of three large signs were attached.

US Government Property – Deadly Force Authorized Beyond This Point, Electrified Fence – DO NOT TOUCH, and *ACTIVE LAND MINES - DO NOT ENTER* were the warnings in both English and Spanish. Behind each fence was a fifty-yard stretch of flat, open ground covered with neatly raked sand that ended at another equally tall fence. Both barriers also had cameras mounted on the top of every post. Beyond were large, paved parking areas that were mostly full of cars, and squat buildings barely visible in the dark. I had been here before and had seen the signs.

On one trip, I had stopped into a local Starbucks and overheard a group of college-aged tourists talking about them. They were laughing and joking, saying they didn't believe them. They thought they were simply a scare tactic and that the government would never put out land mines or shoot a trespasser inside an American city. I had kept my mouth shut and shook my head. I didn't know what government they were talking about or what they thought went on in Los Alamos. Guess they didn't pay attention in history class.

"GPS says it's that building right there."

Martinez pointed at a large, single level structure on our left, hardly visible behind the fencing and full parking lot.

I braked to a stop, staring at our target. My eyes travelled across all the vehicles in the parking area. Lots of cars meant lots of people had been at work. That meant lots of infected inside the fence, and that probably was really bad news in the case of the females. Los Alamos employed some of the smartest people on the planet. If these females had retained their higher brain functions, they were probably still smarter than half the surviving population. Great. I took a moment to share my thoughts with the team, then drove forward, looking for a gate into the complex.

26

We found the entrance gate easily enough, but driving through it was a different story. Actually, there were two gates. The first one was set into the outer fence, the second one, the inner. The narrow driveway between them was fully enclosed on each side. The outer gate was the same twelve-foot chain link mesh with razor wire on top, hinged to swing in towards a small guard shack offset to the side.

If it was just the gate, we wouldn't have had a problem, but it was guarded by half a dozen bollards sticking up out of the asphalt. I was familiar with this type of security measure. The bollards were retractable via hydraulic rams underneath the street and were made of reinforced concrete wrapped in cast iron. They were two feet in diameter and, when extended, stuck five feet up into the air, creating a barrier that not even a tank could break through. Unfortunately for us, they were fully extended and completely blocked our progress.

"I've got this," Scott said from the backseat. "I paid attention when these were being installed at Fort Drum. Just need someone to watch my back."

I glanced at my watch, noting we had about twenty-five minutes before the Russian jet should be back overhead. Looking around, I saw multiple males and several females converging on us.

"How long will it take you?" I asked as I made sure my rifle was ready.

"Two minutes, maybe. There should be a maintenance hatch in the ground next to the guard shack. Once I'm inside, I can release the pressure on the hydraulics and they'll retract under their own weight."

I nodded, checking on Yee before we stepped out to meet the infected. He had been bitten on the arm when we were fighting the infected earlier. The bite hadn't broken the skin, but it had severely bruised the tendons in his forearm. He demonstrated his readiness by holding up the hand and opening and closing his fingers. Telling Martinez to slide behind the wheel, I popped my door and stepped out, Scott right behind me. Yee went out the far side of the MRAP and took up station there, opening up with his rifle a moment after I did.

As we engaged the approaching infected, Scott ran through the bollards and to the gate. He already had a pair of short-handled bolt cutters in hand that he'd dug out of his pack, immediately setting to work cutting an opening in the chain link.

I didn't have time to watch, but could hear him working as I acquired and fired at my targets.

A large group of females was approaching at a sprint and I decided to try a different tactic. If these were smart ones, which I had every reason to expect they were, as soon as I shot the one in the lead, the others should peel off and start trying to flank me. Not that there was room for them to go anywhere with the road fenced on both sides, but I wanted to test a theory. The first female I targeted was running at the back of the group. I fired, and she tumbled dead to the pavement, the ones in front of her continuing their charge without missing a step. I kept firing, working my way forward until there was only the lead female remaining.

She sprinted at me, still not screaming. I held my fire, rifle ready but not pointed directly at her, waiting until she was only twenty yards away. I had been on my knee, in a more stable shooting position. As she approached, I stood, took a step away from the MRAP and aimed directly at her face. She looked around and, not seeing any other females, skidded to a stop no more than ten yards away.

"If you can understand me, turn around and walk away and I'll let you live," I said.

Other than curiosity, I couldn't explain why I was messing around like this. The female just stood, staring at me, opening and closing her hands much like a big cat sheathing and unsheathing its claws before attacking. My aim didn't waiver. My finger was on the trigger, half the travel already taken up. If she even twitched in my direction, she would die. She looked like she was thinking. Weighing her options. But she didn't seem like she had understood a word I'd said. A long moment later, she tensed and opened her mouth with the beginning of a scream. I shot her between the eyes.

While I was testing my theory, Yee had been firing steadily, keeping the infected at bay on his side of the truck. Now, I had to start engaging the males that were approaching. There were a lot of them, a rough guess putting the number at over a hundred. I worked on thinning them out, pausing and looking to my right when there was a loud explosion. I could see a cloud of smoke and dust hanging in the air in the no-man's land between fences, debris raining down in the area of the blast. It took me a moment to realize an infected had gotten in there and stepped on a land mine.

I went back to shooting, hoping Scott was hurrying, then another explosion sounded from behind me not far from Yee's position. Had to be females climbing the fence from inside the compound. There was no way the males could have gotten in there. I kept shooting, but the mass of males was growing and they were approaching faster than I could put them down. Pausing to change magazines, I glanced around when I heard a metallic scraping sound, relieved to see the bollards slowly descending into the road.

"Mount up," I ordered over the radio when I saw Scott squirm through the hole he'd cut in the gate and run towards us.

We all piled back into the MRAP and Martinez hit the throttle. The truck bounced as we rolled over the bollards. It seems that releasing the hydraulic pressure does lower them into the ground, but the rounded tops had remained sticking above the pavement a few inches. Nothing to even slow us down, she continued to gain speed, crashing the armored front of the vehicle into the center of the gate. I had braced for the impact but didn't even feel it as the fourteen tons of hurtling steel tore through like they were made of tissue paper. Two more land mines detonated to our left as more females tried to reach us.

"Don't ram the gate!" I suddenly shouted to Martinez before she could destroy the last line of defense against the packs of infected that were pursuing us. She jammed on the brakes, the big tires screeching in protest as we came to a sliding stop with the front bumper only feet from the inner gate.

I briefly explained what I was thinking and Scott and Yee jumped out with me. Yee moved to the back of the truck to cover us from the infected while Scott and I checked the gate. This one was hinged as well, opening into the compound. Large hydraulic arms on each side were mounted to the bottom rail of each half of the gate, able to pull it open or push it closed. Scott clicked on his red-lensed flashlight and examined one of them, jerking back when a female slammed into the chain link and tried to force her arms through to grab him.

"They can be released, but I can't do it from out here," he said, raising his rifle and shooting the female that was still banging on the gate.

I looked up at the top of the gate, twelve feet in the air with a thick coil of razor wire attached for good measure, then at the idling MRAP. Issuing orders over the radio, I quickly got Yee moved out of the way, then Martinez made a series of K turns until the vehicle was reversed and backed up with the rear bumper touching the gate.

Scott and I scrambled over the hood and onto the roof, which was about eight and a half feet high. Standing, the top of the gate was just above waist level and Scott used his bolt cutters to quickly dispense with the razor wire.

While he worked, I looked back down the driveway. Yee was racking up a respectable body count, but just like earlier, the crowd was growing. Despite his efforts, the front edge was continually moving closer. Another land mine detonated, much too close, and Scott and I both ducked involuntarily when a piece of shrapnel pinged off the armored side of the vehicle we were standing on.

"Ready!" Scott called, storing the cutters and swinging one leg over the top of the gate. I moved next to him and started taking out infected. There were several in the area, mostly females, and all of them were making a beeline for the rumble of the idling diesel engine.

"Go!" I said, shooting a sprinting female.

Scott grabbed the top rail in both hands, swung his other leg over and again defied his appearance by climbing down the gate with far more agility than I expected. He ran to the arm on the left and knelt over it with his multi-tool. I shot more infected that were closing in on him. It took him less than thirty seconds to release the arm, then he ran to the other side and repeated the process. By now, I was firing nearly every second, the number of converging infected inside the fence increasing. Another land mine detonated and Yee yelped.

"Talk to me, Yee," I said on the radio.

"Took some shrapnel in the leg. I'm fine."

I had to take his word for it and his rate of fire never faltered.

"Done!" Scott called out and yanked the gate open, dropping to a knee to join the fight.

Martinez backed up until the MRAP was fully inside the gate. When she came to a stop, I scrambled over the roof, down across the windshield and dropped to the ground. Scott was keeping the infected knocked back for the moment and I grabbed a length of heavy chain out of the tool box mounted to the side of the vehicle, yelling over the radio for Yee to fall back.

"Yee needs help!"

I heard Martinez in my earpiece and spun to see the young Sergeant sitting on the ground, legs splayed out in front of him, still firing his rifle at the quickly approaching herd. I ran towards him, seeing the spreading pool of blood he was sitting in as I approached. A piece of shrapnel had severed something big in his leg and he was bleeding out.

The closest male was only a few feet away, hundreds more no more than ten yards behind. I gripped the chain tightly, cocked my arm back and swung. The end whipped around and crunched into the male's head, shattering his skull and dropping him in his tracks. Hooking my hands under Yee's arms from behind, I dragged him backwards as fast as I could.

Scott met us at the front corner of the MRAP, plucking the bloody chain out of my hand as I ran by with Yee in tow. Slamming the gates, he wrapped the chain around the two center posts, wedging the ends through the brackets that held the mesh tightly stretched. This wouldn't stop a survivor for longer than it took them to unwrap the chain, but the infected weren't smart enough to figure that out. I hoped. Seconds later, the leading edge of males crashed into the gate. It rattled and moved a couple of inches until the chain arrested its travel.

27

Yee's heart stopped less than a minute after Scott and I muscled him into the MRAP. The shrapnel had severed his femoral artery and even if we'd gotten to him immediately after the injury, there was nothing we could have done to save him. We sat looking at him for a moment, then removed his weapons and piled them to the side. Scott dug through a locker, finding a stash of lightweight body bags that are commonly hidden away and we took the time to get Yee's body zipped inside.

Martinez and Scott were just sitting and staring at the body bag, lost in their own thoughts, but we didn't have time for mourning lost comrades. There would be an opportunity for that later, hopefully. I snapped at them to get their shit together and focus on the mission.

While we were sitting there, infected had arrived, pounding on the sides of the vehicle. I looked up at Martinez and she nodded, turning to grasp the steering wheel and get us in motion. She backed away from the gate that was now solidly packed with infected trying to push through. As she backed up, numerous infected were crushed, but I noted they were all males, the females leaping out of the way. Swinging us around, Martinez started following a road that skirted the perimeter of the parking lot.

It didn't take us long to come to an intersection. The MRAP's headlights reflected off a large sign that pointed to the left for Staff Parking and the right for Loading Dock. I had moved into the front passenger seat and pointed to the right. Martinez turned, crushing a few more infected as she drove along the side of the building. The road was wide, obviously built for large trucks. Immediately to our right was another fence with the same warning signs that were posted along the public road. Behind us, I heard the crump of another land mine detonating, but didn't bother to turn my head to look.

Soon we reached the back corner of the building, the road emptying into a very large parking area. A sign warned drivers to stay in their vehicles until escorted by security. There were no infected visible in the lot, but close to a hundred males and females were following us. At the far end of the building, nearly half a mile away, what looked like a giant, metal barn stuck out from the wall, a pair of tall doors blocking access. It clearly looked like an addition to an existing structure and was exactly what I had expected to see.

Los Alamos does research and development of all types of offensive and defensive military projects. Materials, as well as the completed prototypes being taken to the field for testing, had to come and go. The government didn't want our enemies, or even our allies for that matter, to be able to see what was arriving and departing with their spy satellites, so these types of sheds had been added to any facility that didn't have drive-in loading areas. When a truck arrived, it would pull into the shed and close the outer doors, concealing its activity from prying eyes.

"When we get there, swing around so you can back in when we get the doors open," I said to Martinez, pointing at the shed.

She nodded and accelerated to open some distance from the trailing infected. Scott had been paying attention and raised his rifle to look at the doors through his night vision scope.

"Any idea how hard it's going to be to open those?" He asked, rifle still to his cheek.

"None. But we'll figure it out." I leaned forward to look at our followers in the rearview mirror. "Looks like we'll have two minutes at the most before we have company arriving."

"What do we do if there's already a truck in there?" He asked.

I hadn't thought about that and didn't have an immediate answer for him.

Martinez steered around a parked eighteen-wheeler, slowed to make a sharp turn to line up the rear of our vehicle with the shed and jammed on the brakes. Scott and I were already moving, jumping out and running to the entrance. We took a moment to scan down the sides of the shed and around the corner of the building to make sure there weren't any infected in close proximity. Finding none, we turned our attention to the doors.

They were hinged on the inside but appeared to swing out. We couldn't tell if they were electrically or hydraulically operated as that equipment was inside as well. To the right of the door, a small keypad was set into the wall, a dim, red LED glowing in the center of the number pad.

"Power on, or battery?" Scott asked.

We couldn't tell. None of the parking lot lights were on, but that didn't really mean anything. The building could well have had a generator that was running and we just couldn't hear it. There were no external windows, a security feature, so there was no way to know.

"You've got about ninety seconds."

Martinez' voice over the radio, updating us on the approaching infected. I resisted the urge to look over my shoulder, focusing on searching for an emergency release for the big doors. I told Scott what I was looking for, hoping some safety manager had forced the issue when they built the shed, and he started checking to the right while I looked over the left.

"Sixty seconds," Martinez said.

Her voice sounded rock solid calm. But then she was sitting inside a fourteen ton, armored vehicle. Why shouldn't she be calm?

Seemingly forever later, but before we received our thirty-second warning, I found what I was looking for. A heavy, metal plate, nearly two feet tall, a couple of inches above the pavement on the left side of the shed. It was painted the same color as the building and set flush with the surrounding metal. At the bottom, a small finger hole was filled with dirt and debris. Jamming my finger in, I cleaned it out enough to hook the edge of the plate and lifted it up. The hinges were stiff with age, old paint and I suspected a complete lack of maintenance.

"Thirty seconds!"

Martinez finally sounded a little stressed, calling out the time as I shouted for Scott to bring his flashlight. He skidded to a stop on his knees next to me and aimed the red light into the opening, revealing a thick lever, hinged at the bottom. I grabbed the top with one hand and pulled, but it didn't budge. Sitting my ass on the pavement and bracing my feet against the wall, I grabbed with both hands and pulled for all I was worth.

"Twenty seconds!" Martinez was getting antsy now.

Sweat popped out on my forehead from the exertion, and I was about to stop and have Scott grab on to help when I felt the lever begin to shift. As it moved, there was a loud, metallic squealing sound from the area of the doors. My back and arms were on fire, but the lever was still moving, slowly, and I wasn't about to stop and give up the progress I'd made.

"Danger close!"

Martinez shouted on the radio, and a heartbeat later Scott started firing at the swiftly approaching females. The lever had traveled perhaps a third of the way to full extension, the screeching sound from the doors growing louder.

"Might want to hurry it up there, sir. They're coming faster than I can shoot!" Scott shouted, never pausing his steady rate of fire.

With a scream of effort, I pulled with my arms and pushed with my legs, the lever moving faster until it suddenly hit a release point and flopped free into a horizontal position.

"Doors are open. Bay's empty. Let's go!" Martinez shouted as she goosed the throttle and the big truck roared backwards into the shed. I rolled, coming up on my knees and raising my rifle to face the infected.

"Oh, shit!" I breathed involuntarily, immediately acquiring and firing on a target. There must have been close to a hundred females sprinting directly at us, the closest ones inside fifty yards. A world class athlete could sprint forty yards in just a hair over four seconds. I was willing to bet an infected female could outrun them.

"Legs!" I shouted at Scott, flipping my rifle to burst mode and aiming for knees.

I knew this wouldn't kill the infected, but right now I would be happy to slow them down so we could dash around the corner of the building and through the open doors. Each of us pulled our triggers repeatedly, sweeping through the front ranks of the infected. The females crashed to the pavement when our bullets shattered knees, femurs, and hips. They didn't give up, starting to crawl towards us, but we were slowing the advance.

"The doors are closing!" Martinez screamed at us over the radio. Time to go!

Scott and I each fired a final burst, leapt to our feet and ran. Rounding the corner, I saw the twenty-foot tall doors swinging in towards each other, gaining speed as they closed. I sprinted, tracing the path in my mind that I needed to follow to run around the moving door and through the rapidly shrinking opening. Screams from very close gave me an extra burst of speed and I dashed through with inches to spare, slipping and sliding on the smooth concrete floor inside the shed as I tried to stop.

As soon as I cleared the door, I turned my head to check on Scott. A step behind, he crashed into the right door as he made the turn, losing momentum. He was trying to get his body moving forward again when a female slammed into his back, popping him through the opening and coming along with him. Another one slipped through the narrow gap, spotted me and changed direction to attack. A third one tried to make it, but wedged herself in the space, reaching through with her arms and screaming for a moment before the doors completely closed with a solid boom and crushed her between them. Blood and other bodily fluids splattered across the floor where she died.

I was completely off balance from sliding on the smooth concrete and couldn't bring my rifle around as the female leapt at me. Instead of fighting my own momentum, I let my body skid, pulling the Kukri and preparing for the fight. Before I could engage the female, a dagger suddenly appeared in the side of her head and she dropped lifeless to the floor. Martinez strode forward, retrieved the blade she had thrown with perfect precision and turned to help Scott.

He was on his back, infected straddling his chest. He had both thick hands wrapped around her throat, holding her at arm's length as he choked the life out of her. Martinez ran up, grabbed the female's hair from behind to control her head and thrust the dagger deep into her brain stem. She immediately went limp and Scott tossed the body to the side with a disgusted grunt. I was on my feet by now and walked over, extending a hand to help him up. Martinez bent to clean her dagger on the infected's lab coat.

"Captain, if you're half the pilot that you are fighter, the Russians are fucked," I said, clapping her on the shoulder. She smiled, slipping the dagger into a sheath hidden in her clothing.

"Where did you learn to use a blade like that, ma'am?" Scott asked her, checking over his equipment.

"I grew up in Juarez," she replied with a smile. "You think this is dangerous? You should have tried walking home from school in my old neighborhood."

28

The lights were on inside the shed, which was a relief. Without NVGs, we would have been severely hampered in our movements by complete darkness. There was a constant banging from the doors, the infected we had escaped pounding their frustration. What would the Russian pilot think if he flew back over and saw them clustered around an entrance to the building?

Hopefully, if he did spot them, he would dismiss it as likely that a survivor was in the building, and the infected were trying to get in for a snack. But even if it didn't immediately raise an alarm with the Russians, how long would it take him to mention it to someone who would think it was worth investigating? Maybe I was worried about nothing, but the faster we got our hands on the nukes and got the hell out of there, the better.

We each took a moment to check over our gear and for Scott and me to load fresh magazines into our rifles. The MRAP had held a cache of ammunition and we replenished what we'd already expended. Weapons ready, I pulled out the paper Captain Blanchard had given me on the flight from West Memphis to Little Rock.

It was written in a precise hand, detailing the information from an inventory register that had been read to him over the phone. The SADMs were in a sub-basement of the building we were in. They were stored in vault W, five levels beneath us. Great. I was getting tired of big buildings full of infected.

The shed was long enough to take an eighteen-wheeler, with plenty of room to spare. The inside was nothing more than smooth walls and floor leading to a huge, roll-up door that accessed the main building. To the right of the door, a small electrical box was mounted to the surface of the building's wall, metal conduit running straight up and disappearing into the ceiling. I lifted the opaque plastic cover, happy to see two large buttons, the lower one red, the upper green. Thanking whoever had decided that a keypad on the outside of the shed was adequate security, I checked to make sure both Martinez and Scott were ready, then pushed the green button.

A moment later, rotating orange lights set on either side of the door, high above the floor, started turning and a strident alarm began blaring. I looked around for the siren, spotted it hanging from the ceiling and shot it into silence. We had already made too much noise. The last thing we needed was a damn 'door in motion' alarm to alert all the infected inside the building to our presence.

The door moved slowly, Scott on his knees and bent to look under with his rifle aimed at the widening gap. I watched him closely, thumb on the red button, ready to send the door back down if he saw more infected than we could handle. I didn't have a plan B if that happened and breathed a sigh of relief when he just knelt there, raising his body up as the door continued to open.

With six feet of clearance, I hit the green button again, stopping its motion and holding it in place. We didn't need more clearance than that to easily pass through, and if we were being pursued by infected when we returned to the MRAP, I didn't want the door all the way up. The damn thing moved slowly and the farther open it was, the longer it would take to close.

On the other side was a large open area. The same smooth concrete floor reflected the overhead lights. Far off to the left were several electric forklifts, neatly lined up and plugged into their charger. Next to them were a dozen hand carts, but other than that, the space was empty. We stepped under the door, spread out in a line, rifles up and ready. Scott and I were on each flank and turned to scan our sides, but there weren't any infected and there was no place for them to hide.

In the far wall of the room was another large rolling door, and to its right were four steel doors with narrow windows set into their upper halves. The glass was reinforced with wire mesh and no more than four inches wide. On the wall, next to the right-hand door was a large plaque. From a distance, it looked like a map of the facility. When I approached, I was glad to see it was. Our current location was marked with a red dot and a "you are here" note, just like a directory in a shopping mall. Unfortunately, the map only showed the level we were on, none of the sub-basements, but it did show the path to a bank of elevators and stairs.

The sub-basement access was labeled as "Purple", and I glanced down. Different colored lines were painted on the floor, several going through each of the four doors. The purple line disappeared under the second from the left and I pointed at it, making sure my small team saw it.

Moving to the door, I looked through the narrow window into a well-lit hallway. More smooth floor with a three-inch wide purple line running directly down the center of the shiny tile, eventually turning a corner to the right and going out of sight. The walls were featureless with no doors. Nothing moved.

"OK," I said in a low voice, turning back to Martinez and Scott. "We're going to follow that purple line and take the stairs down to the fifth sub-level. I'm on point. Scott, you've got the rear. Two meter spacing. Ready?"

"Why the stairs?" Martinez asked.

"This place has power, which has to be from a generator. I don't really want to be stuck in an elevator, below ground, if the damn thing runs out of fuel."

She nodded and I carefully pushed on the crash bar mounted on the door. There was a soft, metallic click as the lock released, the door swinging open as I stepped into the opening. The hall in front ran farther than I could see, but the right turn dictated by the purple line was about fifty yards away. A yellow, blue and green line continued straight down the hall. I hadn't noticed where they led and didn't really care at the moment.

Stepping fully into the hallway, I braced the edge of the door against my back to hold it open, rifle up and aimed down the corridor as Martinez and Scott slipped through. I signed for them to watch our front and when they both had their rifles up, turned my attention to the door. When I'd pushed on the crash bar, I had heard and felt the lock release. I didn't want to let the door close and get locked out of the cargo loading area.

The hallway side only had an elongated, U-shaped handle for pulling the door open. Next to it was another of the small, electronic keypads that would unlock the door if you had the right key card. I didn't, but I did have some duct tape. Tearing off a strip, I wadded it into a sticky ball and shoved it into the steel recess on the frame to prevent the lock from snapping into place when it closed. Satisfied with my effort, I kept a hand on the door, letting it silently come to rest inside its frame. The lock didn't snap and when I tested the door, it pulled open easily.

Attention back on the hall, I signed that we were moving and stepped off with my rifle tight to my shoulder. We moved fast but quiet, quickly reaching the turn. I stopped us with a hand signal, lowered my rifle and pressed my shoulder to the wall. Taking a few moments to listen, I couldn't hear anything other than the sigh of air flowing out of vents in the ceiling and the quiet breathing of the two people behind me. Not hearing any danger, I carefully poked my head around the corner, scanned the new corridor, then pulled back.

The new hall was clear. Nothing but more shiny tile, smooth walls and a purple line running twenty yards to a bank of elevators. Stepping around the corner, I moved to the elevators and paused by a steel door that was marked as stairs. It was secured with another keypad, and there was no way for us to open it. Well, we could have broken out the C-4 and blown the door open, but there was little that could have convinced me it would be a good idea to make *that* much noise. The facility was absolutely quiet. Too quiet. The little part of me that could still get scared watching a really good horror movie was jumping up and down, telling me nothing good ever happens in big, seemingly empty buildings.

Resigning myself to trusting that the generator wouldn't pick the very moment we were on an elevator to run out of fuel, I reached out and pressed a button. There was only one since there was only one way to go. It lit up and half a second later a large red arrow pointing down began glowing next to the elevator doors. When the arrow lit, there were also two loud *dings* as the metal doors slid open. In the absolute quiet of the hallway, they sounded eerily like a dinner bell. From somewhere deeper in the building, screams echoed down the halls.

29

Lee Roach pulled to the side of the road, looking at the sign ahead. Oklahoma City - 23 miles. He was on the shoulder of Interstate 40. It had been surprisingly easy to find his way off the levee in Arkansas, follow the grid of small agriculture roads to the freeway and head west. He had seen the occasional infected, but only in very small groups and too far from the pavement to present him with any problems. That had been good, because he was only armed with a small pocket knife.

"What are we doing?" The girl in the passenger seat asked, waking up and looking around. Roach ignored the question.

In Little Rock, he had briefly considered going to the Air Force Base and bluffing his way onto the next flight west, but had dismissed the idea for fear that the Army had already sent out a warning about him. Instead, he had skirted the city, driving past heavily armed work gangs that were burning the bodies of slain infected. The stench was unbelievable and Roach could still taste it in the back of his throat.

West of Little Rock, he had needed gas for the truck he had stolen. Sticking to the back roads, he had come across a small service station at the junction of two minor state highways. Stopping across the road, he had surveyed the small business. He was still dressed in boxer shorts, a white T-shirt with a tactical vest over it and his uniform shoes. Wherever he stopped, he would draw attention and be remembered. Was anyone looking for him? Was life in Arkansas still close enough to normal that the police would be checking businesses like this one, his description in hand? He didn't think so and had to have fuel to keep moving, so taking his foot off the brake he pulled to the pump.

Hopping out of the cab, he had grabbed the nozzle, turned the pump on and shoved it into the truck's filler neck before anyone could come walking out. He had no way to pay for the gas and was prepared to do whatever he needed to get away with a full tank. Nearly ten gallons had been pumped before he got curious about why no one had come out to greet him. Proprietors of old technology pumps like these didn't normally sit inside while someone filled up. There was no way to pay at the pump, or even to monitor or control it from the office, so they would come out to make sure someone didn't drive away with a free tank of gas.

At fifteen gallons, curiosity turned to concern and Roach tried to see through the plate glass windows. The light was just right to make them act like a giant mirror and all he could see was his own reflection. Was there someone in there on the phone with the police right now? Why else wouldn't they have come out? What if they were waiting for him to drive away so they could get the license plate to give to the cops?

The thought of being hunted and run to ground chilled him and Roach decided the person inside had to die before he drove away. Opening the truck's door, he rummaged around behind the seat, finding a tire iron and doubling his arsenal. With the heavy length of steel in his left hand, tucked along the inside of his arm so it was hidden, and the folding knife open in his right, he walked toward the side of the building like he was going to the restroom.

Circling around the back, Roach came across a small structure that had been added onto the rear of the double service bay. Stepping quietly, he went to a window on the addition and looked in, jerking away when he saw an infected male. The male couldn't see him because he was blind and Roach had moved quietly enough that the infected hadn't been alerted to his presence. Deciding he'd found the reason for no one coming out looking for payment, he headed back for the truck. Passing the side windows for the office area, he glanced in and saw a couple of racks of chips and jerky, his stomach immediately rumbling loudly at the sight.

Not remembering the last time he'd eaten, Roach changed directions and walked up to the glass door. Pocketing the knife and sticking the tire iron through a loop on his vest, he cupped his hands around his eyes and pressed his face to the glass. Nothing moved and to his left a door that probably led to the addition where he'd seen the infected was closed. Stomach growling again, he quietly pushed the door open, ready to flee if he heard or saw anything.

When all remained still, he pushed the rest of the way in, letting the door close softly behind him. The two racks he'd seen from outside were stuffed full of cheap, off-brand snacks, but they looked like a five-star meal at the moment. He started to step forward to grab some of the food, pausing when he spotted three more racks lying on the floor, stripped bare. If someone had taken it and left, why hadn't they taken all of it? Had the guy in back been living off the junk food before he turned? Movement from a dark corner caused him to catch his breath and whirl to face the threat, snatching the tire iron and lifting it over his head.

A girl, a teenager, aimed a large pistol at him. She was dirty and skinny with shoe polish black hair. A hot pink stripe ran down the center of her head, nearly neon at the tips, fading into the black before it reached her scalp. She was dressed in skin tight jeans and a crop top that exposed her mid-section from just below her breasts to the waist of her low-slung pants. Tattoos covered nearly all her visible skin and what wasn't inked was pierced. Only her face had escaped the needle and the piercer and even in his surprise, Roach noted how pretty she was. Or could be, if she was cleaned up a little.

"You're getting free gas," she said quietly in a soft, Alabama accent. "Just go on and leave and be glad I didn't shoot you when you walked in."

"I need some food," Roach said, surprising himself that he wasn't already running for the truck. "It's been a long time since I ate."

"Tough shit, asshole. Food's mine." The girl waved the pistol slightly, emphasizing that she wasn't messing around.

"OK, I'm going," he said, starting to back towards the door. "Thanks for the gas."

She said nothing, just watched him, pistol never wavering. They both jumped when the infected began pounding on the door behind her. She moved a few steps closer to Roach, turning her body so she could keep the pistol pointed at him, but watch the door.

"Pig fucker!" She hissed at Roach. "He's been quiet for a couple of days..."

If she was going to say more, she never got it out. The door burst open with a splintering of wood, the infected staggering into the room. He was huge, one of the largest men Roach had ever seen, and he had a bearing on the girl. He snarled as he lunged in her direction, arms stretched out to sweep her into a deadly embrace.

Roach expected her to shoot, but she didn't. Grabbing a small pack off the floor, she turned and ran straight at him. He started to move, but she had a step on him and rammed him with her shoulder as she charged out the door. The infected adjusted direction to follow the noise and Roach caught his balance, dashing out the door behind her. She had already reached the truck, which had finished filling, and yanking the fuel nozzle out she threw it to the ground.

She jumped in, cursing loudly and pounding the steering wheel when she tried to start the engine. There were no keys in the ignition. Roach ran around the back of the truck, skidding to a stop when she stepped out of the cab and shoved the pistol in his face. Behind him, he heard the door slam open as the infected stumbled out of the office.

"Give me the keys!" She said, eyes hard over the pistol sights.

"Fuck you," Roach said, bouncing the tire iron against his empty palm. "If you had any bullets in that thing you would have shot him, not run."

She stared at him for a long moment, finally lowering the pistol and shoving it into her waistband. She glanced to the side to see how close the infected was.

"Take me with you," she said, her voice now plaintive. "Please. I've been running for weeks."

Roach looked at the girl, then turned his head when the infected slammed into the far side of the truck, rocking it on its suspension. Soon it would bump its way around the perimeter of the vehicle and he wasn't confident he could bring it down with just the tire iron. He turned back to the girl and took a moment to look her over.

"Look, I'll do whatever you want. Blowjob. You can fuck me. Anything you like. Just get us out of here!" She begged, head turned to watch the infected fumble his way around the hood of the truck.

The offer intrigued him. She was the right age, but wasn't his type. He preferred them innocent looking. Miss Teen Beauty Pageant looks. Fresh and clean, not ruined with tattoos and studs everywhere. He thought about hitting her with the tire iron and leaving her, then thought again. If the police were looking for him, they were looking for a man traveling alone. Not a couple. She might be exactly the cover he needed.

"Get in!"

He gestured with his head, following her into the cab of the truck and slamming the door. Digging the keys out of a vest pocket, he started the engine and peeled away from the pump just as the infected slapped a meaty hand against the driver's window.

30

We quickly moved into the elevator when the screams rang out. If I'd been thinking, I would have remembered that elevators always make some kind of noise to announce their presence. I'd been distracted, thinking about getting stuck in the elevator, when I should have been thinking a step ahead of my actions. Now we not only had to worry about the power dying and leaving us stranded in a metal coffin, I had succeeded in alerting the infected to our presence inside the building. Getting old, John.

Scott had pushed the button numbered 5, the doors sliding slowly shut. Before they closed completely, the sound of running feet in the hallway reached my ears. Shit, the infected had found us fast. I briefly wondered if the smart females had retained enough memory to recognize the sound of the elevator bell, running straight to it. Was that a possibility? Shaking my head, I dismissed these thoughts, forcing myself back to the moment.

The elevator dinged softly as we passed the first sub-level. A couple of seconds later it dinged again for two, then three. We all felt it slow as four approached, then it jerked to a stop, double dinged and the doors slid open.

The three of us stood abreast, backs pressed against the rear wall of the car, rifles aimed at the doors as they moved. When they opened, we found ourselves facing a woman dressed in a skirt and heels with a white lab coat. She had a short barreled automatic rifle pointed into the elevator. Everyone froze. After a few long moments, the elevator dinged again, and the doors started to close. Taking a chance, I lowered my rifle and stepped forward, reversing the door with my hand. I stood there, holding them open.

"I'm Major John Chase. US Army," I said, glad to note that neither Scott nor Martinez had lowered their weapon.

After a few more moments she slowly lowered her rifle and straightened up. Letting the weapon hang down in her right hand, she reached up and pushed a mane of thick, blonde hair out of her face. She was about thirty with big, blue eyes and smears of dirt on her face.

"I'm Dr. Meredith Monroe. Thank God you're here!" She said, smiling at us. I waved for Martinez and Scott to lower their rifles. "I'm an assistant project director. Well, I was. What are you doing here? Did you get my message?"

"No, Doctor. We didn't expect to find any survivors. We're here for something else. Are there others?"

As cold as it may sound, I hoped there weren't. We didn't have the resources or time to mount a rescue mission for a bunch of scientists. I chided myself for the thought, but facts are facts.

"I'm all that's left," she said, a sad expression crossing her face. "There were a few of us hiding. Six others, but there's no food down here so they went up top a couple of days ago and never came back. I stayed behind and when they didn't return I took this weapon off one of our security guys who had died. I was hoping that was them when I heard the elevator."

I looked at her for a long minute, thinking about what she'd just told me. She didn't look like she had missed many meals. Looked healthy and strong, but it was hard to tell. Underneath the blocky lab coat, her ribs could be threatening to burst through her skin.

"Can you take me with you?" She asked, eyes locked on mine.

"Get in," I said, stepping aside but keeping a hand on the door, so it didn't close on her. She hustled into the elevator, heels clicking on the hard floor, moving to the back wall and standing next to Martinez.

"Watch the doors!" I barked to Scott and Martinez. "Doctor, lose the heels. They make too much noise. You know how to use that rifle?"

"I was a country girl," she answered, stepping out of her shoes and losing about three inches of height. "I know how to shoot."

"Fine. Keep it, but do not fire that weapon unless one of us tells you. It's not suppressed and will make a hell of a racket that will attract the infected."

There was another double ding as we came to a stop again, the doors opening onto a brightly lit hall. No one and nothing was waiting for us and Scott and Martinez moved into the opening, each of them blocking a door with a foot as they scanned both directions. When Scott called a soft "all clear," they stepped fully into the hall and I followed with Dr. Monroe. The doors closed behind me and I turned to face our new companion.

"Do you know where vault W is? Save us some time in having to search for it."

"It's to our left. Vaults are alphabetical, going all the way to YY, which is far to our right. What's in there that you need? We don't do bio or viral work here."

She was far from slow, and the look she gave when asking the question told me she had a good idea what we were after. Oh well. She'd find out soon enough.

"SADMs," I answered. She looked back at me with a blank expression. "Backpack sized nuclear weapons."

I didn't know what type of reaction to expect. Would she immediately start protesting that we had no business taking the nukes? That it was wrong to even think about using them? Maybe she'd try to pull out the "you're not authorized" card. But she didn't do any of that. Instead, she thought about what I said for maybe two seconds, then turned and pointed down the hall.

"That way."

"Thank you, Doctor. This is Martinez and Scott. I want you to stay right behind Martinez while we're moving. And don't forget what I said about not using that weapon unless one of us tells you."

She nodded, and I led the way she had pointed. Martinez fell in behind me with Dr. Monroe on her heels, Scott bringing up the rear. The vaults were exactly that. Vaults. Heavy, steel doors with combination locks and stout, chrome wheels sticking out of a central bolt that operated the locking pins. They were also clearly marked, each door with a two-foot tall label attached. I was glad that Captain Blanchard had been able to obtain the combo for our target. I didn't think we had brought enough C-4 to blow one of these doors open.

We passed vault EE and came to a four-way intersection. Signs on each corner pointed the way and I turned left after peeking into the new hall to make sure there wasn't a reception committee waiting for us. The first vault on our left was X, W a few feet farther along on our right. The door was four feet wide and looked as substantial as anything I'd ever seen. From the outside, it reminded me of the vault door in Fort Knox in the James Bond movie, Goldfinger. Except this one had *two* large combination dials. Shit. I only had one combination. I waved the doctor forward to where I was standing.

"I have what I was told was the combo, but I only have one. What's the deal?" I asked, waving my hand at the door.

"You have the vault specific combination. There are a few that require a second, master combination be dialed in by a facility administrator. Not surprising now that I know there are nuclear weapons in there."

"I don't suppose you have that combination?" It was more a rhetorical question, and I wasn't a bit surprised when she shook her head in the negative.

I stood there looking at the door, thinking. Other than the combination dials and the big, chrome spoke wheel, the outside was completely smooth. No hinges visible. The door itself was flush and tight in its frame and I suspected it was probably at least a couple of feet thick. No way were we getting through by force.

Giving up on the door, I started looking at the surrounding walls and ceilings. Was it possible? Would they really have installed multi-ton steel doors and left the walls un-armored? This was the US government we were talking about, so anything was possible.

Waving everyone back, I aimed my rifle a few feet to the right of the door and fired two bursts. The walls weren't soft drywall like in a modern office or home, rather smooth plaster over wooden laths. They were from a different era and had been built tough and intended to last. But they couldn't stand up to six rounds from an M4 rifle. The bullets punched through the shiny white surface, blasting chunks of plaster loose.

Stepping up to the new hole, I unclipped the flashlight from my rifle's rail and shined it into the cavity. I could see the edge of the mounting frame for the vault door, welded to a steel I-beam, but beyond that, there was nothing more than wood and plaster between me and the interior of the vault. I pulled out my Kukri and started hacking away, quickly breaking through the plaster and lath on the hall side. When I had a three-foot by five-foot section cleared, I called Scott over.

Behind the opening I had cut was wooden framing consisting of four by six timbers. Beyond them, the backside of the lath that finished the inside of the vault was clearly visible. I needed two of the vertical framing timbers out of my way and hacking through them with my twelve-inch machete wasn't a good option. Scott had some C-4 plastic explosive in his pack, which I had him dig out for me, along with some detonators and a wireless trigger. The C-4 was in a long, ropelike tube, pre-formed to focus the energy of the explosion towards whatever surface to which it was attached. In other words, a shaped breaching charge.

Cutting off four short lengths, I peeled the wax paper off the adhesive and placed some at the top and bottom of each of the two exposed timbers. Next, I inserted the detonators, then we all moved down the hall and around the corner. I activated the trigger, hitting the 'fire' button with my thumb. There was a sharp clap as the C-4 detonated, the wall I was leaning against vibrating for a moment. I looked around the corner, but all I could see was a cloud of dust filling the hallway.

"This is an old building. How much asbestos you think just got blown into the air?" Scott asked, standing next to me looking at the dust cloud.

"You're little Mary Fucking Sunshine, aren't you?" I turned my head and looked at him. Grinning, he went back to keeping watch on our rear.

The ventilation in the hall was good, the dust cloud clearing quickly. One of the timbers had been neatly cut at each end and was lying across the floor. Shoving it out of the way with my foot, I looked in the hole and saw the other one still attached by less than an inch-wide sliver of wood at the top. The bottom was swinging free, so I grabbed and pulled. The splinter snapped and the big board crashed to the floor. I kicked it over next to the first one, drew my Kukri and started breaking through the damaged lath and plaster that formed the inside wall. Less than a minute later, I stepped through the opening into the vault.

31

The vault was about the size of a large self-storage unit. Roughly twenty by fifteen feet. Looking around with my flashlight, I found a switch on the wall next to the inside of the massive door and flipped it on. Overhead fluorescent tubes buzzed to life, bathing the space in a cool light. Along the side wall of the room were five stacks of two crates each. They were three feet tall, about 18 inches across and deep. Using the blade of the Kukri, I pried one of them open and looked inside.

There it was. An innocuous looking, oversized, olive drab, canvas backpack. Just like I remembered from training so many years ago. Reaching into the crate, I tugged open a flap on the top of the pack. Under was a small, red LED screen. I had once been told the screens for the SADMs had been cannibalized from prototype Texas Instruments calculators the military was evaluating in the nineteen-sixties, long before the first electronic calculators had come to market for the average consumer. Well, the average consumer that could afford a three-hundred-dollar device that did nothing more than four basic math functions when it was released in the very early seventies.

Below the screen was a small, mechanical keypad that looked like it had been stolen from an old touch tone phone of the same era, next to that a brass lock. The device required a key to enable it before a user could select the yield of the detonation and set the countdown timer with the keypad. The lock had three positions; off, enable, and activate. To use the bomb, I'd need to turn the lock to enable, punch in the number of minutes until detonation, then turn the lock to activate which would start the countdown. An extremely simple system. No command authority codes required. As long as you had the key, you were a nuclear power unto yourself.

The key was going to be the next hurdle. These devices might be old technology, but they had been constructed so that if you opened them up and tried to bypass the key, the trigger that fired the bomb would be permanently disabled. That was pretty much the limit of the built-in security. Of course, there was also the possibility that the batteries were dead. We were banking on the probability that the devices had been maintained since they were sitting in storage at the lab where they had been built, but until I could get my hands on the keys, there was no way to know.

Each bomb had its own unique key, and the inventory records showed they were locked in vault XX, which I now knew was at the opposite end of this level. If I hadn't spent time in the military, I would have been shocked at the minimal security measures being taken to protect nuclear weapons. Chain link fencing, mine fields, and a few armed guards wouldn't stop a well-trained team determined to reach the vaults.

I used to be friends with a SEAL whose team was tasked with testing the Navy's security. On several occasions, they had managed to penetrate a variety of environments; armories, submarines, aircraft carriers, and walk right up to nuclear warheads. They would leave large, round, yellow smiley face stickers on each device they had successfully accessed. Needless to say, they weren't too popular with the Naval commanders in charge of the facilities they had breached. What had always frightened me was the thought that if it was that easy in the US, where we actually paid attention to security and had well-trained guards, what was it like in places like Pakistan?

The sound of a suppressed rifle firing in the hallway brought me back to the moment and I stepped to the hole in the wall. Martinez was right outside the opening, rifle pointed back toward the elevators, a small wisp of smoke rising from the suppressor screwed onto the end of the barrel. She saw me out of her peripheral vision but didn't turn her head.

"Two males," she simply said.

"OK, I'm coming out," I said over the radio. "We're going to move to the next vault to get the keys before we hump these things upstairs."

Perhaps I should have retrieved the keys first, but I had wanted to make sure the SADMs were actually here before I bothered with them. Now that I knew they were, they could sit right where they were until I had the keys securely in my possession.

Martinez moved a couple of feet to give me room to step out. Down the hall were the two infected she had killed. Scott was maintaining watch in the other direction and the doctor was between them, huddled against the wall. At least she had her rifle up and across her chest. I reminded her not to fire unless told, then headed for the other vault. The rest of my small team fell in behind me.

I shot another male as we moved to the far side of the level. He had stepped out of a maintenance closet with an open door as I approached, snarling and lunging in my direction. Dr. Monroe had let out a small cry just as I pulled the trigger, coming forward to stand next to me when the infected fell dead to the floor.

"Know him?" I asked in a quiet voice; rifle trained on the dark doorway he had just come through.

"That's Dr. Ben-Jarvis," she said. "He's the assistant director of the facility."

I glanced down at the body and noted the key card hanging from a lanyard around the man's neck. Moving past, I cleared the small closet then pointed at the key card and whispered for Martinez to take it. She bent down and sliced the lanyard with her dagger, slipping the card into a pocket on her vest.

We kept moving, turning several corners in what was quickly becoming a maze, finally coming to vault XX. It was the same set up as the first one we had breached, including the dual combination dials on the heavy, steel door. I repeated the process I'd used earlier and a few minutes later, squeezed through the ragged hole in the wall.

This vault was much larger, at least thirty feet wide by more than fifty deep, and was nearly full of stacked crates of all different sizes. The ones closest to me were stenciled with black spray paint and the most current date I saw was January of 1964. In the back, my light played across a wooden crate large enough for both me and Scott to stand comfortably inside at the same time. On its face was a faded, but clearly recognizable, black swastika. What I wouldn't give to open that up and see what piece of technology we'd captured from the Nazis and brought to Los Alamos for evaluation, but I wasn't here to sightsee.

Where the hell would they store the keys? I scanned with my rifle mounted flashlight and spotted a small safe set in the wall immediately adjacent to the main door. Walking over, I dug out the paper Captain Blanchard had given me, but there wasn't any notation of a safe or what the combination might be.

Shrugging out of my pack, I dug out two small chunks of C-4 and molded them around each of the safe door's exterior hinges. Inserting detonators, I climbed back out through the hole I'd cut in the wall and moved away from the opening.

"Fire in the hole!"

I warned the rest of the team a moment before pressing the trigger. There was a muted crump from inside the vault. I felt the vibrations in my feet and dust drifted down from the ceiling. Back in the vault, I found the door to the safe completely blown off its hinges and lying on the floor.

Shoving it out of the way, I looked inside. Two stacks of small, black boxes waited for me. Grabbing one off the top, I opened it and looked inside. A large, tarnished brass key was securely held in a foam cutout. A five-digit number was clearly stamped across it. I knew that number would correspond to one of the SADMs in the other vault.

Scooping all the boxes into my pack, I took another look around the vault before leaving. All the crates were stenciled with an inventory code and a date which I assumed was the date they were packed. Still seeing nothing less than fifty years old, I shouldered the pack and went back to the hallway. Martinez and Scott were keeping watch, both on a knee with their rifles up and ready. Dr. Monroe stood peering into the dark vault, waiting for me.

"Find what you needed?" She asked, stepping aside as I pushed through the hole.

"Good to go," I said, answering her and letting the team know it was time to move.

"What are you going to do with those bombs?" The doctor asked.

I paused a moment to look at her, trying to determine if I was about to have a problem. I couldn't read her expression.

"Not now, Doctor," I replied. "We need to get out of here."

I lead the way back to the first vault. We reached it without encountering any more infected. I took a moment to shine my light through the hole in the wall to make sure there weren't any surprises waiting, then turned to my team.

"Martinez, you're on guard. Have the doctor watch your back. Scott and I are going to hump these to the elevator."

When Martinez nodded and grabbed the doctor's arm to give her instructions, Scott and I moved inside.

Each device weighed ninety-eight pounds with its pack. The crate probably added another fifteen or twenty, so we took a few minutes and quickly uncrated all of the bombs. Picking one at random, I pulled its top flap open and read the code stamped into the brass under the keyhole. It only took a moment to find the corresponding key. I wanted to make sure these things were ready to go before we carried all of them up to the waiting MRAP.

Matching key in hand, I inserted it into the lock, took a deep breath and turned it ninety degrees to the right to enable the trigger. There was a loud click from the mechanical lock, then a faint, high pitched whine from the primitive electronics within. The LED screen lit up after a long moment, displaying three zeroes.

Now came a two-step process. First, set the yield from 0.1 up to 1.0 which represented kilotons of explosive force, with 1.0 equaling one thousand tons of TNT. Next, the timer could be set for a maximum of 999 minutes, or just over sixteen and a half hours. Sounds like plenty of time, but making a successful, stealthy getaway is not a fast process.

I was holding my breath and when I glanced at Scott, I could see he was too. We were one button press and one key turn away from detonating a nuclear bomb. Not a trivial thing. Still not breathing, I turned the key back to the left and the display went dark when the lock clicked into place.

Both of us let out a long sigh as I returned the key to the cutout in its box before returning it to my pack. The first random test passed, I decided we'd assume the rest were operational and get the hell out of there. Two shots from an unsuppressed rifle startled me.

"Martinez. Report!" I called on the radio, Scott already moving toward the opening.

"Two males came around the corner and Doc took them out," she answered, the surprise evident in her voice.

"Copy. We're coming out. Movement to the elevator. Ready?" I responded.

"Ready."

I bent my knees, squatted and grabbed the strap of a bomb in each hand, straightening up and moving aside for Scott to pick up two more. In the hall, Martinez was ready to lead the way, having positioned the doctor to bring up the rear. Scott and I walked between them, bombs swinging from our hands and banging our shins. We reached the elevator without incident and Martinez thumbed the call button, the doors sliding open with the double, dinner bell ding.

Four bombs stacked in the elevator, we headed back to the vault, me leading this time. Rounding a corner, I stopped as two females stepped into the hall a dozen yards away at the next intersection. They froze when they saw me, but I've had enough of the damn smart ones. My rifle was already up to my shoulder and I snapped off a shot that dropped the one on the left. The other leapt out of sight into the hallway they had just come down and I sprinted forward. I didn't want to leave her running around loose somewhere behind us, waiting to attack.

By the time I reached the turn, she was out of sight and I pulled to a stop. For all I knew there were more of them and she wanted me to come charging after her, right into an ambush. I may not be the brightest bulb in the chandelier, but I'm not that dim. The others caught up and we started moving as a group again, rifles up on high alert.

32

When we reached the vault, I exercised a great deal of caution before entering, but the room was unoccupied. Again, leaving Martinez and the doctor on guard, Scott and I entered the vault.

"Major, how much shit do you think is in this facility that the Russians could use against us?" Scott asked, voicing a thought that had been going through my head.

"Probably a lot. The rub is, how much shit is in here that we could use against them?"

I had been contemplating setting the timer on one of the nukes and leaving it behind to destroy the facility and everything in it. But, and there's always a but, what if I wound up destroying something that could give us the upper hand? That would mean there had to be someone left alive and uninfected that could tell us what it was and where it was. It also meant someone would have to make another trip in here to retrieve it. Then there were the infected and the large presence of Russians only seventy miles away. Fuck it. This was our one shot.

Grabbing one of the bombs, I moved it to the far side of the vault and lifted the flap. Finding the correct key, I inserted and turned it to enable.

Click, whine and finally the screen lit up. Surprised my hand wasn't shaking, I punched the 1 key followed by the star key then the 0 on the keypad, the screen now reading 1.0. I pressed the pound key and the bomb beeped once, softly. The screen flashed, then reset to all zeroes.

Pressing the 9 key three times changed the display to read 999, then another press of the pound key. This time, I received two soft beeps and the screen started alternately showing the two settings, switching between 1.0 and 999 every second. With a deep breath, I rotated the key another ninety degrees to the right and pulled it out of the lock. No beeps, but a flash of the screen and a solid display of 999. In the top right, a small, red dot began pulsing once per second, counting down the time to detonation.

"Looks like you know what you're doing," Scott said, staring at the display.

"Ever hear of the Cold War, Tech Sergeant? There was a two-year stretch when Reagan was President that everyone expected we'd be using these in Western Europe, BEHIND Russian lines. Maybe that would have been better than what we're dealing with now."

Folding the flap back in place, I hid the device amongst the discarded crates. I didn't really expect anyone to stumble across it before it went off, but at the same time didn't think it wise to leave it out in the open and visible. Hopefully, if the Russians did happen to visit the facility, and found the breached vault, they would look in and see the trash and not look any farther. Even if they did find it, I doubted they had the technical personnel with them that would be able to disarm it.

"That timer may say sixteen and a half hours, but let's get the fuck out of here!" I said to Scott, picking up another two bombs.

"No shit. Sir," he said under his breath, grabbing two more and following me out into the hall.

It didn't take us long to make the final trips and get all the bombs loaded into the elevator. Now I had a decision to make. Did we all pile in and ride up with the nukes, or did we send the car up and take the stairs? I've never been a fan of putting myself into a confined position that I may have to fight out of, so I decided on the stairs. Reaching inside, I hit the button for the ground level, stepping clear as the doors slid shut. Martinez used the key card she'd taken off the infected I had shot, tripping the lock on the stairwell door. She pushed it open with her foot, rifle up and ready, but the stairwell was empty.

We all moved through the door, Scott holding it so it closed softly behind us. The stairs were poured concrete with metal handrails and when I leaned into the center, I could look all the way up and down. I cautioned everyone to watch their rifle fire. Bullets would bounce off the hardened concrete and ricochet around the stairwell.

I had a degree of trust in Martinez and Scott, knowing they had been trained. But, I really didn't feel like becoming the victim of friendly fire, so I made Dr. Monroe hand me the magazine out of her rifle and cycle the action to clear the round in the chamber. She might know how to shoot, but that didn't mean she would make the right decision when it really mattered.

Loading the loose round into the magazine and tucking it into my vest, I happened to look at the narrow window in the door we had just come through. The female infected who had escaped earlier stood with her face pressed to the glass, watching us with her red eyes. Her lips were peeled back, revealing blood stained teeth. Occasionally, her tongue would dart out of her mouth and lick the glass.

"Doctor, any way to open that door without a keycard?" I asked.

The others noticed the female and Dr. Monroe gasped and stepped behind me.

"Not unless you have a traditional key," she answered.

Nodding, I glanced around to make sure everyone was ready and started climbing the stairs. We hadn't even reached the next level's landing when the lights flickered. Uh oh. I started running up the stairs as fast as I could move and still keep an eye above us for any threats lying in wait. Behind me, I could hear the rest of the team following, then as we reached the landing at the third sub-basement the lights flickered again, staying off for almost two seconds this time. Just before they came back on, there was a loud bang from the stairwell below, just like a heavy metal door being shoved open and slamming into a concrete wall.

Stopping on the landing, I leaned out and looked down, but couldn't see anything. I couldn't hear anything either, but that didn't necessarily mean much. The females can move pretty quietly when they want to.

"Hey, Doc. I thought you said there was no way through the door without a keycard or a key," Martinez said, leaning over the rail and aiming her rifle at the stairs below us.

"Or a power outage. The door locks are magnetic. Electromagnets. No power, no lock."

Dr. Monroe sounded a bit sheepish as well as frightened. A few seconds later the lights went out and didn't come back on. Moments after that, there were two more bangs below us and another above.

33

The stairwell was pitch black. As black as the deepest, darkest night I could imagine. I ran my hand along my rifle and found the switch for the mounted flashlight and turned it on. The beam was bright and focused and let me see, but only what was right in front of me. It didn't spread out enough to afford me much, if any peripheral vision. Fortunately, we were in a stairwell and any approaching infected would be funneled into a narrow corridor right in front of me.

A moment later Scott and Martinez clicked on their lights, and everyone breathed a small sigh of relief. I've never been afraid of the dark. In fact, I prefer to work under the cover of night, but the infected had changed that dynamic.

"I'm on point. Sergeant Scott on rear. Let's move!" I said and started climbing, rifle up and aiming the flashlight ahead of me.

I heard them before I saw them and it sounded like a lot of feet coming fast. I stopped on the second sub-basement landing and before I saw the ones coming down, I heard a suppressed rifle start firing behind me. A moment later a second one joined in. The first female rounded the turn above me at a run. I had her spotlighted and immediately pulled the trigger. She crumpled, but two more came into view before her body hit the ground. Muttering a curse, I started firing as quickly as I could in single-shot mode.

I drilled one of the two through the head with my first shot, but the second was really moving fast and jumping to clear the body in front of her. She wasn't an easy target and my first round punched through her shoulder with no apparent effect. I followed up with a second shot that tore out her throat before severing her spine. The body crashed to the stairs, tumbling down and I had to jump to the side so it didn't take my feet out from under me. Then a solid mass of infected moved into the beam of my light.

The group was an even mix of males and females. The females were aggressively pushing the males out of their way as they tried to reach me. I flipped the rifle's fire selector to burst and kept firing. Bodies were dropping every time I pulled the trigger and the stairwell was quickly filling with corpses. This slowed the infecteds' advance, but it was also blocking our path to the surface. There were already enough corpses on the stairs and landing above me that we'd have to waste precious time moving them just to climb up.

"Sit-rep!" I shouted over the din of battle, not wanting to take my attention off the seething mob above me.

"We're holding them, but don't see an end. Ammo's going to be a problem. Fast."

This was Scott, speaking in a staccato between rifle bursts. He was right about our ammo. We had come well-armed with a good supply, had been able to replenish when we found the MRAP, but in this target rich environment we were burning through it like a drunken sailor goes through his paycheck when he gets to port. I wasn't seeing any indication the number of infected was thinning and I momentarily wondered if the outside doors into the loading dock had been breached. At the moment, it didn't matter. We didn't have the time or ammunition to keep standing here and fighting.

Behind me was the door into the second sub-level. Since it hadn't slammed open to admit a horde of infected, I hoped it was a safe assumption that level was clear. At least clear near the elevators.

"Doc, is there another set of stairs?" I shouted, shooting a female that leapt over the pile of bodies.

"At the other end of the building," she shouted back, sounding absolutely terrified.

"How far?" I asked, changing magazines.

"I don't know. A long way. It's a big building."

I could hear the fear in her voice and was afraid she was about to completely lose it.

"Martinez, take the doc and see if there's an air shaft or any way up. Scott and I will come through behind you and hold the door.

"Copy," she replied, then a moment later over the radio. "We're clear."

Scott and I backed up, stopping when our backs touched. We were both firing nearly as fast as we could in burst mode, really burning through the ammo. When our backs touched, I kept firing with one hand and reached out with the other and grabbed the vertical metal handle on the door. Yanking it open, I yelled for Scott to go through and I followed a split second later, nearly tripping over the threshold.

In the second sub-level hall, I let my rifle drop to the end of its sling, took two grenades off my vest and pulled their pins. Tossing them through the still open door, I wrapped my hands around the handle and pulled it closed, maintaining my grip and sitting down on the floor with my feet braced against the wall.

Almost immediately infected were at the door, pounding on it and screaming. A few seconds later, the two grenades detonated in the stairwell with a bone-jarring thump that traveled through the floor, my ass and up into my back. The pounding on the door ceased and the mesh reinforced window shattered, the broken glass held in place by the wire.

Grenades are devastating weapons in enclosed spaces. They are designed to fragment into hundreds of pieces of steel that is propelled in all directions faster than the speed of sound. Then there's the concussion from the blast. In a small area with hard walls and ceilings, such as a concrete stairwell, either one of those two factors will absolutely destroy a human body. Combine them and carnage is assured. So, for a few moments, all was quiet and no infected were at the door.

Scott rushed up next to me and I looked up when I heard a ripping sound. He was tearing a long strip off a roll of duct tape. He quickly used it to cover the shattered window, pulled off two more strips and added them, completely blocking the opening. Smoothing the torn end back onto the roll and returning it to his pack, he squatted down next to me.

"Maybe the grenades killed all of them that saw us go through the door. Maybe, if we're quiet enough, they won't know we're here and try to force through the door. Maybe," he whispered into my ear.

I nodded my head. Damn good idea. Not the first time I was glad he was along.

I tipped my head down the hall in the direction of Martinez and the doc who were checking doors by the light of a flashlight. Scott turned and trotted to them, his feet silent on the hard floor. I made sure I had a solid grip on the handle, keeping my body tensed so constant pressure was on the door. Yes, the door opened *into* the stairwell and I'd yet to see an infected smart enough to *pull* one open, but I wasn't about to take any chances.

It wasn't long before I could hear them on the other side. There had to be bodies and bodily fluids everywhere, making the footing difficult. They were stumbling and banging into the metal railing. A few times a body crashed into the door. I was pulling so hard against the handle that my back and hamstrings were cramping, but none of the infected tugged on the door. I worked hard to keep my breathing under control, afraid they would hear me panting if I didn't.

It was completely dark in the hallway, other than the small pool of light from the flashlight attached to my rifle. To my right, I heard a scraping noise, much like someone walking with their shoulder rubbing the wall. Had to be an infected male. I glanced to the left and could see the lights my team was using to look for another way out, but they were too far away to hear the approaching noise. Oh shit!

"I got company down here," I said quietly into my radio's throat mic.

No response.

"Martinez. Scott. Do you copy?" I said a little louder, cringing internally at the noise I was making.

Still nothing back from either of them. I wasn't speaking loudly enough to activate the radio. I didn't want to yell for them and alert the infected in the stairwell to my presence. So far, Scott's duct tape trick was working. They weren't paying any attention to the door. But I didn't want to release the handle. Even though my rifle was suppressed, it would still make enough noise for them to hear. Could they open the door? Did I really want to take the chance?

There was another bumping sound and the scraping stopped for a moment, then resumed. I looked in the direction the noise was coming from as hard as I could, but couldn't see anything even though the sounds seemed to be no more than a dozen yards away. I had next to no night vision at the moment due to the light from my flashlight.

The only thing I had going for me was that the males are blind. I might not have been able to see him, or them, but they couldn't see me either.

They had obviously been drawn to the fighting, and the grenades I'd used had hardly been stealthy. At least they couldn't see me sitting there waiting to get munched, but they might smell me. I'd seen both males and females tip their heads up to sample the air, much like a dog. Another bump, closer this time, and now I could hear footsteps. More than one pair.

I sat there frozen, holding the handle with my head turned in the direction of the approaching infected. Straining my eyes, I could finally make out a pair of feet dragging along the smooth floor. A moment later I could see a second pair, then a third. Thankfully, they were all following the wall on the far side of the hall from where I sat, but it was only ten feet wide at the most. Wide enough for small forklifts or pallet jacks to get crates in and out of the vaults, but not nearly wide enough for my taste at the moment.

The infected continued to approach at a steady pace and for a moment I thought they would walk right by me, but a thump against the door from inside the stairwell caused them to pause. They stood there, swaying, and even though the light didn't let me see above their knee level, I could picture them tilting their heads back when I heard one of them sniffing the air. Shit.

I was five feet away from the closest one, sweating enough that I could feel it running down my sides and back, underneath my shirt. How the hell could they fail to find me? Time seemed to stretch out as they stood there, not making a sound other than sniffing. Watching the feet, it took me a minute to realize they were rocking slightly, side to side. Then the one in front took a step forward and stopped directly behind me.

I could no longer see him just by turning my head. I needed to reposition my body so I could keep an eye on him, but was afraid to move and risk making even the slightest sound that would bring an almost instant attack. The flesh on my back puckered and I could feel the goosebumps run up and down my arms. I was so tense I nearly broke my silence when a drop of sweat suddenly ran down my side.

The infected continued to stand there, sniffing and rocking back and forth and I was to the point of ready to release the door handle and draw my Kukri when one of the team made a noise down the hall to my left. The infected stopped sniffing and a moment later the three pairs of feet started moving in that direction. A long, silent breath escaped my lungs as they moved away from my position.

OK for the moment, I desperately tried to come up with a way to warn the team of what was approaching. The males couldn't attack with the speed and force of the females, but if they suddenly appeared out of the dark and grabbed you, you could be just as dead. I didn't dare try the radio again as the infected were still close enough to hear even a whisper.

34

At first, Oklahoma City was shockingly normal. There was civilian traffic, people seemingly going about their lives. Then they came around a curve in the road and encountered the first roadblock. A dozen police officers and more than twenty soldiers stood in the road, Humvees and a Bradley backing them up.

The police wore respirators and the soldiers were dressed in military MOPP – Mission Oriented Protective Posture – gear from head to toe, including full hoods with masks. They looked like something out of a cheesy Science Fiction movie, but there was nothing cheesy about the weapons they trained on all approaching vehicles.

Roach hit the brakes, the truck coming to a stop with a metallic squeal. He thought about turning around and running, his mind immediately going into a panic at the sight of the police, but another truck had come to a stop behind him and he was stuck. After a few moments, one of the officers waved him forward and he eased off the brake.

Coming to a stop, he watched as the policeman walked up and gestured for him to roll the window down. Roach complied and the man looked at him for a long moment, then shifted his gaze to check out the girl in the passenger seat. Her name was Synthia. Roach suspected her parents had christened her Cindy, but she had made sure he knew the correct spelling when she told him.

Roach had taken her up on her offer of sexual favors in exchange for bringing her along. She was younger than he had thought at first, but he didn't care that she was only sixteen and he was committing more felonies than he could count every time he touched her. He found that he enjoyed her more than he had expected, taking pleasure from being as rough as he could be. She had the bruises on her legs, ass and breasts to attest to some of his fetishes.

"Where are you coming from, sir?" The officer asked, voice muffled by the respirator he wore.

"Tennessee," Roach answered, figuring the truth was best, hoping the cop knew what had happened in Tennessee and he would get some sympathy. "Is there a problem?"

"No problem, sir. We just need to check you for any signs of infection before you proceed. Please pull over there."

The officer pointed at a dirt lot to the side of the road where a large tent had been set up. More Humvees with mounted machine guns guarded the tent and were in position to prevent any vehicles sent their way from proceeding without permission. Roach nodded and turned off the road, bumping across the rough ground.

A soldier met them in the parking area and told them to stay in their vehicle. He backed a few feet away and kept watch, rifle up and across his chest. Ten minutes later, a figure dressed all in white protective gear like a scientist from a biohazard lab, emerged from the tent and shouted. The soldier waved Roach and Synthia out of the truck, telling them to leave the keys. They were escorted to the tent flap and entered a small area that was completely draped with clear plastic. Two more soldiers in full MOPP gear and the figure in white were waiting for them.

They were handed a red plastic bag and told to strip naked. Roach started to protest, but one of the soldiers stepped forward and roughly gestured at the bag. Synthia didn't hesitate to strip and in moments was completely naked. Roach saw the person wearing white notice her bruises, but nothing was said and no questions were asked. With a sigh, he stripped his clothes off and added them to the bag which was tied shut and tossed back out the entry. The soldier handed Roach a small plastic tag with a number on it that he had snapped off the rim of the sack.

Next, they were moved forward into a second curtained area. Here, there was a floor made of slats of metal with a shallow catch basin beneath. Plastic pipes ran straight up eight feet, then bent to create an overhead lattice to which several shower heads were mounted.

"You'll want to keep your eyes closed," the man in white shouted a moment before turning a valve built into the thickest pipe.

The shower heads sputtered to life, a chemical smelling liquid raining down on them with some force. It was cold and Synthia started to shy away from the stream but was told to stand still.

"Rub all of your body," they were told, both complying in hopes the cold shower would end faster.

After almost two minutes, the shower heads were shut off and a flap in the curtain to their front was opened from the far side.

"This way."

Another figure, also in white, waved them forward. They stepped into yet a third curtained area. Two more soldiers guarded another flap that appeared to open into the main tent, but this plastic wasn't clear and Roach couldn't get a good view of what lay beyond.

A small table sat to the side, various instruments resting on it. First, their temperature was taken with a probe that went into their ears. Next, the man held up a device that looked much like a test meter that a diabetic would use to check blood sugar levels. He held his hand out and took Roach's right index finger.

Finger inserted into a slot, he pushed a button and Roach felt a sharp stick. The man released his hand and stared at the device until it beeped twice and flashed. Snapping the slot off the unit, he tossed it into a red biohazard bag before clicking a fresh one into place. The process was repeated with Synthia. A minute later, each of them was motioned forward again, the soldiers stepping aside when the flap was pulled aside.

"This way, please."

A middle-aged woman in surgical scrubs stood waiting for them inside the main area. They stepped through the flap which she carefully resealed behind them. From a cart, she picked up two thin paper gowns and handed them over. Roach gratefully pulled his on, happy to cover his nudity. Despite his predilections, he was far from an exhibitionist and didn't like being seen naked, even by his victims.

"What was that all about?" Synthia asked as they were escorted to the woman's desk where she waved them into chairs before sitting down and looking at a computer monitor.

"Decontamination and check for infection. You're both clean, or you wouldn't be in here."

She waved around the room where several more identical desks were occupied by workers wearing scrubs and people wearing paper gowns. Several police officers, without respirators, stood around the perimeter, keeping a close eye on everyone and everything.

"Now, I'll start with you," she said, looking at Synthia over a pair of reading glasses perched on the end of her nose. "Name, age and social?"

Roach tensed. Immediately started thinking about how he was going to handle the situation when it came out that Synthia was only sixteen. He looked around for anything he could use as a weapon, but there was nothing. Synthia surprised him, solving the problem by lying. She gave a different name, claimed she was twenty and said she didn't know her social security number. The woman looked her up and down, nodded and punched the information into the computer and watched the screen for a moment.

They're running background checks right here! Roach felt himself flush with anxiety. Had anyone flagged him in the system? Had the Army or the Nashville police put an alert out for him? If he gave false information, what would happen? The woman would call one of the cops over. That's what would happen. Then he would be fucked.

What about the information Synthia had given? The computer beeped and the woman looked at the screen, then up to Synthia, then back to the screen. After a moment, she seemed satisfied and clicked something with the mouse. Did a picture come up? Had Synthia been lying to him about her name and age? If so, why would she say she was younger?

"Sir? Name, age and social."

The woman was staring at him over her glasses, fingers poised above the keyboard. Roach didn't know what to do. Did he roll the dice and give his correct info? Did he have a choice? She was asking for a social security number and he didn't think he'd get away with playing dumb. There were probably very few adults in America that didn't have those nine digits burned into their memory. Could he give fake information and bluff?

"Sir?" Roach saw the woman glance over at one of the cops and from the corner of his eye, he saw the man start walking toward them.

"Lee Roach. 33 years old. US Air Force Captain." He said it all in a rush, then rattled off his social.

The woman started typing, the cop walking up and standing behind Roach before she had finished inputting the last bit of information. He could feel the stare of the police officer on the back of his neck, forcing himself not to turn and look up at the man. He was certain his face would betray something.

Instead, he maintained a calm façade and watched the woman watch the computer. When it beeped, she leaned forward slightly to stare at the monitor, then shifted her gaze to Roach for another inspection before turning back to the photo on the screen. After a bit, she nodded and clicked the mouse.

"Thank you, Captain. What are you doing here?" She asked. Roach noted that the cop hadn't left.

"I was at Arnold Air Force Base in Tennessee when the second wave of infection hit. The base fell and we made it to Nashville, onto the evacuation train and out of Tennessee. There were some problems in Arkansas and we set out on our own. I'm trying to get to Tinker Air Force Base to report."

Some of it was the truth and some of it was bullshit, but it was the best Roach could come up with on the spur of the moment. Enough truth to match events and there was no way for them to double check or prove he wasn't really trying to get to Tinker, a few miles outside of Oklahoma City. As long as there weren't any flags in the system put there by the Army, he felt he was good.

"And who is Tammy to you?" She asked, using the fake name Synthia had given and looking between the two of them.

"She's my girlfriend," Roach answered quickly before Synthia could say anything.

The woman nodded and started typing some notes into the computer. The cop finally got bored and wandered off. Roach wanted to heave a sigh of relief but resisted the urge. Finally, she finished typing, clicked twice with her mouse and looked up at them.

"Thank you, Captain. Do you know how to get to Tinker?"

"Yes, I do," Roach lied.

"Good. You can get out right through there. Have a nice day." She pointed at a sealed flap guarded by two of the cops.

"Our clothes?" Roach asked.

"You have the tag?" She asked. Roach held it up for her to see. "There will be a stack of bags outside the door with a soldier guarding them. Give him the tag and he'll give you your clothing."

Not wanting to spend another minute being questioned about who he was or what he was doing, Roach quickly got to his feet and led Synthia to the exit. One of the cops pulled the flap open and they walked out into bright sunshine. To the right was a soldier with a pile of red bags on the ground behind him. Roach retrieved their bag and they quickly dressed there in the open, no options for privacy available.

"Where's my truck?" Roach asked the soldier.

The man just pointed across a large lot, Roach looking until he spotted the vehicle. Two minutes later they were in the truck and back on the road.

"Who's Tammy?" He asked when they were clear of the roadblock.

"My sister. She was killed by an infected. I figured they wouldn't know that and if I told them I was only sixteen they'd probably take me away from you."

Roach was surprised at the answer. It sounded like Synthia actually wanted to be with him. She could have gotten away easily, just by telling the truth. There would have been nothing Roach could have done. She would be free and he'd be looking at the inside of a jail cell. Or worse.

For the first time in his life, Roach felt something akin to fondness for another human being.

35

The males continued to scrape and bump their way down the hall towards my team. I was concerned, but not desperately so until I heard more noise from my right. More infected coming. Enough already. I had to move and had to move now. Taking a quick mental inventory of what I had on my person, I came up with an idea. All it needed to work was for me to be able to release the door handle without a flood of infected pouring out of the stairwell.

As quietly as I could, I let go and climbed to my feet, pulling my rifle sling over my head. Careful to stay quiet and not bang against the door, I inserted the muzzle of the rifle through the handle. It was pointing to my left and lighting up the three infected that had already passed. I pushed the rifle past the door jamb and into the handle until it would go no farther. Wrapping the sling through the handle, I tied it in a knot so the weapon was held in place. With it wedged against the steel frame around the door and through the loop of the handle, it should be impossible for the infected to pull the door open. Should be.

Not wasting any more time, I drew my Kukri and moved into the light to follow the three infected. The first one I came to had been a security guard and was still dressed in light duty body armor. I raised the Kukri and stabbed down into the back of his neck, avoiding the collar of his vest. He died instantly and collapsed to the floor. The other two heard him go down and turned with snarls.

I stepped in, buried the blade in the heart of the one closest to me, stepped over the falling body and stabbed up through the third one's mouth into his brain. He dropped like a sack of wet laundry and I turned to meet the other infected that were coming up behind me. As I completed the turn, I heard running feet, had time to realize at least one female was attacking and stepped sideways to put her between me and the light.

She was almost on me, coming fast and quiet. Body silhouetted by the flashlight mounted to the rifle that was holding the door shut, I sidestepped again and slashed with the Kukri. The blade opened her throat and almost decapitated the body. She crashed to the floor and I continued the motion to spin and bury the point into the chest of another female that was close on her heels.

I missed the heart and she opened her mouth to scream, but only a gurgle of blood from her lacerated lung came out. She tried to wrap me in an embrace, snapping teeth lunging for my face and I shoved her back with my free hand, Kukri coming free as she staggered away. Not waiting for her to recover, I attacked, charging in and slashing across her exposed throat and severing both arteries and her trachea. She fell to the floor, twitching and gurgling as she died.

Four more males were right behind her and I slashed and stabbed my way through them until all were dead on the floor. The polished tile was now slippery with blood and I nearly went down when there was a sound behind me. Catching my balance, I spun, Kukri up and dripping blood from its razor sharp edge, but it was my team, standing there staring at me in the bright flashlight beam.

Martinez looked around at the dead infected for a moment, said something under her breath in Spanish and gave me a big smile. Doc looked pale as a ghost and Scott glanced from body to body, cataloging the carnage. I bent and wiped the blade clean on one of the corpse's pants, sheathed it and stepped up to them.

"What'd you find?" I asked in a quiet voice.

"No other way up," Scott answered, still looking at the bodies. "But we got the elevator doors open and we have a problem. The car didn't make it all the way up before the power went out. It's stuck between the first sub-level and this one."

Shit. Why couldn't anything ever be easy? Or at least go according to plan? For probably about the thousandth time in my adult life, I grudgingly acknowledged the old axiom that says even the best-laid plans don't survive contact with the enemy. So, fucking, true. OK, on to plan C. Whatever the hell it was.

"Alright. We can get into the car from above. We've just got to get to the ground level. What about the elevator shaft? Was there a ladder built in for maintenance?" I asked.

They all looked at each other and I could tell without them saying anything that they didn't know. That was the first thing we needed to check.

"Did you find anything we can use to block that door so I can get my rifle back?" I asked, not wanting to have to leave it behind.

Martinez reached to her left wrist and unbuckled a survival bracelet.

"Got thirteen feet of five-fifty paracord here. Anything on the opposite wall we can use as an anchor point?" She asked, holding the bracelet out.

Paracord bracelets are a cleverly woven length of nylon line with a breaking point of five hundred and fifty pounds. They can be unraveled in an emergency and you have a short length of rope that is very tough and strong. I took the bracelet and headed for the stairwell door, motioning for everyone to be as quiet as possible.

For once, I was in luck. Across the hall from the stairwell was a vault with one of the heavy, chrome wheels in the center of the door. I quickly unraveled the bracelet, straightened the rope out and tied an end securely to the vault. Stretching it across the hall, I made several loops around the door handle, stretched the cord as tight as I could and tied it off. I felt good about this option. I didn't see any way possible the infected could exert enough pulling force on the door to break the paracord. Retrieving my rifle, I led the way to the elevator doors.

Scott and I pried the doors open and while he held them in place, I leaned in with my rifle and looked around with the flashlight. Just a couple of feet above the top of the opening was the bottom of the car with the bombs in it. Shining the light to the side, I wasn't surprised to find that the shaft was wider than the car. Vertical steel girders were in place for stability as it moved up and down, but there was another three feet of space beyond. That space was there for maintenance as well as rescue if the car got stuck, and iron rungs were set into the concrete wall, creating a ladder that ran the full height of the shaft.

"We've got a ladder," I said, pulling my head back into the hall. "I'm going up, then the doc and Martinez. You OK holding the doors while you get on the ladder?" I asked Scott.

"No problem."

I nodded and slung my rifle with the muzzle and flashlight pointing up so I could see what I was climbing into.

I may have mentioned I don't like heights. I can jump out of a perfectly good airplane. I can fast rope out of a helicopter. I can even repel down very tall buildings or cliff faces. Just don't ask me to climb a ladder and clean out the gutters or check the roof. Yes, it's an unreasonable fear and for a moment, I actually considered going back to the stairwell and fighting my way through the infected rather than stepping across that open space and onto the narrow iron rung.

Forcing myself to only look at where I was going to place my hands and feet, I reached into the shaft, grabbed a rung, stuck a leg in and stepped onto the ladder. Taking a deep breath, I started climbing, every step feeling like I was going to miss and fall into the yawning darkness beneath me. But I didn't slip and I didn't fall. I kept climbing until I was above the top of the elevator car. Beneath me, I could hear the others on the ladder.

"Does your light really need to be shining directly up my skirt?"

"Relax, Doc. Nothing I haven't seen before," Martinez answered.

"Knock the shit off and stay focused!" I hissed at them.

This wasn't the time or place to be worrying about personal dignity, or whether someone was getting an eyeful of your goodies. I started climbing again, worried about the infected that were on the ground level. When we had called the elevator to come down, we had heard screams from females in response to the ding from the call button. Had we gotten away cleanly and they moved on in search of us, or were they waiting to pounce as soon as the doors slid open? There's only one way to find out; I thought as I continued to climb.

36

I reached the doors at ground level, having climbed the last few rungs as quietly as I could. If I wasn't cautious, my boots would make a ringing sound when I took a step and I was worried about my rifle or other piece of equipment banging into something. With both feet on the same level, I hooked an arm through a rung and stood perfectly still, listening. After a few minutes of hearing nothing, I reached out and tripped the door's release lever. This didn't open them, just released the mechanism that kept them securely closed when a car wasn't in position.

Pausing again to listen, I kept my hand on the lever, ready to relock the doors if I heard any indication of infected waiting for us in the hallway. I gave it a few minutes, but other than the doc's heavy breathing below me in the darkness, I heard nothing. Taking a deep breath and making sure I had a solid grip on the ladder, I grasped one of the braces on the shaft side of the doors and very slowly pulled it open a few inches.

Still no sounds, and with a death grip on the iron rung, I swung one foot off the ladder and onto the narrow concrete ledge in front of the doors. Stretching my body, I tried to see through the opening, but it was pitch black on the other side of the doors. Staying in that position, I listened hard for a few more minutes. Reaching above my head, I fumbled around until the flashlight was in my hand, detached it from the rifle and aimed the beam through into the darkness.

Shiny, linoleum flooring and a white painted wall opposite the elevator was all I could see through the gap, which was no more than three inches wide. Still no sound. No females lunging at the sudden appearance of a light. No males stumbling and scraping their way down the hall. Where the hell were they? The only way to answer that question was to keep going, so I placed the flashlight on the floor, aimed to illuminate the hall, and pulled the doors farther open.

When I had them open wide enough to pass through, I stopped pulling, picked up the flashlight and leaned into the hall. I quickly scanned in each direction, not finding anything to worry me, then took a more careful look around. The hall was just as stark and empty as it had been when we had entered the facility.

I swung my other foot off the ladder and stepped fully through the doors, reattaching the flashlight and raising my rifle. Silently, I padded to each of the corners, carefully checking the other halls that ran perpendicular to the one I was in, but still found no sign of any infected. Back at the door, I poked my upper body through the opening and waved the team up.

Doctor Monroe was first and was moving gingerly on the iron rungs in her bare feet. When she was level with the door, I reached into the shaft and firmly grasped her upper arm to help her transition off the ladder and into the hall. The lab coat she wore was bulky, masking the body beneath, and I was mildly surprised when I felt hard muscle in her arm. She smiled her thanks and stepped nimbly into the hall.

Martinez and Scott followed quickly, moving to set up a crude perimeter. Now we just needed to get the nukes out of the elevator car and up, but before we started that I wanted to make sure we'd be able to get them to the waiting MRAP. Retracing our earlier steps along the line painted on the floor, we quickly reached the large loading area. Peering through the tall, narrow window in the door, I couldn't see any problems waiting for us, so I stepped in with rifle up and scanning.

The room was still empty, which was good news, and I checked the metal rolling door that separated us from the shed where the MRAP was parked. It was still open six feet; just like I'd left it, which was even more good news. I started to think this was going to work out, quickly shutting down the thought before I jinxed us.

We moved across the open space and ducked into the shed. Scott and I each took a side of the MRAP and cleared the area as Martinez checked underneath the big vehicle. All clear, I motioned them to come into a tight group so we could talk quietly.

"Here's what we're going to do," I started, speaking in a very low voice. "Doc in the MRAP where it's safe. The rest of us are going to take two of those carts and go get the nukes. Scott and I will bring them up the ladder one at a time. Martinez, you'll be on security at the top of the shaft. Questions?"

I half expected Doctor Monroe to protest being left behind in the vehicle, but she seemed more than happy with the arrangement. She was a scientist, not a soldier, and had probably seen enough blood and mayhem to last a lifetime. Scott and Martinez nodded and we quickly got the doc situated, cautioning her not to touch anything.

Back inside, Scott and I each grabbed a hand cart. I abandoned mine and selected another when the wheels squealed as it started to move. The carts were large and flat with four wheels and a metal loop that stuck up at one end to make a handle. If they were painted orange instead of white, I would have thought the US Government had swiped them from a Home Depot.

I was the first one back in the shaft, climbing down and stepping onto the roof of the stalled elevator car. A hatch that could be used for emergency rescues was held closed with a simple spring lock and I popped it open, raising the door and carefully resting it against the wall of the shaft. Aiming my rifle into the opening, the flashlight lit up the inside of the car and I saw the nine remaining SADMs sitting where we'd left them.

Glancing up to make sure Scott was on his way down the shaft, I squatted next to the open hatch, grasped the frame on either side of it and swung my legs into the opening and dropped to the floor of the car. A moment later I heard Scott's boots on the roof and I grabbed one of the bombs, hoisted it over my head and held it up to the opening. He pulled it through and set it to the side as I reached for another. Soon we had all of them on the roof.

Unslinging my rifle, I passed it up and gave Scott a moment to get out of the way. Arms extended, I jumped and grasped the hatch frame, pulling myself until my upper body was through and on the roof. Scrambling the rest of the way, I got on my feet and took my rifle back. Scott already had one of the bombs on his back and he swung onto the ladder and climbed for the opening above. Grabbing another one, I followed.

We were on our next trip down the shaft. Six bombs spread between the two carts, when Martinez' voice came over the radio.

"Contact! Multiple males."

Scott and I froze for a moment. Each of us had a bomb in hand, preparing to swing the pack onto our backs, but if we had to go fight we didn't want to be weighed down by the nukes. A heartbeat later I heard Martinez start firing, her suppressed rifle quiet but still clearly audible in the tomblike silence of the building.

I dropped the bomb I was holding and grabbed onto the ladder, quickly climbing and stepping into the hallway behind Martinez. I glanced in the direction she was firing and saw a large group of males heading our way. She was dropping them efficiently, making each shot count, but they just kept coming around the corner. Rifle up, I scanned the other direction, towards the loading bay. For the moment, it was clear.

Fuck it. We had six bombs. Better to leave now, with six, than try to get the last three and wind up trapped with dwindling ammunition and no other way out. Scott had made it back into the hall and had added his fire to our defense. For the moment, the two of them were holding the infected at a static point, but it was taking a lot of ammo.

"OK, we're moving to the MRAP! Scott, grab a cart. Martinez on security!"

I grabbed one of the carts and rested my rifle over the handle so it was pointing in the same direction I was pushing. Moving fast, I didn't slow for the turn into the hallway to the loading bay. There was four feet of metal in front of me with almost three hundred pounds of bombs on it. If there were any infected waiting around the corner, I would take their legs out before they could attack.

Making the turn, I took a big chunk out of the wall with the front corner of the cart and kept pushing hard as I dashed for the loading bay. Behind me, I could hear Scott making the turn and the nearly continuous fire from Martinez' rifle. Sliding on the floor, I got the cart stopped and yanked the door into the loading bay wide open.

Scott had room to get past and I waved him on, shoved my cart through one handed and turned to back up Martinez. She was right behind us, running backwards and firing into the group of infected that completely filled the width of the hallway.

"Behind you," I said before placing my hand flat on her upper back to guide her to the door.

She fired three more rounds, then stepped through the door, rifle bolt locking open on an empty magazine. Following, I pulled on the door's crash bar to close it. At first, I didn't think the pneumatic arm was going to allow me to close the door before the infected reached us, but it released its pressure when the opening was down to two feet. I held the bar with both hands and looked around, but Scott was already on the job.

He had dashed across the room to get another cart. When I spotted him, he was running towards me, pushing the cart with the squeaky wheels. Arriving, he flipped it onto its side and shoved it across the door I was still holding. The cart was longer than the width of the door and he jammed it tight against the metal door frame.

The infected had arrived, en masse. Loud thumps started up as they pounded on the door, and in the dim light from my flashlight I could see snarling, bloody faces pressed up against the small window. Stepping back, Scott dropped his pack and dug out a roll of duct tape. Pulling a couple of very long strips off the roll, he quickly compressed them into a shape resembling a rope. Feeding these through the crash bar, he wrapped them around the body of the cart, pulled them taut and tied them off. I had no idea how strong duct tape was when used like this, but knew it was damn tough stuff.

Releasing the door, I took a step away. Again, securing a door so the infected couldn't *pull* it open was probably unnecessary, but I sure felt better knowing they didn't have an easy path to get to us. Scott and I trotted across the room, carts wobbling slightly as we moved them faster than they were intended to travel. I was first into the shed, ducking slightly so I didn't scramble what little brains I had on the bottom edge of the rolling door.

Scott came through right behind me, followed closely by Martinez. The back doors to the MRAP were open and waiting for us. Not what I expected. Doctor Monroe should have been buttoned up tight inside. I pulled on the cart's handle, dragging it to a stop as she stepped around the back corner of the big vehicle. Scott and Martinez slid to a stop on either side of me. I cursed when two more figures stepped into view on the far side of the vehicle.

I still had Doctor Monroe's rifle magazine tucked away in my vest, but she had found a fresh one in the MRAP. She stood next to the heavily armored bumper and aimed her rifle directly at my face. The other two figures were wearing uniforms in a camouflage pattern I didn't immediately recognize, but I was familiar with the AKMS rifles held steady on Martinez and Scott.

"Yobanaya suka!" I said to Monroe.

Fucking bitch in Russian.

"Da," she answered with a sweet smile.

37

Rachel couldn't sleep. Heavy storm clouds had moved into the West Memphis area just before sundown, trapping the day's heat and humidity. The air was heavy and, try as she might to relax on the cot she was using, she couldn't get comfortable or turn off her racing mind. Dog lay next to her, panting in the dark. He wasn't enjoying the weather either. She was in the same hangar John and Jackson had slept in before he went off to New Mexico and Jackson was sacked out a few feet away. His snoring, which reminded Rachel of a poorly idling Harley, wasn't helping her situation either.

Finally, she surrendered. Sitting up, she slipped her feet into her boots without tying them and headed outside for some fresh air. Dog fell in beside her, nails clicking on the concrete floor. Leaving the hangar, Rachel was disappointed that the air was just as oppressive. There wasn't even a breeze to help cool her off and fresh sweat popped out on the back of her neck. Taking a moment, she whipped her long hair up into a ponytail, trying to get even a bit of relief. She looked up, hoping to see stars, but the sky was black. No star or moonlight could penetrate the thick layer of clouds.

Strolling aimlessly, she wondered if John was OK. She had gotten Jackson to tell her the details of the mission John was on. To be accurate, she'd gotten him to tell her where John was and how he had gotten there. He wouldn't tell her the details of what he was doing while he was there, or if he was coming back. She didn't know if she'd ever see him again and her heart ached. She had hoped that confessing her feelings would have somehow let her resolve the conflict she was dealing with. Frustration that she had fallen for a man who was married and couldn't return her love. Genuine hope that his quest to find his wife would be successful, yet also wanting him all to herself.

"What a fucking stupid little girl you are," she muttered to herself in the dark.

"Good evening, ma'am."

Rachel jumped and let out a small shriek when Colonel Crawford spoke. It was so dark, she hadn't seen him approach and still couldn't recognize him by sight even though he was standing right next to her. Only his distinctive voice told her who was speaking. Why did these fucking Army guys enjoy sneaking up on her so much? They were like little boys who'd never grown up in so many respects.

"I'm sorry. Didn't mean to startle you," he said, sounding anything but sorry. She heard a rasping sound that was Dog getting his head scratched.

"Can't sleep either?" Rachel asked.

"No. Waiting for word on our boy. I heard from the bomber crew that they jumped about two hours ago."

Jackson had let the Colonel know he'd given Rachel more details.

"When do you expect to hear something?"

"Could be an hour. Could be a day. These types of operations are fluid. He could be having to deal with any number of things that will cause a delay, so we just wait."

A match flared as the Colonel lit a cigarette, the light seemingly brilliant and clearly illuminating his face.

For a moment, Rachel could see his tired eyes and the stress etched into his features, then he shook the match out and darkness descended again. She asked for a cigarette, not really wanting one as they stunk and tasted like shit, but she had found that smoking helped her relax. No wonder the damn things were so addictive.

"Is he coming back here?" Rachel couldn't stop herself from asking.

"You know I can't tell you that."

He sounded genuinely sorry. Rachel reached out towards him and put her hand on his arm.

"Who am I going to tell?" She asked, a pleading tone in her voice.

She hated herself for sounding like she did, but couldn't help it. Crawford was silent for a long moment before taking a deep drag on his cigarette and blowing out a big plume of smoke.

"You'll most likely see him again," he finally said. "Not here, though. We're going to move soon, and if all the plans work out he should be waiting for us at our destination."

Rachel stood silent for a moment, then started crying. She tried to stop, but the more she tried, the harder she cried. Finally, Crawford reached out and folded her into a fatherly hug. She buried her face in his shoulder and let the emotions come out.

The fear of the past weeks of constant fighting and running. The pain over the death of Nora, the young girl who had died helping her save John from The Reverend. The guilt she still carried over how she had behaved towards Melanie Fitzgerald, the brave woman who had died on the train saving her life when the infected attacked. The heartache of love given that couldn't be returned.

She eventually got herself under control and stepped out of the Colonel's embrace, wiping her eyes. Dog was standing next to her and pushed his body against her leg in his attempt to comfort her. A match scratched in the dark and Crawford handed her another cigarette. The first one had burned down, un-smoked. She took it gratefully and reached down with her other hand to rub Dog's head.

"Bird Dog, this is Crow's Nest."

Rachel heard the Colonel fumble in his cargo pocket for his radio.

"Go for Bird Dog," he answered.

"Sir, you need to see this."

The voice on the other end of the radio sounded stressed.

"On my way," Crawford replied, returning the radio to his pocket. He started to walk away, then paused and turned back.

"Why don't you come with me? You probably shouldn't be wandering around out here in the dark. Perimeter security is taking down about half a dozen infected every hour. Only a matter of time until one of them makes it past our lines."

He stood waiting, a slightly darker outline against the dark horizon.

"I'm coming," Rachel answered, tossing her cigarette down and crushing it under her boot.

She and Dog followed him across the tarmac to the control tower. Looking up, she could see a faint light glowing at the top, silhouetting a figure visible through the glass, watching them approach. The guard at ground level snapped to attention then held the door open. She followed Crawford's broad back up the spiral, metal stairs.

In the control area, Captain Blanchard greeted them at the top of the stairs and motioned Crawford to where a soldier sat hunched over an armored laptop. The Colonel fished a pair of reading glasses out of his uniform blouse and bent to see what was on the screen. Rachel moved in behind him and stretched up on her toes to see.

"What am I looking at?" Crawford asked.

The screen looked to Rachel like the weather radar she used to see on the evening news.

“Radar image from our north picket, sir,” the soldier answered.

“An Apache holding station fifty-five miles north of us, sir,” Blanchard clarified.

“I was absent the day they taught us how to read radar at West Point,” Crawford said drily. “What am I looking at?”

“One hell of a bad ass storm. Sir,” the soldier answered.

He reached out and pointed at a spot on the screen. Rachel could make out a vortex in the colors of the region the man had indicated. Tornado? Then he moved his finger and pointed at another spot. Then another, and another.

“Tornados, sir. Four of them on the ground with clearly defined eyes at the moment. I’ve seen as many as seven, but not fewer than three since the storm came into radar range. This doesn’t happen, sir. Not this many, not this close together and lasting this long. And they’re heading our way.”

“What do you mean, this doesn’t happen? This part of the country is tornado alley, isn’t it?” Crawford’s eyes were glued to the screen and, as he watched, another vortex appeared even closer to them.

"Technically, sir, Tornado Alley is a little west of us. North Texas into Oklahoma, but this part of the country does have them fairly often. What I mean is, that it's kind of normal to see one tornado a night at the peak of storm season. Two happens, but that's rare. Five and more? At the same time and as strong as these look? Not since we started tracking the weather a couple of hundred years ago. There's always been speculation about what multiple nuclear warheads going off would do to the weather patterns. Increased violence and duration of storms was one of the theories."

The room was quiet for a minute as everyone watched the screen.

"How strong are these?" Rachel spoke before she realized she should stay quiet, but neither Blanchard nor Crawford chided her for asking.

"Best guess, ma'am, is these are all at least F-4s. And I'm pretty sure that one right there is an F-5," he answered, pointing at the largest vortex.

"English, Sergeant," Blanchard said.

"Sorry, sir. An F-4 is winds greater than two hundred and seven miles per hour. F-5 is greater than two sixty. Either one will wipe this airport right off the map."

As he was talking, another vortex appeared on the radar even farther to the south, closer to West Memphis.

"How long do we have?" Colonel Crawford asked, removing his reading glasses and standing up straight.

"Maybe forty-five minutes, sir," the soldier answered, looking up over his shoulder at the Colonel. "But I wouldn't bet on it."

"Recall all the pickets, Captain! Get the evacuees loaded onto the train and get it rolling. I want us out of here in less than half an hour! And, send a runner to warn the locals. There's not many left and there's room on the train if they want to come with us, but I want that train rolling in under thirty minutes!"

"Yes, sir," Blanchard answered, turned and told the soldier that had given them the weather report to issue an immediate recall to the pickets.

He stepped away and raised a radio to his mouth to continue issuing orders. Within a very few minutes, the quiet airport became a scene of controlled chaos. Soldiers dashed around, packing equipment and supplies and loading it onto the C-130s. The helicopters flying picket began returning, swooping in to flare out in combat landings, the air crews hopping out and grabbing refueling hoses. With the pickets recalled, they lost their view of the approaching storm on the radar and the soldier shut his laptop down, packing up the equipment he had been using.

Rachel heard the door below bang open and a moment later heavy boots rang on the metal stairs. Jackson rounded the last turn and ran over to where Rachel and Dog stood with the Colonel. He had his pack on, rifle slung and carried Rachel's gear and weapon. He handed them to her and asked what was going on. Rachel filled him in while Crawford watched the progress on the tarmac below through the big windows.

"Sir, I'm going to check on the train, unless you have somewhere else you need me," Jackson called out.

"Good, Master Sergeant. Go!" Crawford answered before yelling at Blanchard to get one of the air crews on the radio and tell them to get their asses in gear.

Jackson dashed for the stairs and Rachel decided to go with him. They raced down the stairs and banged out the door onto the tarmac. Dog wasn't sure what all the excitement was about, but he was ready to go, ears up as he danced around Rachel's legs while they ran to a civilian pickup parked behind the tower. Jackson jumped in, Rachel and Dog running around to the passenger side and squeezing into the cab with him.

The drive to the evacuee encampment was short, less than two minutes. As they approached, Rachel could tell the Rangers that had been guarding the camp were doing a good job of getting people up and onto the train. They had turned on floodlights and everyone was already queued up in a line waiting to board, all of their worldly possessions clutched in their arms.

Jackson screeched to a halt and jumped out, not bothering to even shut the truck's engine off. Rachel and Dog followed as he started jogging down the length of the train, making sure everyone was up and ready to load. Rachel stopped and turned when she heard her name called. She looked across the sea of faces, finally spotting Lindsey and Madison when they shouted again.

At first, she thought the girls were just yelling to a familiar person. Then she saw the distress on their faces. She trotted over to them, Dog on her heels. Jackson had noticed and came up behind as she knelt to talk to the two little girls.

"Where's your Mommy and Daddy?" She asked, looking around for the parents and trying to remember their mother's name.

"Daddy went into town to find something. I don't know what. When he didn't come back, Ma went to find him." Lindsey was on the verge of tears, Madison already bawling.

"They left you alone?" Rachel asked.

A large, black woman stepped forward and looked down at Rachel. "The babies is with me, and they be safe. Can you find those fool parents?"

The woman wrapped a protective arm around each girl, both of them turning and burying their faces against her as they cried.

"We'll find them. Get those girls on that train!" Jackson said.

Rachel turned her head to look up at him, but he was already running for the truck.

"We'll bring them back!" She said and sprinted after Jackson.

Dog beat both of them to the idling pickup, jumping through the door Rachel had left open and planting himself on the bench seat. They climbed in moments later and Jackson roared away from the train. They bounced over several sets of tracks, Dog yelping when he lost his balance and went nose first into the dash. Wrapping her arm around him, Rachel held him in place as Jackson drove.

It only took a minute to clear the train yard and race across the northernmost section of the airport. Then they turned left onto the highway that ran to town. On the horizon ahead, lightning played amongst the clouds in a nearly continuous show of power. The air blowing in through the open windows had a charged feel to it and there was a nearly constant rumble of thunder. Dog whined and pressed harder against Rachel, who spoke soothingly to him and rubbed his neck.

"You know that train is leaving in less than twenty minutes. Right?" Rachel shouted over the wind noise.

"I know," Jackson answered. "We're still close enough. You want out so you can go back?"

"Drive faster and quit asking stupid questions," Rachel said.

38

Roach and Synthia sat in the truck on the side of the road, half a mile from the heavily guarded main gate to Tinker Air Force Base, just outside Oklahoma City. They were tired, hungry and didn't know where to go. A few hotels and restaurants were still open for business, but they didn't have any way to pay for a room or food. As they had driven around the city, it was obvious that the residents had settled in for the duration. Everyone they saw on the street was armed and Roach didn't like their chances if they tried to steal anything. Including gas for the truck, which was down to less than a quarter of a tank.

"What are we doing?" Synthia asked.

"Why are you still with me?" Roach asked, ignoring her question. "You could have told the woman at the roadblock the truth and there was nothing I could have done."

"Maybe I like the way you fuck me," she said.

Roach turned to look at her in shock.

"What? You *like* that?"

Synthia was one of very few women that Roach had not killed after having sex. He was a brutal and violent partner, using his fists on the girl as he penetrated her.

"Yeah. I do. Pain makes it better. Maybe sometime we could..." Her voice trailed off.

"We could what?" Roach asked when it was apparent she wasn't going to continue her thought. She remained silent for almost a minute before speaking again.

"It's just that I thought it would be kind of cool to maybe have another girl that we could, uh, do things to while you were fucking her. Maybe share the pain. Maybe even more than that."

She looked him in the eyes and at that moment he recognized a kindred spirit. Roach was shocked. Intellectually, he had always known there were others out there like him. He had always wondered about trying to connect with another that had the same predilections, but had been too afraid of using any of the internet chat rooms. There were too many stories in the media about cops posing as anything from underage girls to hit men for hire for him to take the risk. Now, Synthia had dropped into his lap, and he was stunned that he'd found a like-minded spirit in a girl's body.

"I shouldn't have said that," Synthia said and looked away when Roach didn't react to her statement.

"Yes, you should have. I think that would be cool, too," he said and smiled. She smiled back and reached for his hand.

"You've done... stuff? Before?" She asked, still hesitant to freely talk about the topic.

"Yes," Roach smiled and squeezed her hand. "I have. For years. It's the biggest rush in the world."

He surprised himself how quickly he was opening up to her. How much of a need to share his adventures with another person that he'd been suppressing for years.

"So how do we do this?" She asked.

"We appear as normal as possible. Hide in plain sight. Don't do anything on impulse, and never do it to anyone that can be connected back to us."

The advice spilled out without Roach even thinking about it.

"And how do we do that? We don't have any money or any place to sleep. Not even food. Nothing."

"Yes, we do," Roach said and pointed through the windshield at the Air Base. "Keep using your sister's name. You're my wife. We met and were married last week in Nashville before evacuating on a train that we got off in West Memphis, which is where we took this abandoned truck. Whirlwind romance. No details. Play the frightened and traumatized girl. Got it?"

"Got it," she said with a smile.

Shifting the truck into drive, he drove slowly up to the gate, stopping where indicated by a large Security Forces Sergeant. Three Humvees with mounted machine guns sat in a semi-circle just inside the wire. The guns were trained directly on the cab of the pickup. The Sergeant walked up to the driver's side window as another with a dog on a short lead walked along the passenger side.

Roach identified himself and asked to be taken to the Sergeant's commanding officer. He was told to stay where he was as the man stepped away and started speaking into a radio attached to his vest. It was a short conversation and he quickly returned to the truck.

"You and the passenger please step out of the vehicle, sir" he said.

Roach turned the engine off and nodded for Synthia to get out of the cab. She came around the hood of the truck and walked very close to Roach as they were led through a small walk gate to a waiting Hummer. A young, female Airman was behind the wheel and the Sergeant opened the back door and waved them in. Closing the door, he climbed into the front passenger seat and told the driver where to go.

Roach and Synthia were separated as soon as they walked into the Security Forces office. They were taken to interrogation rooms and left alone after each being given an MRE and two bottles of water. Sometime later, an Air Force Major walked into the room where Roach sat waiting. The Major had a file folder in his hand, dropping it onto the stainless steel table before sitting down across from Roach. Getting comfortable, he opened the folder and looked from Roach's face to what must have been a file photo he had printed out.

"I'm Major Thomas. You say your Air Force Captain Lee William Roach. Correct?" He got straight to the point.

"Yes, I am. Scan my hand into the system if you don't believe the photo, sir."

Roach wondered why that hadn't been done already. Maybe the system was down with no one left to maintain it. He knew the military used a civilian contract service to tie into literally thousands of different databases around the world. It would probably be a minor miracle if the service was still up and running.

"All in time," the Major replied, Roach taking that as a confirmation the system was no longer operating. "First, you need to answer some questions. You are assigned to Arnold in Tennessee. What are you doing here, out of uniform in a civilian vehicle?"

If Roach hadn't been on the other side of the table a hundred times at least, he might have experienced a moment of panic. But he knew the drill. Ask the questions to which there is an obvious answer first. See if the person you're questioning tries to lie about something that there's no need to lie about. That will set the tone for the rest of the interrogation.

Roach spun his story. Mostly truth. He talked about the second wave of infection that had devastated Arnold. He embellished how he had helped in an emergency evacuation of the base onto a Globemaster that had crashed on takeoff. He told how he had escaped in a Hummer, as the infected overran the base, and drove to Nashville where he'd helped with the evacuation. Meeting "Tammy", which was the name Synthia would have provided, falling in love at first sight and seeking out a preacher to marry them just before boarding the last train out of the city.

The Major sat quietly, not asking any questions as Roach talked, just jotting notes on a spiral notepad. When Roach finished, the man started asking for details. He jumped around the timeline Roach had laid out, looking for any inconsistencies. Any change in the story that would indicate a lie. But Roach was a master of deception, having perfected that particular skill while still a teenager and the Major couldn't find any loose threads in the story to start unraveling.

"Thank you. I've got a few things to go check out."

The Major stood abruptly, collected his notebook, file folder and left the room. Several hours passed. Roach was starting to get concerned when the door opened and a Security Forces Senior Airman walked in with a bulging duffel bag.

"Captain, I'm here to escort you and Mrs. Roach to housing. Please come with me, sir."

Roach smiled and stood up.

39

It really pisses me off when I get fooled as completely as the Russian bitch had managed. Her English was perfect. Not a trace of an accent. Not an incorrectly used idiom, nothing. And she had played the role of frightened scientist to a tee. But I still chastised myself for having been duped.

I knew that Los Alamos would be a huge temptation for Russian intelligence. Knew it well enough that I had armed a nuke to destroy the place after we were gone, but the idea that Dr. Monroe wasn't who she claimed to be had never entered my little pea brain.

Now we were in a world of shit. Three rifles trained on us and, even though we had ours in our hands, they weren't aimed. If one of us started to move, I had little doubt we'd all be shot without any further hesitation. But then, why hadn't they just shot us as we ran up? What did they want? Did the woman know about the armed and ticking bomb five levels beneath our feet and need me to disarm it?

I didn't think she knew. She'd been outside the vault when Scott and I had our brief conversation, and I had set the timer on the SADM. So, if that wasn't it, what the hell did they want? I'm cute, but I'm not that cute.

"Lower your weapons, Major," the woman said, rifle not wavering in the least.

"Indanahway suka bluut!" Was my answer in Russian, which I've found is a wonderful language for cursing.

Translated, I said 'Fuck off bitch slut', which sounds stilted to American ears but is considered very offensive by Russians. Other than a brief widening of her eyes, she didn't react. One of the men snorted, but I couldn't tell if it was in humor or offense for the honor of the woman.

"Why don't we try English," she said. "Your Russian is horrible. Where did you learn it, anyway? US Army's language school? I always thought they did a better job."

Actually, I had never learned Russian. I had wanted to rotate through the Army's language school in California, but it seemed there was always one more mission and never time for me to go immerse myself in a foreign language. Besides, we'd always had someone on our team that could speak the language in whatever region of the world we were operating in.

My few, crude Russian phrases came from a drunken leave in Bangkok where I'd run into some Russian soldiers on leave. After we sorted out who could fight better, known as who has the bigger dick, we became drinking buddies for two days.

They'd taught me how to curse in Russian. I'd taught them how to not scare off the Thai bar girls. We'd not exactly become friends, but had reached a friendly truce for a long weekend. Détente, I think they used to call it.

"What do you want?" I asked her.

"I want to help you," she said. "I'm going to have my men lower their weapons so we can talk. First, I want your word that you won't fire on us as soon as we do."

I stared at her for a long moment, trying to figure out what she was up to. They needed something from us. Otherwise, we'd be dead already. She had us cold and she knew it, but was willing to compromise her position to gain my trust.

"You have my word," I answered, ordering Martinez and Scott to stand down.

She looked in my eyes for another moment before lowering her rifle. The two Russian soldiers followed her example without having to be told.

"My name is Captain Irina Vostov." She introduced herself, stepping closer to me. "I am with the GRU. I'm sure you know what that is."

The GRU is the largest intelligence agency in the world. The KGB, and its successor the SVR, was made popular in movies as the Russian bad guys, but they were small in comparison to the GRU. Part of the Russian military and also the directorate that controlled all Spetsnaz troops, they were responsible for Russian military intelligence. It made sense that the GRU would be very interested in the toys housed at Los Alamos.

"I know what you are," I answered.

"We were here ahead of you," she explained. "We watched you approach in the truck; MRAP you call it? Something like that? When it became apparent you would make it inside, I found these clothes and ID in an office so I could find out why you were here. What are you planning to do with those bombs?"

"Planning to fuck you with one of them, caja," Martinez said under her breath, but the Russian Captain heard and turned to look at her.

"What is that? Caja?" She asked.

"It's not important." I interrupted before she found out Martinez had just called her a cunt in Spanish. No reason to keep poking the Russian bear. At the moment. "We need them to fight the infected. Leave them in the path of the herds to slow them down and thin them out."

She looked at me, blue eyes locked on mine. Would she accept my lie? I was pretty sure she was smarter than that. A woman became an officer in the GRU one of two ways. Either she was incredibly beautiful and willing to seduce and sleep with any man who had information her service needed, or she was very smart and ruthless.

Captain Vostov certainly had the looks to be used as what is known as a honey pot, seducing and using foreign men, but she wouldn't be here with two Spetsnaz soldiers if that was her specialty. That meant she was even smarter than she was beautiful. Great. A smart and beautiful woman. How many of those had changed the course of world history?

"I do not think I believe you." She smiled. "But we can discuss that further after I tell you what I have to offer. Perhaps we can make a trade."

She moved cautiously, slinging her rifle and holding her hand out to her soldiers. One of them reached into his pack and handed her a small box, about the right size for a pair of children's shoes. She held it in front of her in both hands.

"This is enough vaccine to inoculate one hundred people against the Chinese virus. There is also a flash drive with the technical information needed to allow your scientists to synthesize more vaccine. This is what I have to offer."

I was stunned. I don't know what I expected, but this was as about as far from it as possible. A vaccine? But did we need it? There had been a second outbreak already. I kept hearing that there were people that were immune to the virus. Wasn't that what was left alive?

"I don't understand," I said. "We've already had the nerve gas kill or turn millions. Then there was a secondary outbreak from the virus. Those of us that are left are supposedly immune."

"No, they are not. The virus acts faster in some people than others. There will be another outbreak in less than a week. The virus is airborne. Everyone is infected now. When the next outbreak happens, there will be no one left that has not been vaccinated. Russia will rule the world, or what's left of it. All we will have to do is clean out the infected. Then everything is ours."

Was she telling the truth? A third outbreak? A thrill of fear ran up my spine and on either side of me I could see Martinez and Scott exchange worried glances.

"Why?" I asked. "Why would you give this to me? Isn't this what Russia's always wanted? Wipe out America and rule the world?"

"Why? You confuse Russia with the corrupt, power-mad few that rule our country. You think this is what the Russian people want? To see millions, no, billions of innocent people turned into raging monsters for us to gun down? To watch the world die around us? Nyet!"

As she spoke, I could hear the anger in her voice and see it flash in her eyes. Was she sincere, or was she just one hell of an actress?

"As it has been for generations, you Americans do not understand the Russian people. Does your current president accurately reflect the hearts of the American people? Does he care about what is best for America, or is he as corrupt as I think he is? Power hungry and making decisions that only stroke his own ego and promote his personal agenda?"

I thought about what she was saying and found I couldn't disagree with her. But just because she had a good picture of American politics didn't mean she wasn't running a game on me.

"Say I believe you. That there really is another outbreak coming and there is a vaccine in that box that will save what's left of America. What do you want in exchange?" I asked.

She smiled. This time a genuine smile, not the one from earlier that reminded me of a shark getting ready to bite off a chunk of my ass.

"I want the nuclear bombs and their keys," she said, gesturing at the two carts Scott and I were standing behind. "They are what we came here for, but had not found them before you arrived."

"What do you want them for?"

I was confused. Russia had at least as many, if not more nukes than the US. These bombs were fifty-year-old technology. What could they possibly need them for?

"It is time for a... what do you Americans call it? Regime change? Yes, regime change. It is time for that in Russia. But the Kremlin is heavily guarded and we cannot get close enough to arrest or kill our corrupt leaders. Neither can we gain access to Russian munitions. Too many people who would betray us in an attempt to curry favor. So, we decided to use American bombs. Poetic justice to use bombs from America, is it not?"

The information she had given me raced through my head. Did I believe her? Yes, I did. Everything rang true, right down to the emotion in her voice as she spoke. Besides, she didn't need to trade anything for the SADMs. They could have shot us and taken them without saying a word, but they didn't.

"And that's why you were here when we arrived? To get the bombs?" I asked.

"We knew there were bombs here. We have been here for two days looking for them. I had hoped to find some scientists or military still alive in the building that I could make the trade with, but there were only infected when we arrived."

I had a decision to make. The plan, the mission, my orders were to retrieve the SADMs for use against the Russians that were on American soil. We were supposed to penetrate Kirtland AFB and leave two surprise packages for the Russians before beating feet to rejoin the Colonel at Tinker in Oklahoma City. From there, other teams would be dispatched with nukes for Montana and South Dakota. If I agreed to Captain Vostov's proposal, none of that would happen.

But what if I didn't agree and there was a third and potentially final outbreak? Other than killing a few thousand Russian airmen and soldiers, what would we accomplish by deploying the nukes only to fall victim to the V Plague virus? When I laid it out in its simplest terms, it was an easy decision to make. For not the first time in my career, I decided to willfully disobey orders.

Colonel Crawford might stand me up against a wall and put a bullet in my head, but I had to take the opportunity the Russian woman was offering. But, first things first. My dad had always told me to never trust a beautiful woman making an offer that sounded too good to be true. Once I was in my thirties and realized Dad wasn't the dumbest person to ever inhabit the planet, I understood what he'd been trying to tell me.

"How do I know there isn't a vial of saline and a flash drive full of Russian folk tunes in that box?" I asked.

She smiled and slid the lid open and held the box up for me to see. Inside was a foam block with cutouts for four large vials of a reddish tinged liquid. A small USB flash drive rested on top of the foam between two of the vials.

"What can I do to prove it to you?" She asked.

I was stumped. Even researchers would need specialized equipment and training to know what was in those vials and to make sense of the data on the flash drive. I was in way over my head and had two choices. Trust the Russians, which went against everything I'd ever believed, or turn them down and start a firefight that most of us wouldn't survive. But could I risk passing on the opportunity of a vaccine?

I decided to trust my gut. I'm usually right when I do. I had known Katie less than three weeks when I asked her to marry me. Still don't know if that was my gut, or another part of my anatomy a little bit lower, but it was the right decision.

The worst case scenario was that she was playing me and I lost all the nukes. Best case, she was telling the truth and if I didn't have that vaccine there really was no point in worrying about Russians on American soil. Time to listen to my gut.

"Three of them," I said. "That should be more than enough for your purposes."

"And what do you really plan to do with the rest?" She asked, closing the lid on the box. "You really do not expect me to believe they are for the infected. Perhaps you are planning to sacrifice a few American air bases and their Russian captors along with them. No?"

"Three for the box, or we can see who has the faster trigger fingers," I said, staring into her eyes. She stared back for nearly a full minute, then smiled.

"Agreed," she said. "As long as I have your word that they will not be used on Russians. Our troops have been told that they are here at the request of the American president because the military is trying to take over. It is not the fighting men; it is the Kremlin. We have a common enemy, Major."

"How is it you know the truth?" I asked.

"I am GRU. I know everything. Besides, my uncle is... well, he is very high up and is helping with bringing down the madman that occupies the Kremlin. Barinov makes Stalin seem like a disciple of Gandhi."

The look on her face told me she was afraid she'd said too much about her uncle. No one is that good of an actor.

"How long for you to get this done and your uncle to seize power?" I asked.

"My, but you are smarter than you look." She laughed. "Yes, my uncle plans to step into the power vacuum left when the Kremlin is destroyed. Four days. That is what we need."

"Then you have my word that I won't use these on Russian troops for four days. Tell your uncle that he has that much time to either begin removing every last Russian from American soil, or to place all the troops and equipment that are here under American command to help knock down the infected and retake the country."

After a moment, she smiled and nodded her head. "Agreed. And I will be sure to communicate your message. Word for word."

She held the box out toward me.

Removing my rifle from where it rested on the cart's handle, I held a calming hand up to the Russians when they started to raise theirs. Lowering my weapon to hang on its sling, I shrugged out of my pack and placed it on the cart on top of a bomb. Removing the boxes of keys from the pack, I picked out three, then stepped forward and held them out to Captain Vostov.

"Do you need me to show you how to use these things?" I asked.

40

Rain suddenly started pounding on the windshield. Not a few drops to warn of what was coming. Not even a steady downpour. Torrents. Like someone turned on a fire hose and aimed it directly at them. Jackson cursed and hit the brakes to slow down as visibility went from the limit of the headlights to zero in less than a second. Dog whined his anxiety as the rain pounded the roof of the truck with a ferocity that neither Jackson nor Rachel had ever experienced.

Fumbling for the wiper controls, Jackson finally got them going, but to little effect. Now he could see the end of the hood instead of just the curtain of water on the windshield. He glanced down at the speedometer, unhappy they were only going fifteen miles an hour, but had to slow even further because he couldn't see the road in front.

"How are we going to find anyone in this?" Rachel asked, holding Dog tight and staring at the water being pushed around by the wipers. Jackson checked his watch and shook his head.

"How long?" Rachel had seen him look at the time.

"Seventeen minutes. At the most. They'll leave sooner if they have everyone loaded."

"What do we do? I want to find those girls' parents, but we aren't going to find anything in this storm," Rachel said.

"We've got a full tank of gas," Jackson said after checking the dash. "If we miss the train, we drive. They're heading to Oklahoma City. We just get on I-40 and head west."

Rachel nodded, not thrilled with the idea of being on their own for a several hundred-mile trek across the country. She trusted Jackson, knew he was probably just as capable as John in a fight, but wasn't sure he had the same resourcefulness they might need to survive the journey. Dismissing the thought, she focused her attention on trying to see through the storm.

"Light ahead," Jackson said a couple of minutes later, leaning forward over the steering wheel to peer through the windshield.

Rachel saw it too. At first, she thought it was a car approaching with only one weak headlight, but as they slowly drew closer she could see that it was bobbing up and down. What the hell was it? She reached over and turned the defroster on high to help see through the glass.

As suddenly as the rain had started, it stopped. It didn't lighten up or trickle out, it just stopped. Rachel remembered tropical storms roaring through the Carolinas where she grew up, and how bands of clouds would pass over and bring sudden downpours that would stop just as quickly. Grateful for the relief, she could suddenly see clearly and the light resolved into two figures on the side of the road carrying a flashlight. One of them was large and bulky, the other tall but thin.

"No way we get this fucking lucky!" She said as Jackson accelerated to cover the final distance to the people walking.

He slowed as they approached, headlights picking out the two pedestrians. It was the girls' parents! The woman had a flashlight in one hand as they walked side by side on the shoulder of the road. Rachel smiled and gave Dog a hug in celebration of something being easy for a change. He returned the affection with a big, wet lick across her face.

Rachel cranked her window down and leaned out when they were only a few yards away.

"Am I ever glad we found you! We're pulling out ahead of the storm and your girls were afraid you'd get left behind," she called out.

There was no response from either of them. The brakes squealed as Jackson brought them to a complete stop, the parents standing a few feet beyond the right front fender of the truck. There was enough light from the headlights to see and recognize them, but little more. Rachel frowned, thinking they were scared and didn't recognize her. The mother's name finally popped into her head and she opened the door, stepping out onto the road.

"Mary Alice, it's Rachel. I found your girls..."

She never finished her sentence, starting to turn to the truck when she realized something was very wrong. The instant she looked away, Mary Alice leapt with a scream, tackling her to the ground and lunging for her throat with bared teeth.

Dog responded instantly, launching off the truck's bench seat and slamming into Mary Alice's side, ripping her off the top of Rachel. They rolled across the shoulder and into a ditch full of water, Dog's snarls and Mary Alice's screams loud in the night. Her husband stepped forward and reached for Rachel, who was already scrambling away.

When the female attacked, Jackson threw the transmission into park and jumped out of the cab. By the time his boots hit the ground, the male was stumbling towards Rachel. Jackson ran around the hood of the truck, drawing his pistol. Coming up from behind, he fired a round into the back of its head and the body crashed down on top of Rachel's legs.

Whipping the pistol around when he heard a noise, he lowered it as Dog clambered out of the ditch, blood dripping from his muzzle. Rachel was trying to kick the dead infected off her legs and he bent and lifted the body with one arm and tossed it into the ditch with the dead female. Extending his hand, he hauled Rachel to her feet and looked around for any more threats.

"What the fuck was that?" He hissed. "Another outbreak? And *when* the fuck did they get smart enough to use a flashlight?"

Rachel's blood ran cold at the thought, but he had asked a damn good question. These people had been fine a few hours ago. Why the hell had they turned? And they could use tools now? Then she thought about the two little girls. How the hell was she going to tell them?

"We've got to go," Jackson said, grabbing her arm and shaking her.

Rachel nodded and spared a glance at the ditch with the two bodies before turning back to the truck. When he saw she was moving, Jackson headed back to the driver's side, climbed in and called Dog. Dog looked at Rachel and she motioned him into the cab, then followed him in and slammed the door. Jackson turned the wheel and floored the accelerator, heading back to where he hoped the train was still waiting.

41

I had just finished instructing Captain Vostov on how to enable, set the yield, timer and arm the SADMs when I noticed one of the soldiers with her turn his head slightly to the side and raise a hand to his ear. The universal, automatic reaction to a voice coming over a radio headset stuck in your ear. She saw where I was looking and straightened up, watching him. He started speaking in rapid-fire Russian, carrying on a conversation with whoever was on the other end. I checked on Martinez and Scott, who were also watching him intently.

After nearly two minutes he lowered his hand and turned to the Captain and filled her in on his conversation. Or he could have been discussing the weather in Moscow for all I knew. They were speaking Russian and my knowledge of the language was limited to how to curse someone or tell a woman I wanted to see her naked. Hey, I'm a guy. What do you expect?

"There is a patrol on the way. Approximately thirty minutes out," Vostov said to me. "One of our pilots noticed the infected massed around the gates you came through and called it in."

"Thirty minutes means they haven't started climbing up onto the mesa yet," I said. "Do you think they'll come inside?"

"Da. They go inside," one of the soldiers answered in heavily accented English.

Shit! We had time to break out and slip away before the patrol arrived, but the damn infected would just follow. Might as well put a flashing red light and siren on top of the MRAP to make it easier for the Russians to find us.

"How are you extracting?" I asked Vostov.

She looked at me for a moment, probably trying to decide if it was a good idea to share that information.

"We have a comrade who is a helicopter pilot scheduled to fly a patrol in a few hours. He will pick us up on the roof. He is how we got here."

"How many hours is a few?" I asked.

She looked at me for a moment before checking her watch.

"His patrol starts at 1500 hours local. Why?"

"You have to be out of here before then," I said after doing the math in my head. "This whole facility is going to turn into a smoking crater before that."

"Pizda na palochke!" She said in her native tongue.

I didn't understand the words, but got the meaning from her tone.

"Whatever that means, I probably agree," I said. "We go out of here together. We'll get you to a safe location and you can wait for your buddy to pick you up. I'm sure you have a way to get in contact with him to change the pick up point."

She thought about it for a moment before turning and having a brief conversation in Russian with the two soldiers. The thing about Russian, if you're an English speaker, is that you can't tell if they're pissed off and ready to start shooting at you, or if they're professing their love for each other. The soldier who had spoken in English earlier ended their discussion with a nod of his head.

"Thank you. We accept your offer," Vostov said, turning back to me.

The first order of business was to get the nukes loaded into the MRAP. The two Russians took care of that under the watchful eyes of Martinez and Vostov. While they worked, Scott and I checked out the big, exterior doors at the far end of the shed. We'd gotten in by tripping the emergency release on the outside, and even though there should have been one inside, we couldn't find it.

A steady drumming was coming from the heavy, steel doors. Infected outside that wanted to come in for dinner. The doors were hydraulically operated, as most things large and heavy are, but instead of rams pushing on the frames of the door, the mechanism was housed in the massive hinges that ran up each side of the opening.

"Can you release the pressure and we just push them open with the MRAP?" I asked.

"Don't see a release," Scott answered, shining his flashlight up and down the hinge for the right-hand door. Finding nothing, he moved to the other side, but came up empty there as well.

"There has to be a release," he said. "They can't do maintenance without it. Change the hydraulic oil and you have to open a valve to bleed out any air that got into the system."

He was back to the right-hand hinge, climbing the skeletal framing on the inside of the shed to get a better look at the upper section of the hinge.

"You've got one minute to find the release. Then we're going to ram our way through, Tech Sergeant," I said.

"Yes, sir," he answered, climbing higher.

I returned to the MRAP and looked in the back. The nukes were neatly stacked along one wall of the vehicle and Yee's body had been pushed under a bench seat that ran along the other. The three Russians stood at the side of the vehicle, watching Scott try to find the release and Martinez had climbed behind the wheel.

"Can we not just break through with this big vehicle?" Vostov asked.

"I think we probably can, but if we can get the doors to release I'd feel a whole lot better. There's a few thousand infected waiting on the other side of those doors and if we damage or disable the vehicle trying to break through, our goose is cooked."

"Goose?" The big Russian soldier asked, looking at me curiously.

"Means we're fucked, Ivan," I answered, calling him the name everyone in the Army uses when referring to any Russian soldier.

"Igor," he said and thumped his chest. I ignored the impulse to say "Tarzan" and thump mine.

"Got it!" Scott shouted.

I turned and watched him perform an aerial ballet, keeping one foot and one hand on the shed's frame while extending the rest of his body out to reach the valve on top of the hinge. Even from where I stood, the jet of red oil was visible in Scott's flashlight when the valve opened. Moments later he was back on the floor and dashed to the other side and climbed.

This valve opened with an audible pop and a veritable flood of oil shot out, hitting the ceiling and splashing onto Scott and the metal cross member he was holding. He was pulling himself back to the wall to climb down when he slipped. The hydraulic oil had gone everywhere and when he adjusted his grip to take the first step down his hand landed on oil and instantly slipped off.

He had time for the start of a shout of fear before he crashed to the concrete floor. I was in motion before his body hit, Martinez slamming the MRAP's door open to follow a half a second behind me. Scott was unconscious when I reached him. Martinez skidded up next to us on her knees and started to reach for his head, but I stopped her with a hand on her arm.

"Don't move him, yet," I said.

She nodded and placed her hands in her lap, concern creasing her face. Scott was breathing normally, which was the good news. The bad news was a broken arm and blood pouring from a wound under his hair where the scalp had split when his head hit the floor. I heard bare feet walk up and Vostov kneeled beside me.

"Igor is a medic. If you will allow him, he will help your Sergeant."

I looked at her then cranked my head around to look at the chest thumper who stood behind me with a pack in hand.

"I help," he said in his guttural accent.

I glanced at Martinez, but she just shrugged. Moving aside, I kept a close eye on what he was doing. First, he checked Scott's eyes, then gently ran his fingers along the back of his neck. Grunting to himself, he checked the limbs that didn't have obvious breaks, finishing his cursory exam by pushing his hands underneath Scott's vest and checking his ribs.

"Arm broken and, and…"

He switched to Russian and spat out what he was trying to say as he retrieved a small first aid kit from his pack.

"His arm is broken. There do not seem to be any other broken bones. The head wound looks nasty with all the blood, but he does not think it is serious since the eyes check out normal," Captain Vostov translated.

Igor withdrew a vial of blood clotting powder and sprinkled it into the scalp laceration. The flow of blood stopped almost immediately, the powder turning red and swelling to fill the cut. Next, he applied a thick gauze pad and wrapped it to Scott's head with several turns of dark blue medical tape.

Head wound addressed, he moved to the far side and carefully picked up Scott's arm. Using a pair of scissors, he cut in a line up the sleeve, exposing the abnormal bend where the bone was displaced. Probing with his fingers, he grunted and waved me over next to him.

"Hold!"

He placed my hands on Scott's upper arm, just above the elbow, grasped his wrist and gave a sudden, twisting tug. The bulge subsided, the arm looking normal again.

Igor shouted something in Russian to the other soldier who quickly shrugged out of his pack and drew a small dagger. He deftly sliced open some of the stitching on the back, reached into the opening and pulled out two flat lengths of aluminum that were part of the pack's frame. Each piece was about eight inches long and a couple of inches wide, flat and no more than an eighth of an inch thick. He trotted over and handed them to Igor who formed them to Scott's forearm with his thick fingers.

"Hold," he said again, grabbing my hand and placing it on top of the splint he was creating.

As I held the aluminum in place, he wrapped the arm with gauze, not tight, but securely enough for the makeshift splints to prevent the broken bone from shifting. Finishing with the gauze, he wrapped the whole thing with more of the blue medical tape, pulled the shemagh he was wearing from around his neck and fashioned a sling out of it. Slipping this over Scott's head, he gently placed his arm in it and made some final adjustments.

"Good!" He said, looking up at me and smiling.

"Spasiba, Igor," I said, thanking him in Russian and returning the smile.

We quickly loaded Scott into the MRAP, placing him on the bench and strapping him into place. Using Vostov as a translator, I'd asked Igor how long he thought Scott would be unconscious. He just shrugged in response.

Everyone climbed in and we buttoned up the big, armored truck. Martinez was driving as I rode shotgun, the three Russians squeezed into the back. Vostov perched on top of the SADMs, bending her legs to make room for Igor's big feet, which caused her skirt to ride up around her hips.

I looked at her and couldn't suppress a giggle when I thought about Slim Pickens riding the nuclear bomb in Dr. Strangelove. She gave me a dirty look. I guess it's not a good idea to laugh at an attractive woman when her skirt is around her ass. Fortunately, she was familiar with the movie and saw the humor when I explained it to her.

"Ready?" Martinez asked.

She already had the MRAP in gear, holding us back with the brakes.

"Let's go," I said. "Nice and easy on the doors. Just come up and tap them, then push. The relief valves are open, so they'll move, but the oil can only come out so fast. Can't push faster than that."

Martinez let the vehicle idle forward, touching the brakes and bringing us to a stop just as the heavily armored nose banged against the doors. They pushed open a few inches, then sprang back, smashing into the bumper before rebounding back open a couple of inches as the volume of oil in the system dropped. I was glad we had exercised caution. The doors were so heavy, the impact shook the fourteen-ton MRAP when they sprang back and hit us.

She gave it a few seconds, then let us idle forward again and give the doors another bump. This time, when they rebounded, there was a two-foot gap and the infected immediately started flowing through the opening. There were hundreds of them waiting, and I knew there would be many more than that at the chain link gate we'd closed behind us. I heard Martinez' breathing pick up as the infected flooded into the opening we were creating.

"Easy, Captain. They can't get in. We're fine as long as we don't panic and do anything to damage the vehicle," I said in a calm voice.

I could hear the fast breathing of the Russians behind me and the occasional curse muttered under someone's breath.

"Yes, sir. I'm good," Martinez said, sounding a little more frightened than she was admitting. That was fine, as long as she kept it together.

Another bump with the MRAP and the gap widened to five feet. I told Martinez to turn off the headlights so we weren't so easily visible to any Russian eyes that might be overhead. She flipped the switch and let off the brakes to bump the doors again. Enough oil must have finally been forced out of the system because this time, they didn't bounce back against the bumper. They opened another couple of feet each and stayed there, giving us a nice, wide, nine-foot gap.

The infected were pouring through the doors like floodwaters, quickly filling all the open space around us. Fists pounded on the armored sides of the MRAP, but we could barely hear the blows through all the layers of steel. Females leapt onto the hood and attacked the windshield, but they might as well have been trying to claw their way through one of the vault doors below. Human hands, even enraged human hands, were completely ineffective against the multiple layers of ballistic glass.

Martinez took her foot off the brake and let the truck roll. Infected were knocked aside and under the huge tires. She gave a little throttle and we bulled through the throng, brushing bodies aside like dry leaves before a strong wind. Quickly clearing the infected, Martinez accelerated across the open parking lot, steering for the gate. We rounded the corner of the building, the exit ahead to our left, and she brought us to a stop.

The gate was still closed, but bowed inwards under the tremendous pressure of the crush of infected bodies. The fenced road between the inner and outer gates was completely packed with snarling and screaming bodies, the crowd flaring out into and filling the public road that ran through the area. I couldn't even guess how many of them there were, but there was no doubt this horde was what had drawn the pilot's attention.

"Can we push through that many?" Martinez asked without taking her eyes off the seething mass of flesh.

"We can, and we will," I said, intentionally sounding more confident than I felt at the moment.

"We don't have a choice," I said silently, within my own head.

"Fast or slow?" She asked.

"Slow and steady wins the race, Captain," I said.

She looked at me, grinned slightly and turned back to the front as she started to accelerate.

42

It took less than a minute for them to drive back into the rain, Jackson slowing to a crawl when visibility was once again reduced to nothing. Lightning flashed close behind them, the sharp crack of thunder rattling the truck less than a second later. Dog whined and climbed into Rachel's lap, somewhat comforted when she wrapped both arms around him, hugging him to her chest. Out of the corner of her eye, she saw Jackson check his watch.

"Are we going to make it?" She asked.

He shrugged and reached up to adjust his earpiece.

"Crow's Nest, Black Dog. Copy?" Jackson said into the radio.

"Black Dog? Really?" Rachel looked at him with a small grin.

"Don't ask." Jackson snorted a laugh then went quiet to listen to the radio. "What's status of evacuation? I'm inbound from town. ETA, ten mikes."

He listened some more before speaking again.

"Copy. Three souls inbound if you can hold one of them."

Rachel didn't think it was sounding promising. She suspected Jackson was being told they would miss the train and was asking if one of the helicopters could wait. John seemed to be in love with the big, noisy, bone vibrating machines, but she didn't share his feelings. The damn things could go up and down and change direction so fast she always felt like her stomach was having to play catch up.

"Copy," Jackson spoke the single word and let out a breath of frustration.

"What?" Rachel asked when it didn't seem he was going to share the news.

"We've missed our ride out of here. We're going to drive to Little Rock and meet up with them at Little Rock Air Force Base, then continue on to Oklahoma City. The storm's coming fast and the Colonel doesn't want to risk any of our air assets by sticking around waiting for us."

"How far is Little Rock?"

"Maybe a hundred miles. Hours in this shit," he said, waving a hand at the storm raging around them. "Ninety minutes if I can see to drive."

The rain continued as they pushed on to the west. Jackson stopped and reversed when they passed a sign that pointed to I-40 westbound. Neither of them had seen it until they were already past the turn. Following the curving ramp, they climbed up to the Interstate, but had to keep the speed under ten miles an hour. There were wrecks and abandoned vehicles strewn across the pavement. Nothing they couldn't maneuver around as long as they saw the obstacle in time to avoid it.

Within a couple of minutes, the rain eased off from fire hose to bucket brigade volume and Jackson pushed their speed up slightly. Then the hail started. Small at first, the chunks of ice no larger than a pencil eraser, but quickly growing to the size of golf balls. The nearly constant impact of the ice on the roof of the truck sounded like a hundred blacksmiths all beating on the metal at the same time. The windshield cracked when a particularly large hunk of ice smashed into it, the crack spreading as the smaller hailstones continued their barrage. Lightning and thunder were now constant.

"It's a good thing the Colonel didn't hold a helo back for us," Jackson commented. "This kind of storm can put one into the ground in a hurry. Hail and rotor blades are not a good combination."

Rachel just nodded, holding Dog tight to her body, feeling his heart pounding away. He had pressed his face under her chin and she talked to him in a soothing voice, trying to comfort him as much as she was trying to distract herself.

With no warning, the hail and rain stopped like someone had thrown a switch to shut off the storm. Lightning and thunder continued, though, the countryside around them being lit in an electric white strobe every few seconds.

"Oh, fuck me running," Jackson said after one of the lightning flashes.

"What?"

Rachel looked around, but it was completely dark other than the road in reach of their headlights. Jackson pointed to their left, out his window, and a moment later lightning flashed again. The fraction of a second of light was more than enough for Rachel to see the tornado less than half a mile to their south.

It was a brown monster that had to be close to a mile across where it touched the ground. In the instant of light, she had seen huge pieces of debris, frozen in the air by the flash, swirling around the vortex.

"OK, you need to drive really fucking fast!" She said, trying to keep herself from screaming.

Jackson had already floored the accelerator and the truck was gaining speed. Lightning flashed again, the tornado still looming large and way too close. Swerving around a wrecked minivan, Jackson gritted his teeth when a motorcycle lying on its side appeared in the lights. Yanking the wheel, he avoided it, but nearly turned them over. Regaining control, he kept the throttle hard to the floor as Rachel stared out the window, waiting for another flash of lightning. She didn't have to wait long.

"It's closer!" She screamed when the lightning strobed.

"How close?" Jackson shouted back.

"How the hell do I know? Close! Damn close! Just drive!" She yelled back, eyes glued to the spot in the darkness where she'd seen the tornado.

Their speed climbed steadily and, mercifully, there weren't any more wrecks that had to be avoided. Lightning flashed, and it was closer. A roar, much like Rachel remembered Niagara Falls sounding when she had visited, drowned out the truck's bellowing engine. Leaves, small branches and trash started blowing across the road in front of them. The tornado was almost on top of them.

Rachel glanced at the speedometer and saw they were traveling at eighty miles an hour, the needle holding steady. She looked back in time to see another flash, the tornado now close enough that it filled the entire horizon. Chunks of debris larger than the truck were caught up in the swirling winds. She remembered her dad saying that the debris in a tornado was what killed you, not the wind. She didn't know if that was true, or an old wives' tale, but had no doubt it was dangerous enough to end their day in a hurry.

"Faster!" She shouted.

"This is it. It won't go any faster!" Jackson shouted back, hands locked on the steering wheel as he peered forward trying to see farther than the headlights reached.

The truck didn't have a smooth ride to begin with, but it suddenly got much rougher as the wind buffeted against it and pushed them around on the wet pavement. Lightning flashed and the tornado appeared close enough to reach out and touch. They weren't going to outrun it.

"Find a low spot, like an underpass. That's our only chance!" Rachel yelled over the bellow of the storm.

Jackson had grown up in Mississippi and learned about the danger of tornados at an early age. He also knew exactly what Rachel was talking about. Tornados don't follow small changes in the terrain. Ditches, underpasses, anything that was significantly different in elevation than the surrounding terrain would be passed over and left relatively unscathed. He'd seen it happen a dozen times when he was a kid, but the problem was there weren't any places he could see to seek shelter from the storm.

The part of Arkansas they were in was table top flat, and the Interstate ran a perfectly straight line across that table. It actually was built up above the surrounding terrain, which was predominantly flooded rice paddies. All they needed was somewhere to get a few feet below the average ground level.

The buffeting from the wind grew worse. Their speed slowly dropped to below seventy-five, even though Jackson still had the engine wide open. They were in the *suck zone* of the tornado now, the air being pulled into the vortex so swiftly it was slowing their progress. Larger pieces of debris were flying towards them, slamming into the grill and windshield as they were devoured by the hungry storm.

"There!" Rachel shouted, pointing ahead and to the right.

In a flash of lightning, she'd seen a raw scar cut into the earth along the side of the freeway. A construction project of some kind, and it had apparently required the digging of a deep ditch a few feet to the right of the pavement.

"Hold on!" Jackson shouted.

He fought to maintain control of the truck as the wind speed increased. Cranking the wheel hard to the right, he crashed through the safety barricade. They went airborne for a brief moment when the ground dropped out from under them, then the truck slammed down into a water filled ditch.

43

Martinez had us rolling at a steady fifteen miles an hour when the front bumper contacted the gate. The MRAP shoved it open and compressed the front ranks of bodies packed against it, then started to slow. Martinez fed in more power and the truck kept rolling, crushing bodies against the fences that lined the driveway and under its massive tires. The screams of the females were audible even through the thick armor and ballistic glass.

The engine strained in low gear as we continued to bull our way deeper into the crush of bodies. I tried to estimate how much weight was pushing against the front bumper, but quickly gave up. We'd either make it or we wouldn't. Figuring out how much resistance was coming from all those bodies wouldn't help us at this point.

The MRAP slowed more, a glance at the instrument panel showing we were down to less than ten miles an hour. Our Russian guests were cursing and breathing like they'd just run a hundred-yard sprint, and I realized so was I. It wasn't hot in the vehicle, but we were all sweating, filling the air with the stink of fear.

I glanced over at Martinez, who was completely focused on driving. She was also cursing in a steady stream of Spanish, which I understood a little better than Russian. I learned a few new ways to combine words for different parts of the human anatomy as well as a couple of biological functions. I couldn't help but snort a laugh when she got very creative with different Spanish curse words for the act of procreation.

"What the hell is funny?" Martinez asked, wiping sweat off her forehead.

"Not a thing, Captain. Just expressing my appreciation for your heritage."

"Fuck off. Sir," she said.

I grinned despite myself. Maybe she wasn't showing the proper military respect, but I'd take a woman like her, with a fire in her belly when things got rough, any day over someone who was too worried about offending me to act like a human. Guess that's why it took the end of the world for me to become an officer.

We kept pushing, the engine roaring and the grin disappeared from my face when our speed dropped to five miles an hour. A fast walking pace. We were in our lowest gear with the throttle wide open, and we were barely moving faster than I could walk. Much slower and I was going to ask the Russians to get out and push.

The bodies in front kept compressing. The infected that had been on the road rushed forward when we appeared and crashed the gate. We weren't just pushing what was right in front of us, we were also battling against the entire rear of the herd that was trying to reach us. The tires began slipping, losing traction. I looked out my side window and couldn't see pavement. We had to be driving on bodies, not asphalt. Another ten feet and we came to a full stop, engine bellowing and tires making a high-pitched whine as they spun uselessly.

"Don't blow the engine," I said, reaching out and placing a hand on Martinez' arm when she didn't respond.

When I touched her, she lifted her foot off the throttle and the engine settled into a smooth idle. Infected pressed in from every side so tightly I didn't understand how they weren't killing themselves in the crush.

"We are fucked," Captain Vostov said from behind me.

I turned and looked at her and felt a moment of pity. Her hair and blouse were soaked with sweat and her skirt had finally made it all the way up around her waist. The two Russian Spetsnaz looked concerned, but were keeping their shit together.

"Not yet, Irina," I said, using her name instead of rank. "There's one thing you Russians have never understood about us Americans."

"What is that?" She asked in a shaking voice.

For the first time since meeting her, I could hear a trace of an accent.

"We never fucking quit!" I said. "Martinez, rock us back and forth to get some traction, then make a left turn."

"What? Into the mine field?" She asked, the fear apparent in her voice.

"Captain, what do the first two letters in MRAP stand for?" I coaxed her as she wiped more sweat off her face.

"Umm, it stands for Mine Resistant..." Her voice trailed off as she realized what I was saying. "Yes, sir! Left turn coming up!"

I was more worried than I was letting on. Yes, MRAPs were designed and built to counter the use of roadside bombs by Al Qaeda in Iraq and the Taliban in Afghanistan. They are tough as hell. And, I hoped that the land mines that had been used as part of Los Alamos' security measures were the lower powered anti-personnel variety. If that was the case, we should be able to roll through the minefield with ease. If that was the case. Regardless, we were out of options.

Martinez jammed the truck in reverse and hit the throttle. The tires spun, grabbed, moved us a couple of feet, then started spinning again. Back in drive, we moved forward maybe three feet, then started spinning again. She repeated this process a few times, turning us a little more towards the fence every time she went into drive. Finally, it felt like we had all the traction we were going to get, and the nose of the MRAP was at a forty-five-degree angle to the fence.

Now, instead of thousands of infected stacked up and pushing against us, there were less than a hundred crammed between us and the fence. In drive, Martinez pressed the accelerator to the floor and the tires slipped for a moment before grabbing. The infected in front were pushed back and compressed against the fence which immediately started bowing outwards. Steering for the gap between two of the steel support posts, Martinez kept pressure on the throttle and the fence ruptured, spilling crushed and mangled bodies into the sandy no-man's land behind it.

We followed them through the fresh gap in the chain link, shedding infected as we bounced over the concrete curb at the edge of the pavement. The MRAP handled the soft sand like it had been born for it, which it had. The infected from the driveway were pouring through the opening in our wake, but they couldn't keep up. We heard a loud explosion from behind as one of them found a mine that we had somehow managed to miss.

"Get past the back edge of the herd, then through the fence and onto the road," I said to Martinez, pointing out the windshield at the infected filling the road to our right.

Before she could respond, we hit the first mine. It sounded like Thor himself had come down and struck the side of the MRAP with his hammer. Vostov let out with a decidedly un-military, but very feminine, scream. The heavy truck hardly shuddered and didn't slow. If there was any damage, it was to the exterior armor and wasn't a concern at the moment.

We hit two more mines before traveling far enough to get clear of the herd on the road. I pointed, and Martinez turned the wheel, speeding up to crash through a section of chain link fencing. The truck didn't even shudder, slicing through like nothing had happened, then we were back on pavement.

I looked behind and saw the herd in pursuit. As I turned back to the front there was the sound of a hard impact and a spot on the windshield the size of a half dollar, directly in front of Martinez' face, suddenly turned opaque. There was a second impact and another opaque spot before I realized someone was shooting at us with a high caliber rifle.

44

When the first bullet struck the windshield, Martinez had reflexively backed off the throttle.

"Go!" I screamed.

I had no idea where the sniper was or how good he was. If he was good enough to keep putting rounds within a couple of inches of the same spot, he would eventually punch through the ballistic glass.

Martinez immediately floored the accelerator, the diesel roaring as the heavy vehicle surged forward. She didn't have to be told to swerve back and forth between the fences as she drove. She was a combat helicopter pilot. Several more spots appeared on the windshield from bullet strikes, but they were in random spots.

"Looks like your patrol is early!" I shouted to Vostov over the roar of the engine. She twisted around, got her skirt back below her hips and stuck her head over my shoulder.

"Probably a two man scouting party that came ahead of the patrol."

She grabbed my arm to keep from being thrown to the floor when Martinez swerved again before making a right turn onto a side road. I had no idea where it went, but almost anything was better than being a sitting duck for a sniper.

"And they're probably on the radio with the patrol right now," I said. "Will they call in air?"

She turned her head and had a brief conversation with Igor in Russian.

"Igor says that for only one vehicle, they will just track us. They do not know who is in the truck, or why we are running. They will not want the Air Force involved as long as they think they can stop us."

"How big is the patrol?" I asked, running ideas around in my head.

"Usually five men," she answered after another exchange with Igor.

"Are you willing to kill your countrymen to get away with these bombs?" I asked her. "If they aren't going to stop chasing us, we're going to have to fight before they get a couple of helicopters up here to frag all of our asses."

"Frag?"

"Frag, as in fragment. Blow us all to hell. Fire an armor piercing round right up our ass."

She looked at me a moment then turned to the two Russian soldiers. They talked for a couple of minutes, voices raised and getting passionate a couple of times, then they seemed to reach a consensus and nodded all around.

"We will fight," she said, turning back to me. "We don't want to, but this is bigger than a few soldiers. It will just make it all the sweeter when Barinov is turned into a pile of ash."

I looked into her eyes to make sure I saw the resolve that would need to be there. I did. Turning, I locked eyes with the other two Russians and saw the same. Nodding to myself, I turned to Martinez and told her to find us some terrain that would hide the MRAP. Five minutes later the road narrowed significantly and started to wind down into a canyon. Large rock outcroppings pushed in on one side, a steep drop off looming on the other.

"There!" I said to Martinez, pointing at a narrow trail that cut between two massive rocks on the right side of the road.

She jammed the brakes and cut the wheel, driving the MRAP onto the small track. When I said it was narrow, I wasn't exaggerating. Both sides of the vehicle scraped on rock as Martinez pushed on. After only a few feet the trail ended and we came to a stop with our front bumper touching a sheer rock face. None of the side doors could be opened as they were wedged against solid rock, so we popped the rear and jumped to the ground.

"Will the sniper team join up with the patrol?" I asked.

"No. They will follow behind them to provide security," Vostov answered, this time without having to consult Igor.

Climbing back into the MRAP, I picked up Scott's suppressed rifle and tossed it out the door to Vostov, followed quickly by all the spare magazines Scott had on him. Next, I removed his radio and earpiece, jumped back out and handed it to Vostov.

"I'm going after the sniper team," I said. "The patrol is yours."

Martinez looked at me like she wanted to say something, but kept her mouth shut. Vostov looked at me and nodded as she attached the radio to her clothing and inserted the earpiece. Igor stepped forward and placed a big, meaty hand on my shoulder. I waited for him to say something, but after a moment, he withdrew his hand and turned to start setting up an ambush for the patrol. I could only imagine the conflicting emotions that were going through his heart.

"Don't make me regret trusting you," I said to Vostov in a quiet voice before turning and starting to make my way back up the side of the canyon.

I stayed well off the pavement, and the going was steep and difficult. The side of the canyon was packed sand, rock, and the occasional cactus. The only place for the sniper team to set up was at the edge of the mesa, looking down, and I needed to get there before they did. It was almost a certainty that they would have night vision and if I wasn't in place waiting for them, they'd just have a deep, hearty Russian chuckle as they put a bullet in me.

There was still twenty feet of steep, rugged terrain to the top when I heard voices. Russian voices. They were speaking quietly, but the clear, high desert air carried the sound quite well. It was a short conversation followed by the soft sound of a vehicle door closing and an engine starting. A moment later, an American Humvee nosed over the edge and started down the winding road a few dozen yards to my right. They were running dark, no light showing.

I thought about it for a second, wondering why they were driving a Hummer. Once I thought about it, it all made sense. Why transport all the heavy ground vehicles from Russia when there were plenty to go around in America, just waiting to be taken. Plus, all the spare parts they could need were right here, so that's even more equipment they didn't have to put on a plane. Besides, it's not like a Hummer is a specialized piece of equipment. If an eighteen-year-old, American Army Private can drive one, there's no reason the Russian Army couldn't.

Staying very still until the Hummer was below my position, I turned my head to look for the MRAP. I couldn't see it in the faint moonlight, but could see the two rocks far below that were hiding it. I didn't know what type of ambush had been set up for the Russian patrol, but I did know that there was a high probability that some of my team – when the hell did I start thinking of the Russians as my team? – would have to expose themselves to sniper fire from above.

In a straight line, it was less than four hundred yards to where they were waiting, even though the road wound around and covered well over half a mile to get there. That range, for a trained military sniper, is a nothing shot. These guys routinely train at eight hundred plus yards. I had to find and neutralize the two men before they started ruining peoples' evening.

I covered the final twenty feet on my belly, moving slower than I wanted, to stay as quiet as possible. A large tarantula crawled out from behind a rock and scurried across my hand. Flashing back to a mission in Central America many years ago, I remembered a teammate and close friend we called Spider. He was bigger and meaner than me.

A spider, the size of a nickel, had crawled into his bunk one night at Fort Bragg. He'd screamed like a pre-teen girl and tried to shoot the damn thing before we tackled him and took his weapon away. From that day forward, he was known as Spider. He was gone now, having survived the Army but not the heart attack that had taken him a few years ago.

Smiling at the memory of my friend, I kept crawling until I could poke my eyes above the lip of the mesa. Turning my head a fraction of an inch at a time, I scanned the immediate area. Not seeing anything in either direction, I patiently checked a second time. Still nothing. Where the hell were they? I was about to start a third survey when the faint sound of a boot rubbing on sand came from my left.

I froze and listened, but heard nothing additional. Slowly, I turned my head, still seeing nothing, then remembering my training started looking for *what is wrong with this picture*. Rocks are irregular shapes, and so is the human body, especially when concealed and lying on the ground. Cactus are unique shapes unto themselves. What doesn't occur in nature are perfectly straight lines. Those are almost always something man made, like a rifle barrel. Then I spotted him.

His rifle was silhouetted against the night sky from my vantage point, visible even with the camouflage netting that had been placed over it for concealment. Now that I knew where to look, I could see the sniper. Make out his body, his face pressed to the stock of the rifle, eye to the scope. He was at the base of a rock the size of a VW Beetle, lying in the recess where it met the ground. The rifle was extended over the edge of the mesa, pointed down into the canyon at a forty-five-degree angle.

I didn't see his spotter, but he had to be within whispering distance of the sniper. Or so I thought. America fields two man teams, a sniper and spotter, which are usually joined at the hip. I knew that when I had been in the Army and studied Russian tactics, they followed the same doctrine, but had that changed? Was the spotter possibly at another location and in touch via radio? It didn't make sense, tactically, but I sure wasn't seeing the second man.

The clock in my head was ticking. I had to eliminate the sniper before the ambush started. Slowly, I wormed my way onto the mesa, up on knees and elbows now. Crawling straight forward to get behind the sniper's peripheral vision, I turned and worked my way behind him. I was moving slow and silent, each elbow and knee being placed lightly to test for noise before I shifted my weight forward.

Finally, I reached a point thirty feet directly behind the prone man and paused. Now one of the things a spotter is responsible for, in addition to helping identify targets, is providing security while the sniper is focused downrange. I still couldn't find the other man and momentarily worried that he already had a rifle aimed at a point between my shoulder blades. With the thought, a spot on my upper back twitched and began itching.

Moving as slow and quiet as I could, I pulled my rifle around off my back. Settling my cheek into the stock, I peered through the scope, which was overkill at only thirty feet. Using the night vision, I swiveled back and forth, hoping to spot the second man. Still nothing. I swiveled farther to the right, again found nothing and shifted aim back to the sniper. I hadn't heard anything, hadn't detected any movement, but he was gone.

Two loud explosions I recognized as grenades shattered the night, then the sound of unsuppressed AKMS rifles reached my ears. The ambush. I started to raise up onto my knees and elbows to change positions, but a heavily accented voice from behind froze me in place.

"Not to be moving, American. I will be shooting you!"

45

Rachel woke up shivering and in pain. It was completely dark and she panicked momentarily when she realized she was in water to above her waist. She tried to move, but something was holding her in place and there was a heavy weight resting on her. Forcing herself to calm down, she touched the object pinning her legs and felt thick, wet fur. Dog!

It all came back to her in a flash of memory. Fleeing the tornado in the pickup. Jackson driving and crashing them into the ditch she had spotted to escape the devastating wind. Jackson! She reached out with her left hand, fumbling in the darkness until she felt his thick shoulder on the opposite side of the bench seat.

Mind racing, Rachel tried to prioritize what she needed to do. Before she could help Dog or Jackson, she needed to extricate herself from the truck. Why was it full of water? Forcing her hand down by her side, she released the seat belt, then had to shift Dog's body to let it retract and free her. She let out a sigh of relief when she placed a hand in front of his muzzle and felt his breath. He was breathing steady and strong. Alive. Hopefully, nothing was broken and he had just been knocked unconscious like her and Jackson.

Reaching to her right, Rachel's hand banged against the window. Feeling around, she found the door handle and pulled on it, hearing the lock release. She pushed on the door, but it didn't budge. Was the passenger side of the truck stuck against the wall of the ditch they'd taken shelter in? It was too dark to tell.

Rachel moved her hand around the door panel, gratefully finding a crank and not a button for electric windows. She turned the lever and it started moving slowly, the glass beginning to retract into the door. There was obviously damage that was binding either the mechanism or the track it traveled in, but with some effort, she was eventually able to get it all the way down.

It was raining, not torrents like before, but a steady rain that pattered on the roof and came in the open window. Rachel stuck her arm out and felt the muddy wall of the ditch. It was close to her. Very close. Too close for her to squirm through the opening and onto the roof of the truck? She reached up to the top of the window and moved her hand back and forth between the steel frame of the door and the mud. It seemed like it would be a tight fit, but she thought she could make it, not for the first time regretting the implants she'd had put in her boobs. Wouldn't it just be fitting if she couldn't get out of the truck because of a boob job?

Gently shifting Dog to the seat between her and Jackson, she paused when he whimpered. Stroking his muzzle, she spoke soothingly to him, hoping he was waking up, then pulled her legs under her butt and twisted her upper body to pass through the window. She worked her head through, pausing when she could see over the roof of the truck. Even though it was raining, there were large rents in the cloud cover and some moonlight was making it through.

Rachel could see that the roof was a good four feet below the lip of the ditch. That difference in elevation had saved them. The trench was about a third full of water, swamping the truck to a point halfway up the doors. Taking a breath, she repositioned her feet and pushed, popping her shoulders and arms free, but came to a stop when the top of her breasts met the edge of the window frame. She tried pushing her back into the muddy wall. Tried rubbing handfuls of mud on her shirt to make it slippery. Nothing worked.

Cursing, she squirmed her way back through the window and splashed onto the seat. A moan from the other side of the cab caught her attention.

“Please wake up,” she said softly, as much to herself as to Jackson.

She reached across, finding him slumped forward, forehead resting on the top of the steering wheel. Cautiously probing, she felt a large bump on his head where he'd most likely struck the wheel when they crashed. She also noted how hot his skin felt, feeling even more chilled because of it.

Reaching behind Jackson, she pulled on his door handle and the door popped open a couple of inches before hitting the ditch wall on that side. Realizing there was more room on the left side of the truck, she found the crank and lowered the window. Moving onto the floor and getting on her knees, she shifted Dog to her side of the truck. Back on the seat, she climbed over Jackson's back as carefully as possible, afraid of falling on him and hurting him more than he already was. At the window, she repeated the slithering maneuver and again got her head and shoulders above the truck's roofline before getting stuck by her boobs.

"Goddamn it!" She said and slammed a fist on the roof of the truck.

Jackson moaned again, and she called to him to hang on. She didn't know how she would be able to help him. He weighed way too much for her to move and was way too big to squeeze through the narrow opening, but there was no way she could help if she was trapped too.

Squirming back into the truck she almost screamed when something touched her arm, but it was only Dog. He was on his feet and had stuck his nose against her. Relief to have him conscious flooded through Rachel and she took a moment to wrap him up in a hug before turning back to the window. This time, she faced the mud and started levering her body up through the window.

With considerable effort, she managed to force her way clear, momentarily fearful that she was going to pop one or both of her implants. A giggle escaped her mouth when she pictured herself in a tight shirt, lopsided with one big boob and one small one. Pushing the ridiculous image out of her head, she got her feet up on the door and kept squirming, finally getting her hips past the top of the truck. At that point, she was free, quickly pulling her feet up and walking her ass across the roof to the middle before pulling her knees to her chest to combat shivers of cold.

Covered in mud, she sat there trying to figure out how to get Jackson and Dog out of the truck. Seated on the roof, her head was still below the top of the ditch and she slowly stood to get a look at what was around them. Turning a full three sixty degrees, she was dismayed to see nothing other than darkness. Several vehicles lay on the pavement a couple of dozen feet away, moonlight gleaming faintly on their chrome details.

She wasn't sure, but didn't think the cars had been there when they'd driven into the ditch. Had the tornado deposited them as it passed? She well knew the big storms certainly had the power to do so. Looking back down at the truck she was standing on, she heard a thump from below and leaned forward to see Dog pressing his nose to the rear window. She could hear him whining, wanting out of the wrecked vehicle.

The rear window! If she could break it out, then she would have easy access to rescue Jackson and it would be an easy leap for Dog. Sitting down, Rachel dropped into the bed of the truck, splashing into a foot of muddy water. She turned and looked at Dog, who was uncharacteristically frantic, clawing at the mud through the open passenger window in an attempt to escape. Jackson was still unconscious.

Checking around in the bed, she came up empty with anything to break the glass. Climbing back to the roof, she leapt to the edge of the ditch, clawing in the sticky mud to pull herself onto the shoulder of the road. Pausing a moment to look around for any danger, she dashed to the closest vehicle when she didn't see or hear anything.

The car was a newer Cadillac, all the glass missing out of the windows. It sat on its roof at the edge of the shoulder and with a shudder Rachel realized it had only been a matter of blind luck that had prevented the tornado from dropping it right on top of them. Hoping for a tire iron, she moved to the trunk, but it wouldn't release. On her hands and knees, she crawled inside the vehicle, found the button and pushed it to no avail.

Abandoning the Caddy, she moved on to a small Mazda SUV that sat on four flat tires. The body was twisted and none of the doors or rear hatch would move. Next, she came to a Chevy truck on its side. The back window was gone. Not just broken out, but the entire thing was missing out of the frame. Sucked out by the tornado, Rachel mused as she leaned into the cab.

Shoving the rear seat out of the way, she dug around in the darkness until her fingers felt the cold iron of a lug wrench. It held fast when she tugged and she had to run her hand down its length until she felt the large, plastic wheel that secured it in place. Spinning it, she grabbed the tire iron when it clattered free.

As she ran back to the ditch, she could hear Dog's whines and growls as he continued to try and dig his way free. What the hell had him so panicked? At the edge, Rachel paused and composed herself. A poor landing that resulted in a twisted ankle or broken leg would be beyond bad. It would most likely be fatal. Measuring the distance with her eyes, she jumped and landed squarely in the middle of the roof. The rain slick metal afforded poor traction and her boots slipped, legs flying out from under her and she wound up on her ass.

Tailbone hurting, she dropped into the bed of the truck with a splash and turned to look in the cab. Dog had made a lot of progress with his digging and mud coated much of the inside of the vehicle. He was still going at it, whining and snarling as he worked to clear room to squeeze his body through the window. Rachel glanced at Jackson, who was still unconscious with his back to her.

Stepping back, she took a practice swing with the tire iron, turned her face away and smashed it into the window right behind Jackson. The glass shattered, spider webs appearing across the entire surface, but it stayed firmly within the frame. Rachel hit it again, rewarded this time with a hole the size of a softball. She kept beating on the glass, finally reversing the tool and using the rounded edge to rake shards out of the way. Before she could finish, Dog leapt through the window, nearly knocking her down in his desire to get out of the truck's cab. Rachel looked at him standing near the tailgate; head lowered and a loud growl rumbling in his chest.

"What the hell is wrong with you?" She asked him as she knelt in the water.

Turning her attention back to the cab, she saw that Jackson was starting to move. That was a good sign. She leaned her whole upper body in through the window, trying to see his face as he lifted it off the steering wheel. Reaching out, she placed a hand on his powerful back. With a guttural snarl, he turned, reached up and grabbed her neck, lunging for her face with snapping teeth.

46

No matter how good you are, or think you are, there's always someone out there that's a little better. Maybe a little younger, or maybe just smarter and faster. Either way, I felt like an idiot when I heard the Russian sniper's voice. While I was busy looking for his spotter, he'd managed to circle around behind me without making a sound. The son of a bitch moved like a ghost.

"Be turning over," he ordered.

I resisted the impulse to make fun of his poor English. He hadn't shot me right off, so there was nothing to be gained by antagonizing him. Instead, I released my grip on the rifle and rolled over to face him.

He wasn't a big man, no more than five and a half feet tall and very thin. This was obvious even with the ghillie suit he wore, which masked his outline and features. The Dragunov rifle he was pointing at my chest looked huge in his small hands. With the long sound suppressor attached to the muzzle, it was nearly as long as he was tall.

I've worked with a few snipers over the years, and they are truly a different breed of men. Solitary, except for their spotter, they are typically deep thinkers with the patience of Job. They will lie in wait for their target, sometimes for days on end, in situations that anyone else would find intolerable. To them, intolerable is missing their shot. This ran through my head as I lay there looking up at the muzzle of the Russian rifle.

"They shooting patrol?" He asked, meaning the rest of my team.

There was still fighting below, but it sounded like there was only one AKMS still firing. I hoped that was one of the soldiers with Vostov that was still shooting, not the patrol. The firing was sporadic and sounded like mop up.

"Fuck you, Ivan," I said, drawing a confused expression.

"Segrei. No Ivan," he said.

God help me, but language barriers could be fun if someone wasn't pointing a high-powered military rifle at you.

The firing below had stopped and I saw in his eyes when he made the decision to shoot me. I also saw movement in the dark behind him. I shifted my eyes, expecting to see the spotter who had probably been watching me sneak up and warned him via radio. But a moment later I realized it wasn't a spotter. It was two females, and they were coming fast.

He saw my look, but ignored it at first, probably assuming it was a feint. He must have seen something else when I recognized the females because he whipped around, bringing the rifle to his shoulder. He snapped off a shot immediately and I moved while he was occupied.

From the corner of my eye, I saw the first female's head explode. To have turned and fired in the same motion, that was one hell of an impressive shot. He shifted aim and fired again, the second female crashing to the ground at his feet, what remained of her head almost on the toes of his boots. He didn't step back or make any movement other than to give her a brief glance.

By this time, I was five yards away behind a two-foot tall pile of rocks, rifle up and locked onto him. He turned back to where I had been and froze the instant he realized I wasn't there, patiently waiting for him to kill me. The entire engagement with the two females had only taken about five seconds and he had thought I would have stayed rooted to the ground. Not the first time I've been underestimated, by a long shot, and I'm not complaining. Go ahead. Underestimate me all you want. I'll stick a knife in your ribs then twist it while you're trying to get over your surprise that I didn't do what you expected.

Only I wasn't close enough to use my knife. I settled for pulling the trigger. The rifle was in burst mode and three rounds punched into his chest in a fraction of a second. He fell back, landing on top of one of the dead infected, Dragunov flying out of his hands and clattering on the rocks. I stood up and walked over to look down at him, rifle ready.

He wasn't dead, yet. Blood was already soaking the front of his shirt and red, frothy bubbles were forming around his lips.

"Sergei," he rasped.

"Go to hell, Sergei," I said, firing a round into his head.

In the movies, this is where the guy who just pulled the trigger stands there, staring down at the man he has killed while he carries on some internal monologue. Always seemed stupid to me. If I want to think about the man I killed, I'll do it somewhere nice and safe. Standing here in the open, infected running around, Russian planes not far away – this was not the time or place for introspection. It was time to run, and that's exactly what I did.

"Sitrep," I called on the radio as I started down into the canyon.

"Red force eliminated. No casualties, one injury." I recognized Martinez' voice.

"Copy. I'm on my way to you. Get our ride ready to go," I panted back.

I don't care how good your conditioning is, running at 7,300 feet above sea level when you aren't used to it will make you pant. It takes some time to acclimate to physical exertion a mile and a half up in the air.

I used the pavement when it was going in the direction I needed to travel, but mostly I was scrabbling my way down the steep canyon wall. By the time I approached the idling MRAP, my hands, forearms, ass and legs had more than a few cactus thorns in them. Ignoring the pain, I called out on the radio that I was coming in, gave them a moment to make sure no one shot me when I suddenly appeared out of the dark, then ran up to the vehicle.

They were waiting for me, ready to go. Martinez was back behind the wheel, Vostov and the other two Russians crammed into the rear compartment. The MRAP was sitting on the pavement, and they had driven the damaged Humvee in between the rocks and loaded the bodies of the patrol into it.

Yanking open the passenger door, I jumped in and told Martinez to get us the hell out of there. She headed deeper into the canyon and I turned to look at our passengers. Captain Vostov was bleeding from a through and through bullet wound in her upper thigh, but it was in the meaty part on the outside of her leg, well away from the femoral artery or femur.

Igor had already pushed her skirt up and was cleaning the wound. She grimaced in pain as he squirted the Russian equivalent of Betadine into and through the neat hole. Area clean, he numbed her wound and started suturing. Face white with pain and covered in a sheen of sweat, Vostov looked up at me.

"I always thought my legs were my best feature. Now..." She joked as Igor struggled to keep sewing while Martinez cranked us through a hairpin turn.

"Trust me. With legs like those, no one's going to care about a couple of little scars. They'll just make you more mysterious."

I don't know why I said that. Why I cared how she was feeling. Guess I can't be an asshole all the time.

"Did she survive?"

She looked at me and grimaced, pushed sweat dampened hair out of her eyes and pointed at the gold wedding band on my left hand. It was the only possession The Reverend hadn't taken when I'd been captured in Tennessee.

"I don't know," I answered, not knowing why the hell I was having this conversation with this woman. "I haven't seen or talked to her since the day before the attacks. I was not with her when it happened."

"Why not?" She asked, gasping when Igor's needle hit a spot that hadn't been numbed properly.

"I was working. Opposite end of the country."

I didn't feel like going into the whole long story.

"Why aren't you trying to find her?" She rolled up onto her hip so Igor could work on the exit wound on the back of her leg.

"I am. Or I was, until some fucking foreigners decided to invade my country."

I stared at her. She stared right back, not flinching away from my gaze.

"You know I'm going to do something about that. I just killed five of my own."

"I know."

The anger that had been building evaporated instantly when I thought about being put into the position of having to kill your own countrymen when they were being duped just like everyone else. I couldn't imagine it. I felt for her and her two comrades. They were choosing to do the right thing, even if it meant doing some bad things to accomplish their goal.

"Where will you go from here?" She asked me.

"I can't tell you that."

I might trust her to a degree, but that didn't mean I was born yesterday.

"I understand. Maybe this will help. I recognize the pilot badge on her uniform. What does she fly?" She asked, gesturing at Martinez.

Igor tied off a stitch and dug out a flashlight to check his work. I thought about the question and couldn't come up with a reason not to answer.

"Helicopter," I said, looking up when the MRAP hit a big bump then made a left onto a smooth, straight road.

"Good. Then I have a parting gift for you. There are six Stealth Hawks at Kirtland. They are scheduled to be loaded aboard Antonovs and flown back to Russia in a couple of days, but for now, they are sitting in a hangar on the southern edge of the base. Hangar 41."

Stealth Hawks are a completely updated version of the Black Hawk, incorporating all the lessons about stealth aircraft that America has learned in the past twenty years. These are what was flown into Pakistan to get Bin Laden. They had been kept very secret, never flying during the day anywhere near civilian eyes. Quiet operating, low radar profile and a minimal IR signature for heat seeking missiles to lock on to, one of these would be just the ticket to get us out of New Mexico.

"How do you know I'm not going to leave one of these little babies behind at Kirtland?" I asked, goading her a little, but also testing her response.

"You gave me your word," she answered with a strained smile. Igor was sewing again. "If I couldn't judge men, I wouldn't be much good at my job. You'll keep your word."

I nodded, not really wanting to acknowledge that she had nailed me. Am I that transparent? Maybe she really is that good of a judge of character. Not that I have a good character, by any means, but I don't give my word lightly.

"Captain, there should be a crossroads about two kilometers ahead. Please stop there and let us out," Vostov called out to Martinez who looked around at me with raised eyebrows.

"Do it," I said.

The next two klicks went by quickly, Martinez bringing the MRAP to a stop in the middle of the intersection. Looking out the windows, all I could see was dark desert in every direction. Not even a road sign told me where we were. Igor and the other soldier opened the rear doors and stepped out. They had already matched up the keys I'd given them with the appropriate SADMs and lifted those out, stacking them on the side of the road.

Vostov started to stand, letting out a gasp of pain and dropping back onto her ass. I moved around the three remaining stacked bombs and helped her to her feet. Jumping down to the pavement, I turned and lifted her down, setting her gently on the road.

"Turn right and stay on the road. In a few miles, you will pick up the river. Follow it all the way into Albuquerque. I trust from there you can find your way to the air base. You will want to switch to a civilian vehicle as soon as you can. We are not interfering with civilians as long as they do not cause any problems, but this truck will draw attention you do not want." She waved at the big, ugly vehicle.

"Your man will be able to land and pick you up here?" I asked, looking around at the desolate terrain.

"Yes. His father is a friend of my uncle, also very powerful. No one will question what he does." She smiled, her teeth starkly white in the weak moonlight. "I am truly sorry for what my country has done. I know the death of a few old men in the Kremlin cannot make amends, but we shall see what can be done once they are out of the way."

"Be sure your uncle knows what happened here, tonight," I said. "When he's in control, we're going to be calling him for help. If he really regrets what happened, he'll answer when we call."

She nodded agreement.

"One more thing, Major." I was turning to get back into the MRAP, but stopped and looked at her when she spoke. "The timing of the virus is not a precise science. More people will turn. Many more. Any that have not been vaccinated. It would be good if you took the vaccine sooner rather than later. One CC, IM. In a muscle. It burns like acid, so be prepared."

I stood looking at her for a moment before nodding and turning back to the waiting truck. I climbed in the back, shutting the doors behind me and asked Martinez if she'd heard the instructions on how to get to Albuquerque. She answered that she had and stepped on the throttle.

Checking on Scott, I was happy to find he was breathing normally. His color was good, but I expected he would have one hell of a headache when he woke up. Glancing around, a glint of light caught my eye and I looked closer at the top of the bomb where Vostov had been sitting. Three small syringes, still in their sterile wrapping, sat waiting for me.

47

While Martinez drove, I opened the box that contained the vaccine and stared at the four vials. They were labeled in Cyrillic, but I was able to figure out that each contained twenty-five CCs of liquid. In for a penny, in for a pound.

I opened the three syringes and one of the alcohol pads that Igor had thoughtfully included. Cleaning the rubber seal on the top of a vial, I inserted the first thin needle and extracted one CC of the colored liquid. I repeated the process until I had three injections ready to go.

I don't know much about medical procedures, but I do know that if you're going to get a painful shot into a muscle, you're better off taking it in the glutes. Figures. Taking it in the ass, again. Oh well. Never one to hesitate to go first, I stood up, unbuckled and dropped my pants. Twisting around as much as possible, I cleaned a spot on my right cheek, took a breath and stuck the needle in. The needle itself was small and thin, about the same size as I remembered from getting my annual flu shot. It didn't hurt.

I pressed the plunger and forced the vaccine into my body. For a couple of seconds, nothing other than a slight pressure at the injection site. For a couple of seconds. Then, someone jabbed a red-hot knitting needle into my ass and started twisting it around as molten metal flowed into my flesh. I've had about every injection, vaccination, and inoculation that the US Government and civilian medicine could devise to keep me healthy as I traveled the globe. None of them came close to this.

I stood there stoically, resisting the impulse to piss and moan. I've never been one to see the point in dramatizing my pain. It doesn't make it hurt less; it just scares the hell out of the guy in line behind you. Well, let me take that back. I have been in lines where I did a good job of acting like something was incredibly painful, just to mess with the guys coming behind. Hey, I never said I wasn't an asshole.

I rubbed the spot, hard, and after about a minute the pain began to subside. The burning had spread to most of the right side of my ass, but it was bearable now. Sort of.

I gave the injection site another swipe with the almost dry alcohol pad and pulled my pants back up. Buckling them, I glanced up to see Martinez looking at me in a mirror.

"No problem, Captain," I said.

"Whatever you say, sir. But I don't know what was more fun. Watching a Major drop his pants, or seeing a big, tough Green Beret grimacing in pain from a tiny little shot."

She grinned and turned her attention back to the road.

"Captain, has anyone ever told you that you're not funny?"

"No sir, never. I usually have them rolling in the aisles."

"Smart ass bitch," I mumbled under my breath with a grin.

I started fumbling with Scott's belt buckle, looking up when he spoke.

"I've heard about you Army guys, but you could at least buy me dinner first."

Everyone's a fucking comedian when the bullets aren't flying. I smiled back, happy to see him awake even though he looked like hell.

"Hell, Tech Sergeant. I'm surrounded by Air Force. When in Rome..."

He grinned and used his good arm to unbuckle, then I helped him work the trousers down far enough to expose his hip. A quick swipe with alcohol and I stuck the needle in and pressed the plunger.

"Fuck me!" He said quietly a couple of seconds later. "What the hell did the goddamn Russkies put in this? Battery acid?"

He couldn't reach the injection site to rub because it was on the same side of his body as his broken arm. I wasn't about to sit there and rub his ass for him, so he dealt with the pain by trotting out some inventive curses.

"OK, Princess. Don't take this the wrong way, but it's time to show me your ass," I said to Martinez.

She slowed, pulling onto the gravel shoulder a moment later and shifting into park, leaving the engine idling. Climbing out of the driver's seat, she worked her way to me, turned her back and lowered her pants to the bottom of her ass.

"Be gentle with me, sir. It's my first time," she said in a little girl voice as she looked at me over her shoulder.

Scott snorted, then let out a guffaw as I cleaned a spot with the last alcohol pad. I stuck the needle in and pressed the plunger.

"Chinga tu madre!" She said a couple of seconds later, reaching back and vigorously rubbing her ass. "I retract any disparaging remarks I may have made about the Green Berets. That fucking hurts!"

"Company coming," Scott said, instantly making us forget about the injections.

He had sat up on the bench, trying to find a way to squirm around and massage the sore spot. Seated, he had a good view through the damaged windshield. I bent to see around Martinez as she quickly pulled her pants up. Less than a mile in front of us were five sets of headlights coming our direction. Had to be Russian military. Civilians don't travel in tight convoys like that. They also don't travel with a helicopter pacing them, providing air support and a bird's eye view.

"Have we passed any trails or turnouts?" I asked Martinez, making sure the vial was safely back in the foam cutout before storing the box in my pack.

"No, sir. Nothing. We can head cross country, but there's no breeze. We'll leave a dust trail that will be noticeable," she answered, slithering over equipment and back behind the wheel. "What do you want to do?"

"Turn around," I ordered. "Our new Russian friends back there will have a hard time explaining what they're doing on foot in the middle of nowhere."

Martinez got us pointed the other direction, careful to keep the big tires on pavement and not create a dust cloud that would alert the approaching troops to our presence. Facing back north, she pressed on the throttle, driving faster than I was comfortable with in the dark, but then we didn't have much time. We reached the crossroads quickly, Martinez jamming on the brakes and bringing us to a halt with a slight squeal of the tires. I popped the latch on the back doors and hopped out onto the pavement, looking around.

Vostov and the two soldiers were already running towards the MRAP, each of the men shuffling along under the weight of the SADMs. Vostov reached me first, limping up as she favored the leg with the bullet hole.

"We see them," she said. "Thank you for coming back. The first patrol or the sniper must have gotten a message out."

"Can you bluff them?" I asked.

"Yes. If the story matches the circumstances."

I got Martinez out of the driver's seat and, after loading his two bombs in the back, Igor slid behind the wheel. Vostov joined him in front, stiffly climbing into the passenger seat. Martinez and I got into the back and joined Scott where he had moved onto the floor. We were crammed in like sardines, Martinez sitting on my lap with her legs extended across Scott. The other Russian slammed the door and took a seat on the bench, rifle across his lap, pointing in our direction but not directly at us.

"I sure as hell hope you're right about her, sir," Martinez mumbled to me as she shifted her weight off the sore side of her ass. With her on top of me, I couldn't do the same, and the pain was an unwelcome distraction.

"Me too, Captain. Me too."

We all shut up as Igor put the vehicle in gear and turned us around. Vostov said something in Russian and he turned the headlights on and accelerated down the road, directly at the oncoming convoy.

It only took a couple of minutes for us to meet them, Igor braking gently and bringing the big MRAP to a stop, straddling the line down the middle of the road. I looked through the windshield and saw a row of Humvees completely blocking our progress, each of them with a manned machine gun pointed at us. The helicopter came into a hover directly overhead and a spotlight turned night into day.

At a command from Vostov, Igor opened his door, stood up on the running board and started shouting at them in what sounded like angry Russian. Of course, all Russian sounds angry to me. A voice shouted back and Igor grew animated, shouting louder and waving his arms in a manner that was telling them to get out of his way.

None of the Hummers moved and after a moment, three men approached. Two carried rifles, not quite aimed at Igor, but only a few degrees off target. The one leading them didn't have a rifle, only a holstered pistol. I hoped he didn't outrank Vostov.

The officer walked up to Igor's side of the vehicle and I could see the variety of colors and insignia on his uniform. My knowledge of Russian uniforms was rusty as hell. I hadn't done any formal study of their military in a lot of years, more years than I cared to acknowledge, but I was reasonably sure he was a Captain in the Russian Air Force.

He started to speak to Igor, but Vostov barked out a rapid-fire stream of Russian and he moved to her side of the vehicle. She opened the door and stepped down, doing an admirable job of disguising her injury. She pulled an ID case out of the now dirty lab coat she still wore. Opening it, she flashed it in front of his face, talking a mile a minute in an aggressive tone. I recognized the Russian words for the full name of the GRU and the word for prisoners. She continued to hold the wallet open as she started waving her arms, voice growing louder as she continued to berate the man.

The Captain had stiffened when he'd seen what I assumed was her GRU ID. As she screamed in his face, he pulled himself into a rigid position of attention. Vostov paused in her tirade, barked out a single word, slapped her wallet shut and returned it to her pocket. The Russian officer held himself at attention for a brief moment, snapped off a salute and turned to bark orders at his men. Two of the Humvees moved, opening the road, and Vostov gave the man a glare before climbing back in the MRAP and slamming the door hard enough to rock the heavy vehicle on its suspension.

Igor was already back behind the wheel and floored the throttle, roaring through the opening in the roadblock and narrowly missing two Russian soldiers who had to jump for their lives. A full minute passed while Vostov leaned forward to watch in the outside mirror. Finally, she relaxed and turned to me.

"No one wants to interfere with a GRU operation."

She smiled and I was relieved to see the Russian sitting in back with us lower his rifle so the muzzle was pointed at the floor. He met my eyes and winked.

I was impressed with her performance, but then Russian soldiers are just like soldiers everywhere else in the world. When confronted by an angry officer, that also happens to belong to a very powerful intelligence unit, you don't ask questions. You mind your own business and hope to God the spook didn't write down your name.

As we approached Albuquerque, we began encountering more Russians patrolling in captured Hummers. Twice we were stopped, but Vostov showed her ID and the soldiers couldn't apologize and wave us on about our business fast enough.

"With that magical ID, why didn't you want to just ride to the base with us?" I asked her after the second time we were questioned.

"Because now I am drawing attention to myself. And it will be noted that I came through security at the base with a captured American vehicle and three prisoners. If my superiors happen to notice, which is definitely possible, I will have a difficult time explaining my actions and why you are not available for interrogation."

"But, it does not matter. Because of my uncle, they will be afraid to take any action against me without concrete evidence. They may start an investigation, but like everything internal to the GRU that is political, it will take weeks. Well before that, if everything goes according to plan, things will change at home, and I will be untouchable."

"And if things don't go according to plan?" I asked, but I already knew the answer.

"Then I will be arrested, tried, convicted of treason and shot."

She answered more calmly than I thought I could have if I were in her shoes. The conversation died out and within ten minutes we had crossed the outer edge of the city and turned off the highway, following signs that pointed the way to Kirtland Air Force Base. When the main gate was in sight, Vostov spoke to the two Spetsnaz in Russian. They nodded and she turned back to the front. The man in back with us moved his rifle into a guarding position as we slowed for the gate.

My legs were asleep from the pressure of Martinez sitting on them. She turned to look at me and I could see the fear in her eyes, but also resolve. Like me, she still had her pistol, hidden in her clothing. Unlike me, she also had several blades concealed on her person. I knew she had one strapped to each forearm and I could feel the one in the back of her pants digging into my leg. Scott looked like he was dizzy and in pain, but ready to fight as well.

I was proud of these two. They thought like warriors. If things went bad, they would fight. There was no possibility of surrender to the Russians. But if we had to fight, I needed my legs to function. Wrapping my hands around Martinez' slender waist, I lifted her, spread my legs apart and lowered her to the metal deck between them.

Pressure off, the pins and needles hit as normal blood flow resumed. I flexed the muscles in my legs and swiveled my feet around, loosening the joints.

A moment later we came to a stop and Igor opened his door to speak with the guard. There was a question in Russian from the guard and I could see three more men standing in a semi-circle to our front, rifles ready. I suspected there were more behind us. Also, it was more than likely that the Russians had something pointed at us with enough power to penetrate our armor and turn us all into pulp.

Vostov leaned across the front and handed her ID to the guard, speaking much more calmly than she had to the Captain at the road block. The guard's tone was deferential, but he apparently insisted on inspecting the vehicle and all the passengers. He kept Vostov's ID and took Igor's as well. Coming to the back, he banged on the door. After a nod from Vostov, the Russian guarding us reached out and opened it.

The gate sentry looked in, two more men with rifles aimed at us backing him up. He said something and the soldier across from us fished out an ID card and handed it over. Three ID cards in hand, he disappeared around the side of the vehicle, but the rifles pointing in at us didn't waver. I spared a glance at Vostov, who looked completely at ease as if she went through this daily. Perhaps she did.

A long five minutes later, the guard stepped back to Igor's open door and handed all three IDs to him. He said something that sounded respectful to Vostov, then turned his head and shouted to the men behind us. Rifles lowered, one of them stepped forward and slammed the rear door shut. Igor closed his door, waved at the guard and a moment later drove us through the gate onto Kirtland.

"Was everything about that normal?" I asked once we cleared security.

"Yes. Completely," Vostov said, smiling.

"They don't inspect equipment coming on the base?" I asked, patting one of the nukes sitting next to me.

"Not when there is a GRU officer in the vehicle that just told them she was returning with captured technology and American prisoners. Not if they value their futures. All they did was check to make sure our IDs matched with the list of personnel assigned to this base and were valid. Once everything checked out, their job was done."

"How long do you think you have before someone starts asking questions?" Martinez spoke up.

"Two days, maybe three. Maybe less when one of the Stealth Hawks disappears. No matter. The bombs will be on a cargo flight to Moscow in a little over twelve hours."

She turned to Igor and gave directions, pointing towards a road that followed the perimeter fence and would take us to the far side of the base where our ride was waiting.

48

It's around five-hundred air miles from Albuquerque to Oklahoma City. The Stealth Hawk's cruise speed was lower than a standard Black Hawk, but it still only took a little over six hours to make the flight. It had been surprisingly easy to steal the helicopter from the Russians. Well, can you really *steal* something that was yours to begin with? Anyway, there had been no security posted at the hangar when Igor pulled to a stop.

When the Russians captured Kirtland, they had transported all the Air Force personnel at the base to the Bernalillo County Jail, which was only a few miles away. Throwing the doors open, they had released all the prisoners, unconcerned with turning loose murderers, rapists, arsonists, and all other variety of felons. Jail cleared of civilians, they had stuffed the facility with every American who had been unlucky enough to be on the base when they arrived.

A platoon of infantry was assigned to guard the jail, and with security around the perimeter of the base, the Russians hadn't felt the need to expend manpower guarding locations within the fence. This just made it easier for us. For that matter, as we had driven the perimeter road, I had noted that it would have been simple to breach the fence and gain access to the hangar if we hadn't had Vostov to escort us through the gate.

The helicopters were exactly where she had said they would be. Sitting in the hangar, they looked more like something out a science fiction movie, but this was due to the design changes necessary to make them stealthy to radar. I heard Martinez catch her breath when we walked into the hangar. I looked at her and the look on her face reminded me of a child in a toy store. Walking to the closest helicopter, she checked it over, shook her head and moved to the next. After checking all of them, she came over to where I stood with Vostov.

"None of them are fueled. We'll have to wheel one out to fuel it before we can leave."

"Pick the one you want and let's get going. We've only got about five hours of darkness left," I answered, checking my watch.

Martinez nodded and trotted off to a small tractor parked against the wall of the hangar. Moments later she had it running and pulled up to the nose gear of the aircraft she had selected. They all looked the same to me, but after checking each one carefully, something about that one had gotten her attention. Tractor hooked to the front landing gear, she waved at Igor and me and we rolled the massive doors the rest of the way open.

Helicopter out in the open, Martinez parked it next to an in-ground fuel point and wasted no time in connecting a hose to the Stealth Hawk. While she monitored the fueling, the two Russians helped me load my three bombs and secure them with heavy, rubber bungee cords. Igor assisted with the loading of Yee's body, then Scott climbed aboard and settled into a web sling, rifle across his knees. I tossed my pack in next to his and Martinez' and turned to Vostov.

"We've made a good start, Captain," I said. "When this is over, I just hope our two countries can work together to rebuild, not continue fighting each other. There're enough enemies in the world."

"We will meet again, Major."

She leaned in, and in very Russian fashion, kissed me on each cheek before turning and climbing aboard the MRAP.

When the fueling completed, Martinez and I had boarded and she'd started the engines. The first thing I noticed was how quiet this bird was compared to a standard Black Hawk. Then she lifted us into the air and I was even more impressed when the noise of the rotor didn't threaten to rattle my brain into mush.

We exited Kirtland to the east, almost immediately flying over nothing but empty desert.

She kept us low, flying nap of the Earth. I climbed into the co-pilot's seat and pulled on the helmet that was tethered to the control panel with a long cable. When I lowered the visor, a screen flared to life in front of my eyes showing the view from the front in glorious HD night vision. In the top right, I could see our speed, heading and altitude, surprised that we were traveling at a hundred and thirty knots, only fifty feet above the ground.

Looking back at the forward view, I got a knot in my stomach when I remembered that telephone poles, cell phone towers and all kinds of other things were taller than fifty feet. But as I watched the ground rush under us, I realized that Martinez would be able to clearly see any obstacle in plenty of time to avoid it. Leaving her to it, I returned to the back, checked on Scott and stretched out on the gently vibrating deck. I think I was asleep in less than a minute.

I woke up with a start when Scott kicked my foot. I looked up at him, and he grinned back through obvious pain.

"We're ten minutes out of Tinker," he said.

I nodded and stifled a groan when I stood up. The body was tired and sore, and sleeping on a hard, steel deck hadn't helped anything. And my ass still hurt from the vaccine injection. Rubbing my backside, I climbed forward into the cockpit, squinting at the early morning sun shining directly into my eyes. I worked the helmet onto my head and lowered the visor. My view changed to the HD cameras mounted on the exterior of the aircraft, the electronics automatically compensating for the blinding sunlight.

"How we doing, Martinez?" I asked on the intercom, stifling a yawn.

"No worries, sir. I've been on the radio with Tinker for half an hour and they're expecting us. Seems there's a Colonel Crawford mighty anxious to see you."

Great. I still believed I had done the right thing in making the deal with the Russians. I just hoped the Colonel agreed.

"We've got an escort," Martinez said and I looked to the side to see a pair of F-35s flying in formation with us.

As I turned my head, the helmet seamlessly transitioned across several cameras and I could see two more on our left. I watched in the display as we descended, then looked ahead and saw the sprawl of Oklahoma City. It looked so fucking normal. There was traffic on the freeways and surface streets. Not much, and I was sure nothing close to pre-attack volumes, but there were people down there going about their daily lives.

But for how much longer? Could we take the data in the flash drive and synthesize enough vaccine to save them? And even if we pulled that off, there were still tens of millions of infected roaming around the country. What happened when they decided to come to dinner?

The four fighter jets peeled off with a roar, leaving us to descend the final two thousand feet on our own. We cleared the perimeter of Tinker Air Force Base and Martinez cut our speed to under fifty knots, flying over row after row of barracks, then down the length of a runway. At the far end, a row of hangars sat with their doors rolled open. Two Humvees, an ambulance and an Air Force staff car waited for us.

Martinez cut our forward speed to zero and made a sedate landing, though I suspected she would have preferred to execute a high-speed combat landing. Every pilot I've ever known does. Descending that last twenty feet to the tarmac, I looked towards the waiting vehicles and saw Colonel Crawford and Captain Blanchard step out of one of the Hummers. The other disgorged four Rangers and three Air Force officers stepped out of the staff car. Where was Jackson? Was he still searching for Rachel and Dog?

"Good to see you, Major," Crawford said after I climbed down out of the Stealth Hawk and walked forward to meet him. "Your pilot said you have some special packages on board."

"Yes, sir."

I had already taken the keys out of my pack and handed them to Blanchard. He headed for the side door of the aircraft, Rangers close on his heels. They would take possession of the nukes and make sure they stayed secure.

"Where's Jackson, Colonel? Did he find Rachel and Dog?"

Now that the mission was over, I let myself think about them. Think about Rachel. Acknowledge the ball of worry that I'd kept tamped down in my gut for the duration of the mission. When I thought about her, a pang started deep inside me and threatened to strangle my breathing. Was this just fear for someone I cared for deeply, or was this love?

She had wanted to know my feelings when she'd professed hers, and I still didn't know the answer. All I knew was that it was just as important to me to find her now as it was to find Katie. Was that my answer? Was I in love with two women? I shook my head, telling myself I was being ridiculous and focused on what the Colonel was saying.

"There's a lot to tell you, and I suspect you have a lot to tell me. I only see three packages coming off that aircraft."

I followed his gaze, watching as the Rangers loaded the bombs into the back of their Humvee.

"Yes, sir. There is. But you didn't answer my question. Where's Jackson? What's going on with the search?"

49

Rachel tried to scream when Jackson's hands went around her throat, but he squeezed so hard she couldn't move any air in or out. He was still wearing the seatbelt and strained against it, trying to turn and move his jaws to her, but it held tight. She felt her feet leave the bed of the truck as he pulled her closer and put her hand on his chest to brace against him. He was incredibly strong and it did no good. Snapping teeth only inches from her face, Rachel remembered the iron lug wrench in her right hand and jammed the end of it into Jackson's mouth.

Teeth broke and his lips were torn, but he didn't flinch. She started pounding on his head with the tool, splitting his face and scalp open, but having no other effect. His grip was still like bands of steel around her throat and she could feel the edges of her consciousness starting to close in. She could no longer hear the snarling, only a roar like the ocean in her ears. She felt his bloody lips brush her cheek.

Suddenly one of his hands was no longer constricting her neck and she gulped a ragged breath. Her hearing returned and she panicked when she heard additional snarls in the truck with her until she realized it was Dog. He had leapt in through the missing window and had clamped his powerful jaws onto one of Jackson's arms.

Jackson waved his trapped arm, strong enough to drag Dog around the cramped cab. Rachel renewed her attack with the tire iron, this time pounding on the wrist of the arm that was still holding her. If she could break it, he wouldn't be able to maintain his hold. She hoped.

The third blow did the trick, his grip slackening. Rachel put her hands on the window frame and pushed, tearing her throat out of his damaged hand. She stumbled backwards in the bed of the truck, losing her balance and falling to her ass in the muddy water. Dog was still inside, savagely ripping at Jackson's arms, but the confined space prevented him from getting the advantage and tearing his throat out.

"Dog! Come here!" Rachel shouted, her voice hoarse.

Dog disengaged and in a flash, jumped through the window and splashed into the water next to Rachel. He pressed his body against hers, facing the front of the truck and she could feel him shaking. Or was that her shaking so hard it only felt like Dog?

They sat that way for a long time, Rachel's arms locked around Dog, his head against her chest. Jackson could hear them breathing, continuously trying to turn his body, but the seat belt was stronger than he was. He was trapped. Stuck in the seat and only able to snarl and flail his arms. Tears started rolling down her cheeks. Then deep sobs racked her body as she buried her face in Dog's matted fur.

Rachel was in shock. And she was cold. The cold finally got her moving. Cried out, she sniffed back her tears and slowly got to her feet. The sun was coming up behind her, but the first light of the day provided no warmth. Looking around, she saw that the ditch behind them had a gentle ramp up to ground level for the heavy equipment that did the digging to drive in and out.

Jumping over the tailgate, she splashed into waist deep water and waded up the ramp. Dog joined her, having to swim a short distance before he could reach a location shallow enough for him to stand. Together, they climbed the ramp into the sunshine. Looking around, Rachel was dismayed. In every direction, the land was flat to the horizon, and nothing was standing. Not even vegetation.

The tornado had sucked everything out of the ground, leaving only raw mud in its wake for as far as she could see. There were even chunks of asphalt missing from the road. In a daze, Rachel wandered over to the cars that had been deposited by the storm. She ignored the Cadillac, Mazda and Chevy truck. Beyond them was another tangle of vehicles and she dismissed them when she saw the amount of damage they had sustained.

Walking past them she spotted two more, both sitting on their tires. A Mercedes S-Class sedan sat in the sun, tires and glass intact. Other than a mud covered exterior, it appeared to be in perfect condition. Rachel pulled the door open and looked inside. It even smelled new. But there weren't any keys in the ignition.

The vehicle next to it was a battered Ford Bronco. Like the Mercedes, its tires and glass were intact. As she got closer, Rachel could tell it was painted orange underneath all the mud. Pulling the door open, she looked and found the keys dangling from the switch. Reaching in, she turned the key and the starter whined, then the big V8 engine rumbled to life. She waved Dog inside, climbed behind the wheel and turned the heater all the way to hot.

Pulling the gear selector into drive, Rachel paused before taking her foot off the brake. Looking down, she saw the pistol still holstered on her belt. With a sigh, she took her foot off the brake and slowly drove to the top of the ditch. She stepped out of the Bronco, leaving the door open, and could immediately hear Jackson's snarls coming from below. Drawing the pistol, she checked it the way John had taught her. Made sure nothing was obstructing the muzzle. The slide operated smoothly. A round was in the chamber.

Pistol in hand, Rachel walked down the muddy ramp, wading through the water until she reached the truck. Climbing over the tailgate, she slowly moved towards the back of the cab, Jackson's snarls a constant as he heard her approaching. Stopping a couple of feet short of the opening, she raised the pistol, aimed at Jackson's head and pulled the trigger.

50

Roach was back in an Air Force uniform. He was dressed as a Captain again, clothes perfectly pressed and creases razor sharp when he walked into the offices of the Lieutenant Colonel in charge of the Security Forces on Tinker Air Force Base. He didn't know what was in store for him, but the best thing about the attacks on America was that none of what he'd done the past couple of weeks had been documented or could even be attributed to him. Here at Tinker, he and Synthia would get a fresh start.

He had a lot to teach her about patience and covering her tracks. She had tried to convince him the previous evening to go out and find a woman for them to play with. Descriptions of what she wanted to do to the woman with her knife had sent Roach into a sexual frenzy and he had nearly agreed to her request. He could feel the flesh of the woman as he beat her, taste her blood when he bit her, hear her screams when he savagely penetrated her.

Then he had reached orgasm and looked down to see that it had been Synthia's flesh he was beating, her blood he was tasting and her screams he was hearing. Bruised and bleeding, she had smiled up at him and told him she loved him. Having never heard those words before, even from his own mother, Roach ignored them and immediately began worrying about the noise they had made.

Dressing quickly, he stepped out on the front porch of the small house that had been assigned to them. His neighbor, also a Captain and a cargo pilot, was standing in his driveway looking at Roach's house. Roach apologized for the disturbance and told the man it was his wife having night terrors about the infected that had trapped them in Nashville. The man nodded his head in sympathy and wished Roach a good night before going back into his house.

They would have to be more careful than that. Perhaps a gag for Synthia. Yes, that would work. He'd used gags before and found them quite effective.

"Captain, Lieutenant Colonel Lewis will see you now."

Roach looked up when the young Senior Airman sitting at the reception desk spoke. She was pointing at a door behind and to her left. Roach stepped up to it, knocked sharply, and entered when a voice called out "come."

The Lieutenant Colonel was older than Roach expected, a slight paunch around the middle and thinning hair on top. He looked like he hadn't had a shower, shave or change of uniform in a couple of days. Not bothering to stand, he waved Roach into a chair in front of his desk and picked through a pile of folders until he found the one he wanted. Opening the folder, he leaned back in the chair and looked at it through a pair of gold-rimmed reading glasses.

"Welcome to Tinker, Captain. You and the missus all settled in?"

He didn't bother to look up from the file he was reading.

"Yes, sir. Thank you, sir. We're quite happy with the accommodations."

The man flapped a hand in the air, dismissing Roach's thanks.

"So, here's the deal, Captain," he said, closing the folder and placing it back on the pile. He leaned forward and rested his forearms on his desk. "We're stretched about as thin as we can be, at the moment. Thinner, even. I lost a third of my personnel to the outbreak and another ten percent just lost it. In the rubber room. They're useless to me right now."

He paused, looking around his desk. Shoving some papers aside he found a crumpled pack of cigarettes and pulled one out.

"Do you mind?" He asked, holding one up for Roach to see.

"Not at all, sir. Please feel free."

"Thanks. Now where was I?"

He leaned back and lit the cigarette with a gold Zippo lighter.

"Stretched thin, sir. I'll do whatever needs to be done," Roach said.

"Right. Thin. Anyway, we've got the normal problems of any large Air Force base. Thefts, assaults, rapes, even murders. All of those are on the rise, by the way. But we've also got the goddamn Russians on our doorstep. It's up to us to keep this installation secure from spies and saboteurs."

He paused and drew deeply on the cigarette. It was only through a well-honed strength of will that Roach managed not to make a face at the stink of the burning tobacco.

"I'm ready to jump in, sir. I ran base security at Kadena for 18 months. Learned a lot about defending against espionage and sabotage."

Roach forced himself to keep his hands in his lap and not start fanning the smoke away from his face.

"Good, but I've got a man on that. The other issue that's stretching us is refugees. We're getting a steady stream of people from all over the country that have made it to Oklahoma. General Simonds has graciously opened our gates, but we're falling behind in processing them and getting even the basic necessities issued. That's what I need you to take charge of."

Refugees. Roach tried not to smile as he thought about the possibilities. Women and girls that no one knew who they were or where they were. And they'd be vulnerable and eager to accept any kindness, not recognizing the danger they were in until it was too late.

"Yes, sir. I'm happy to take that off your plate," Roach said, smiling.

The Lieutenant Colonel wrapped up the meeting in a hurry at that point, sending Roach to see the Senior Airman at the front desk. She told him where to go and who to find when he got there. Next, she handed him a two-way radio, its charger, and directed him to the rear parking lot where extra Hummers were parked.

"Just take any one that doesn't have a red sticker on the windshield."

Roach thanked her, found a vehicle and drove across the base to a massive hangar where five Airmen and a Staff Sergeant were trying to deal with a large group of women and children. Roach walked up to the Sergeant and introduced himself.

"Damn glad to see you, sir," the Sergeant said, tossing a clipboard onto a table covered with file folders and loose papers. "I'm sure Lieutenant Colonel Lewis told you how understaffed we are. And we just had another group roll in a couple of hours ago."

Roach looked around the hangar. A dozen women were trying to control what must have been close to fifty, school aged children. The kids were running around, chasing each other, yelling and screaming, while others were sitting by themselves and crying. First thing they had to do was get the children calmed down.

"Who's leading them?" Roach asked.

"I don't know her name, but that's her over there."

Roach looked at the woman the Sergeant pointed out and felt a familiar thrill start at the base of his spine. She wasn't as young as Roach liked, under twenty, but she was beautiful. On the shorter side, he estimated no more than five foot three or four. She was obviously in very good condition.

She wore a pair of khaki shorts with tan desert boots on her feet and a once white but now filthy T-shirt. A large frame pistol was holstered on her right hip, two spare magazines in pouches on her left. Long, wavy red hair spilled down her back. Every time she moved, grabbing a running child or turning to yell at another that was misbehaving, the muscles in her arms and legs rippled.

Nodding to the Sergeant, Roach walked over and stood looking at her, waiting for her to finish scolding a little girl that had just punched her brother. Finished with the girl, she straightened with a sigh and stretched her back, the fabric of the shirt pulling tight across her breasts. No bra. Roach felt himself growing hard. Noticing him standing there, she turned and looked him up and down.

"Hi," she said.

"Hi. I'm Captain Lee Roach. Welcome to Tinker Air Force Base. I'm going to help you."

He held his hand out.

"Thank you, Captain! It's been a while since anyone offered to help." She took his hand and shook it. "I'm Katie Chase."

Continue the adventure in Transmission: V Plague Book 5, now available from Amazon!

Printed in Great Britain
by Amazon

72135696R00241